THE TAO OF HOCKEY

MELANIE TING

Development editing by Jodi Henley

Copyediting by Amy J. Duli

Cover design from Indie Solutions

ISBN: 978-0-9947830-7-3

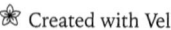 Created with Vellum

CONTENTS

1

TESTED

"HARDER, ERIC," Donna urged me. "Go hard!"

My legs were pumping as fast as I could go, but I could feel the lactic acid burning in my quads. All I wanted to do was stop, but I kept pushing and ignored the pain. Mentally strong.

"Go, go, go! Don't slow down. Ten seconds."

Pedal. Pedal. Focus.

"Five seconds." She was right in my face, grasping the handlebars of the stationary bike, but she was a blur to me. I tried to rise above the excruciating pain.

"Two, one…and you're done."

I groaned and eased off pedalling. Donna undid the Velcro monitor on my bare chest. She looked at my expression and motioned with her hand.

"Bathroom is that-a-way."

I got off the bike and rushed into the washroom. I puked into the toilet and then flushed it. At least this cubicle was clean, unlike the many other places I'd thrown up. I went to the sink and cleaned up, rinsing out my mouth and washing my face.

Donna was inputting readings into her iPad when I came out. She looked up at me.

"You okay?"

"Yeah, fine. Sorry about that."

Her smile was broad and sincere. She reminded me of my favourite teacher in grade school, this gigantic woman from the Prairies who was so kind. "No worries, Eric. At least you made it to the bathroom. I figure it shows how hard you're working. If you're not barfing, you're not trying."

I picked up my technical T and put it back on. "I hate Wingates."

"Who doesn't? But it's the best way to measure anaerobic power. Well, we're done with this portion of the testing, but I'm guessing you don't want to break for lunch right now."

"Yeah, not really hungry at this moment."

"Okay, let's do the psychological testing now."

"The what?" Extra sweat began beading on my skin.

She ignored my question and led me back into the lobby. It was furnished with leather couches and huge framed photographs of hockey players in action. Nobody recognizable, but blurry, arty stuff. Everything at the Tony Sano Institute of Human Performance looked slick and professional. Given how much I was paying for this training, that only made sense. This was unlike any place I'd ever worked out at. But for my big chance, I was willing to go huge.

Donna handed me a clipboard and a pencil. "There are two types of questions. The first set asks you to rate statements on a scale from one to five, one being agree completely and five is disagree completely. The second set presents you with situations and ask you how you would respond. Please fully colour in the circles so we can scan the answer sheet. Tony will want to see the results before he meets with you." She looked at her watch. "I'll check back in a bit and see how you're doing. If you need me, I'll be in the office or the gym."

I nodded and looked down at the question sheet. The first two statements were: *You believe that the past shapes the future. You frequently contemplate the complex nature of life.*

No fucking kidding.

I took a deep breath and began filling in the little circles. There was no cheating on a personality test. I knew enough not to indicate I was a sociopath, but similar questions were worded in slightly different ways, so I had to be consistent.

One hour later, I was done and sitting in an empty lunchroom with Donna.

"Everyone else has already eaten," she explained. She walked over to a large industrial fridge and pulled out two plates. "There's usually a choice at lunch, but I put away stuff for us. While you're working out here, if you need to hydrate or refuel, there's always something in here."

My lunch plate had a kale salad with apple slices and pumpkin seeds. There was a grilled chicken sandwich on dark, dense bread. I tried some of both. "This is great."

Donna chuckled. "No complaints? Guess we won't have to convert you to Tony's dietary rules."

"I've always eaten clean. Kinda second nature in my family, and even in the town I come from."

"Where's that?" The question was muffled through her chewing.

"Nelson." It was only yesterday morning I'd driven the eight hours to Vancouver.

She tilted her head. "Sorry, I'm geographically challenged. That's still in B.C., right?"

"Yeah, up in the Kootenay Mountains—it's beautiful. And there's an alternative vibe—you know, around diet and spirituality."

Donna stared at me. "You're a little different from most of the guys at training camp. How come you're here so late?"

It was early August, and everyone else had probably been here since June.

"I just got a chance to try out for an AHL team. It's a big deal for me, so I wanted to go full out. I've got six weeks before camp. My agent recommended Tony's facility."

"Who's your agent?"

"Lance Bertrand."

Donna whistled. "You must be a big deal prospect."

I shrugged. I used to be, but not any more. My high-profile agent was the only thing I had left from those days.

After lunch, we switched to on-ice evaluations. The rest of the guys were doing drills and skills training at one end of the ice, and Donna had commandeered a corner for us. I finally got to see Tony for the first time. He had dark, short-cropped hair and tanned skin, and he was the shortest guy on the ice, but he had an intensity that I could sense even from across the rink.

Donna was very skilled on skates. I guess I shouldn't have been surprised since she worked here.

"You've played hockey before."

"University, while I was getting my kinesiology degree." She made a face. "And a women's pro team that only lasted one season."

We finished up our session just in time. The guys were switching into full-ice drills. I lingered on the bench to watch. All the players were really good, miles ahead of everyone I'd been practicing with back home.

"Okay, we're pretty much done now," Donna said. "You've got time to shower, hydrate or grab a snack, and then you'll be meeting with Tony around 5:30. He'll probably be late though." She chuckled, and I sensed the respect she had for her boss.

"Okay," I said. I watched the other guys circling the ice, warming up for some complex drill. Since the first moment I hit the ice, I had loved skating and playing hockey. When my parents were fighting, when I was worried, whatever was wrong in my life—all that crap disappeared at the rink. The crisp scraping sound of my skates on ice was like a signal to my brain to shut out everything else.

"I can see you're dying to get on the ice with them," Donna remarked. "Hopefully, that will happen tomorrow."

Hopefully? I frowned. This training was urgent for me. Why wasn't that a sure thing?

I WAS WAITING in Tony Sano's office. It was glass-walled, so he could keep an eye on the gym next door. If he could have, I was sure he would have wedged the office above the rink so he could watch that as well. I wiped my sweaty hands on my shorts.

Tony burst in. He was probably in his late thirties, but he was so fit and healthy it was hard to tell. "Eric. Sorry, I'm late." He shook my hand. His expression was friendly, but I could tell he was taking stock of me.

He settled in behind his desk, unzipped his track jacket, and carefully placed it on the back of his ergonomic chair with muscular, well-defined arms.

"So, what's your timeline here?" He fired up his computer and stared at the monitor.

"My tryout camp starts in the middle of September. I've been training all summer, but Lance told me that if I wanted to maximize my chances, I needed to work with you."

He nodded. "It's late, but six weeks is better than nothing. Did you just find out you were getting a tryout?"

"Yeah. Only 48 hours ago. It's been a crazy two days."

Tony consulted his monitor. My results were undoubtedly in a database comparing me to every other hockey player Tony had worked with. "Well, your fitness test scores are not bad. Usually I have to ride my guys about diet, but your body fat percentage is already at 12%. That's almost optimal, and the season is still over a month away."

He nodded as he scrolled through more results. "Your flexibility is excellent, especially for someone of your build. I see you've been practicing yoga for years."

I nodded. "Pretty much since I could crawl."

"It's probably helped to prevent injuries. Your medical record shows no serious injuries throughout your playing career."

I swallowed. "Nope. I'm like Superman."

Tony turned away from the screen towards me. "When we spoke on the phone, you told me your goal was to make it to the NHL."

"Yes. That's all I want." Admitting that out loud made my stomach flip. Everybody wanted to make it, but my journey had been complicated.

"Well, I'm sure I don't have to tell you that being in great shape is only the first step. Nutrition, rest, preparation— there are literally hundreds of tweaks I can make to your program. But it's the second part of your evaluation I'm really interested in—the psychological testing."

I held my breath.

"When I read your personality evaluation, I feel like I'm looking at the reincarnation of Ghandi. You're calm, controlled, and at peace with mankind. If this is really you, I'd have to question your fire to make the NHL. It's a tough game, and you need more passion than this."

I waited for him to continue.

"But when I read the scouting reports on you, Eric, I couldn't believe you're the same guy." Tony put on some reading glasses and opened a file folder.

"Driving Under the Influence charges, suspension in juniors

for deliberately injuring an opponent. AHL: fined for under-aged drinking, team disciplinary action for intoxication, three trades, 160 penalty minutes for a top six forward. And then when your last AHL team cut you, you disappeared completely. Off the map for nine months until you turned up in Switzerland."

He cleared his throat. "And that's just the official stuff. There are confidential notes as well. Player was seen smoking marijuana. Incidents of binge drinking. Eric was observed to have multiple sexual episodes without regard for team rules or curfews." Tony raised his eyebrows. "I don't even want to know what that means."

My stomach dropped. This guy knew everything. Now I understood Donna's remark. You couldn't just sign up to work with Tony—he had to accept you first. I blew out a long breath to quiet the rising panic in my body.

"I'm not that person anymore."

"That's a start." He took off his glasses. "Look, I want players who are going to reflect well on what I'm trying to build here. Players who screw up and make it appear that I didn't prepare them for competition set me back. I took one look at your history and said 'no way.'"

He stood up and scowled towards the gym where a couple of young guys were fooling around. They noticed him watching and got back to work.

Tony sat down and continued. "Then Lance Bertrand had a long talk with me. He explained how you had changed. In Switzerland, you were not only the highest scorer on the team, but winner of a sportsmanship award. I called your coach from the Swiss League. Mike Guildford sang your praises. It's like you've gone back to the top-grade prospect you used to be."

That was the hope. I had succeeded in Switzerland where the pressure was off, but could I translate that success into something bigger? Making the AHL was the first step in that process.

"Before I commit my time and effort into training you, I want to hear from you. Why are you different now?"

"I've done a lot of work on myself." I motioned towards my chest. "You know—personal, spiritual stuff."

"What exactly?"

"When I got cut from my last AHL team, we had just finished this series in Texas. So, I shipped my hockey gear home, then I went to this retreat in Sedona. They dealt with addiction recovery. It wasn't fancy or anything, just a simple monastery. But there was this shaman there who helped me a lot. We did desert meditations."

A lot of people checked out as soon as I said the word shaman, but Tony was still listening. "Shaman Felix helped me to realize that I could never escape the demons that were inside me. I needed to exist in peace with them. I was there for weeks and at the end, I underwent a fire-cleansing ceremony.

"And then I went home to Nelson. Next season, Lance found a team—Ambrì-Piotta—that would take a chance on me. I had a good season, so I got this offer to try out with the Vancouver Vice."

Tony's forehead creased when I named the Vice. "That's not the team I would have picked for someone in recovery. So, you're not drinking anymore?"

"Felix believed that not drinking alcohol at all meant that you were susceptible to complete relapses. He's a proponent of all things in moderation. I have the occasional drink, but never when I'm driving. I still have an interlock system on my truck—a screening device. My ignition won't start if I have alcohol in my system."

My chest constricted. I took deep, cleansing breaths and

tried to relax. My whole fight-or-flight reaction got triggered by this topic.

"Tell me about the accident, Eric."

His knowledge didn't surprise me. "I was eighteen. I rolled my car. Totalled it."

Tony's intense gaze was fixed on me, but he said nothing.

I felt like a moth pinned to a board. I tried hard to keep my voice normal, but it cracked slightly. "My best friend got injured."

"Gary Lysenko?"

Fuck this shit! If he already knew everything, why did I have to talk about it? Everything always boiled down to this one night of my life. I tried to appear calm, as Gary filled my head. Even sitting here, memories seeped back into my head —the terrible darkness, the sound of Gary sobbing—but I pushed all that crap to the back of my mind. This was my chance and I had to stay in control.

"Yeah, it was Gary. He had some internal injuries, and... his leg got—" I motioned to my thigh.

Tony waited, but when I didn't finish the sentence, he did something on his keyboard. "You guys played junior together, right? What's he doing now?"

I cleared my throat. "He's got his own business back in Nelson. He works as a landscaper."

"So you guys are still friends?"

I nodded. It wasn't the same, of course. How could we be best friends when one of us couldn't play hockey anymore and the other one could—but kept fucking up?

"Do you want to add anything else?" Tony's expression was completely blank. At least he wasn't judging me. But nobody could be harder on me than myself.

"I have changed. I believe that it's a permanent change. I've been in a positive lifestyle for over a year. My performance will reflect well on your program, Tony, if you give me a chance." There was no question I had more humility now.

He turned and searched his computer again. "Your blood work turned up THC. That's got to stop. They're doing random drug testing in the NHL, so marijuana is out, even in moderation."

I nodded.

"I know Nelson is pretty 4:20 friendly, so that goes double for when you're home."

I finally smiled. The fact that Tony was giving me long-term advice meant he was going to work with me.

"What about sex? Are you still having 'multiple sexual episodes?'"

Nothing was off-limits here. "No, I'm not." I had hook-ups, but the normal kind.

"Do you have a girlfriend?"

I shook my head.

"Too bad. I prefer when my players have a stable personal life. But moderation is fine." He pushed back on his ergonomic chair and spun away from the desk.

"Eric, according to your physical evaluation, there is nothing holding you back from everything you want to achieve. You've got size, skills, and you're in excellent shape. So, clearly, the mental side is what we have to work on. Your mental game is going to determine whether you make it back to the AHL—and succeed. I've had to exercise people's mental sides before, but not to this extent. I'm looking forward to the challenge. Welcome aboard."

He reached out and shook my hand. This whole deal made more sense now. I was such a public screw-up. If Tony managed to turn me around, I'd be a shining example of how good he was.

Then he went over to the cupboard, got a stack of books and papers, and handed them to me. "Here's your schedule, a top-line of your results, and some reading I've selected for you. There will be discussion and questions, so pay attention." I leafed through the books. Most of them seemed to be about sports psychology, something I'd already done a lot of reading on.

Tony smiled. "If you do all these readings, you won't have time to get in trouble."

2

A WHOLE NEW WORLD

TONY'S BUSINESS was part of a larger private ice sports facility. Kids and parents surrounded me as I exited the building. My white truck was parked beside a brand new crossover with the hatch and doors open. A young mom was struggling with a toddler, a baby, and a bunch of kid stuff.

"Hey, can I give you a hand?" I offered, grabbing the handle of her double stroller.

She scowled at me. "Please don't touch that. It's all under control." The baby began wailing louder, like he was afraid of me too.

I let go of the stroller and backed away. I had forgotten that I was in Vancouver, where everyone had big-city suspicions and paranoia. My hometown was small and friendly— everyone knew each other in some way. And I'd come back from a village in Switzerland that was so tiny that everyone knew exactly who I was from the moment I'd arrived. But here I needed to mind my own business.

I got into my truck and tried to shake off the feeling of loneliness. Big cities could be great—once I'd made some new friends. The best part of hockey was the instant bonding with your teammates, but that reward was far in the future.

My cellphone rang, and I grabbed it, eager to hear a friendly voice.

"Hello?"

"Eric. How did your first day of training go?"

My voice dropped. "Oh hey, Dad."

"Is this Tony Sano worth the ridiculous amount of money he's charging?"

"It's my money," I pointed out.

"Yes, but who's going to have to bail you out once you don't have a job or savings?"

I sighed. There was no winning this argument. "Actually, I spent the whole day getting tested."

"What? That's ridiculous. He understands what a big deal this is for you, doesn't he? Time is critical. It's your first step on the ladder back to the NHL. Damn it, Eric. You're 23 years old. For a winger, that should be your prime. If you don't make it this time—you'll never make it."

Like there wasn't enough pressure, he had to keep reminding me of the big prize. Thanks, Dad. "It's under control. He tests me now and tests me again in a month so he can fine-tune the program. You should see this place—the equipment, the other players. A thousand times better than anything I could do at home."

My dad mumbled something else about the expense. "As long as you're ready to work. No distractions."

I sighed. I didn't even have to ask what that meant.

"I mean it, son. There's a lot of temptation in Vancouver. Your partying days are over, right? I'm not usually on board with all the woo-woo stuff your mother's into, but that desert place really seemed to straighten you out."

"I'm good. You don't have to worry. Look, I better go. I'm

on the road, and I don't want to get nailed for distracted driving. Bye."

I disconnected and leaned back against the seat. The young mom was just pulling out; our eyes met and she gave me a little smile. I smiled back.

Time to go. I blew hard into the interlock remote and waited. It never took long, but it seemed like an eternity. Too much time to wait and remember why I was in the DUI program. Really, I should have graduated from supervision by now, but playing hockey all over the place meant I couldn't check in every month and prove I was a sober driver. Fuck. Maybe I was lazy or maybe I liked the insurance of not having to take responsibility.

My reading came up "pass." I started up the truck and drove out. Sometimes it felt like all my dad did was think about my hockey career and how I had screwed it up. Too bad he had never remarried and started a new family to take some of the pressure off me.

My move to Vancouver had come together quickly. My mom's boyfriend, Dino, had arranged for me to live in his brother's basement suite. It was free, so the price was right. Tony's expensive training program was going to eat up almost all my savings.

I parked in front of Joe Rossi's East Van house. I'd arrived late last night, so I hadn't had a chance to really look at the place. It was a two-storey house with pale blue wood panelling and white trim. I went through a white gate and around to the back door that was my entrance.

My basement suite was a little dark, with only half-windows on the sides and back, but it was tidy and func-tional. The living room had a small couch, a chair, and a tele-vision. There was a separate bedroom with a double bed and a dresser. The kitchenette had a cooktop, a bar fridge, and a sink. I unpacked the groceries I'd picked up on the way home. The whole place smelled like antiseptic cleaner.

There was a knock on the connecting door. I opened it, and Joe stood there in jeans and a t-shirt. In fact, his outfit was exactly the same as last night, except he had swapped his Led Zeppelin logo for an AC/DC one.

"Hey, Eric. We hardly got a chance to get acquainted last night. You want to join me for dinner?"

"That'd be great." Not only for the food, but the company.

He led the way up the stairs. We went straight to the kitchen where he had laid out two table settings on the small table. His kitchen looked clean and organized. There was a meat sauce simmering on the stove.

"Smells great in here," I told him.

"It's our mama's special recipe. Did Dino never cook this for you?"

I shook my head. "Dino's vegan now."

Joe made a snorting noise that showed his opinion of that dietary choice. "That's why the guy never has any energy. How's he doing?"

"He's good. Still at the bookstore." Dino worked at a metaphysical bookstore on the main street of Nelson. He was pretty quiet, and we didn't talk much. Sure, he had his subjects, stuff like reincarnation and Victorian history. Mostly, he let my mom do the talking for both of them. I liked him though, especially since he really cared about Mom and treated her well.

"Help yourself to a beer," Joe motioned. He had one going already.

I went to the fridge and took out a bottle of Molson Canadian. I twisted off the cap and inhaled that hoppy smell. Then I tilted the bottle. That first cold rush of beer down my throat felt so good. It tasted like the promise of oblivion.

"So, did Dino tell you that you can have the suite until the permits come in? I'm not sure when that'll be though. I'm going to reno the whole thing. My girlfriend thinks I can make more money with this Airbnb thing, but first I have to move up from student grade."

"Whatever. It's all good. I'm training now, but my camp starts in mid-September, and I'll know by the end whether I need a place for the season. But if you need it sooner, I'll work something out." If I made the team, I'd rent a place for the season, or more likely share with a teammate. "Dino told me there was no charge, but are you sure I can't pay you for this?"

"For a couple of months, no way. Plus you're a friend of Dino's." He hesitated over the word "friend," but it wasn't like Dino was my stepdad. I had moved out before he moved in.

"Well, thanks. I owe you one, for sure."

Joe squinted at me. "Actually, now that I see how big you are, maybe I'll get you to help me out with a few things. I'm putting in new kitchen cupboards in here, but it's a two-man job. We could do it on the weekend, if you're free."

"Sure. Sounds good."

He put the pasta in to cook and started talking about housing prices in Vancouver. That seemed to be a favourite topic for people here. From looking at rental units, I already knew it was crazy town.

"Where's the bathroom?" I seemed to have polished off the beer without even realizing it.

"Down the hall, on your right."

Before I could shut the door, there was flash of white and this fluffy white cat sat on the bathroom rug and looked at me expectantly.

I held open the door. "Out, kitty." She completely ignored my hint and began licking herself. I shut the door, lifted the seat, and took a piss. As soon as I flushed the toilet, she was right here, front paws on the rim, watching the water swirl down. I washed up, and we left the bathroom together.

"I see you met Misty." Joe laughed as we both walked into the kitchen.

"She's got a toilet fetish."

"Yeah. I hardly notice anymore, but guests are always a little shocked." Misty rubbed against Joe's legs, and he slipped her a piece of sausage. She crunched it and then disappeared again—probably to stake out the bathroom.

We sat down at the table. Joe served up the spaghetti in a big platter with a salad alongside. We both dug in, and at first we were too busy eating to say much.

"This is delicious," I told him. While I ate clean, home-cooking was always a welcome treat. I'd be burning a ton of calories at Tony's facility, so I could eat a lot.

"Thank you. You live on your own long enough, you have to learn a few dishes." Now I realized why I felt at home in Joe's place. It was like my dad's house: neat and tidy, but kind of Spartan. None of the little feminine touches that my mom added to our house.

"Dino said you're an athlete, right?"

"Yeah, I play hockey."

"So, are you trying out for the Millionaires?"

I shook my head. Trying out for Vancouver's NHL team was the dream. "No, the Vice."

Joe's eyebrows went sky-high. "Jeez. You know about them—the bar brawl last year?"

"Yeah." Unfortunately this was the reaction of most people when I mentioned the team.

"I work in the film industry as a carpenter. I was between gigs, so I went to help out a friend who got the call to fix up the place they trashed. It looked like they ran a fucking tractor through there. And the bar owner told me that some of the team were in there regularly hassling every woman in the joint. Are you sure that's the kind of team you want to be a part of?"

I shook my head. "To be honest—not really. But it's my only chance."

Joe nodded. "Yeah, I had to work on a lot of schlock when I first got into the film business. But once you make it, you can choose to work with people you respect. You'll get there too."

Since Joe hardly knew me, his prediction didn't hold much weight. Yet it sounded like a good omen.

––––––

THE TRAINING DAY started at 7:00, so I made sure I was at the facility fifteen minutes early. To my surprise, everyone else was already there. Obviously, Tony wasn't the only one whose intensity level was dialled up.

My first day was a blur. Donna took me through a weight program that she assured me Tony had designed. I'd already been working out hard in preparation for a new season in Switzerland, but this was more detailed and muscle-specific than anything I'd done before. I was playing catch-up since everyone else had been working out for months.

The guys were all friendly, but there wasn't much time to chat. Even during our lunch hour, there was a nutritionist giving a talk on optimum mealtime scheduling.

We wrapped up the day with a long scrimmage, then hit the dressing room—our day finally done. I was exhausted.

The guy beside me had been one of the best players out there. He was a d-man, but he could rush the puck up ice and score at will.

"Hey, I'm Jack Baumgartner. Bomber." He offered a huge, sweaty paw, and I shook it.

"I'm Eric Fairburn," I said. "You play in the NHL, right?"

"Yeah, for Columbus. But I grew up in Vancouver. Where'd you play last season?"

"Swiss A League," I told him. My team was in a tiny village that nobody had ever heard of, so I didn't bother explaining further.

"Shit. The Swiss League must be better than I thought," he said. "Where're you playing this year?"

"Depends. I'm trying out for an AHL team, so we'll see."

Bomber nodded. He wasn't nosy. Guys who played at a high level understood that players who looked good in scrimmages and at camps might not be the best in games. No matter how skilled I looked now, it came down to real-life competition.

"Which team?" Another guy called out to me. He was a good-sized winger like me.

"The Vice."

The big winger snorted. "They're a shit storm inside a blender full of shit." Not poetry, but it matched everything I'd heard so far. The Vice were the worst team in the AHL and had been for the past couple of seasons.

He continued, "The coach is a huge bastard, and their captain is a fucking asshole."

"Who's that?" asked a redheaded guy. They all seemed to be friends, since they changed in the same corner.

"Captain's a guy called Daniel Ramsey. Coach is Robert Pankowski."

"Never heard of either of them." The redheaded guy shrugged.

"Count yourself lucky. Ramsey bullied some rookie right off the team last season." The winger looked at me. "Don't let him push you around."

I nodded. This was exactly the kind of information I was hoping to get before training camp.

"I'm Dirk Smith. I play AHL too, but out on the East Coast."

The red-haired guy introduced himself too. "I'm Reeds. Frederick Reid. I play for Florida." I would have guessed that too. Reeds was an NHL-quality centre. It was easy to tell who the best players were once we hit the ice. The NHL guys all had an economy of movement and an effortless speed. They could get away impossible shots. "So, I heard you talking to Tony about yoga?"

I nodded warily. I was used to getting hassled about this stuff when I was in junior.

"Maybe you could help me with a few things. I'm trying to improve my flexibility, so I've been going to a class with my wife. But I don't think the instructor gets that the positions aren't the same when your quads are this big." Reeds motioned to his tree trunk thighs.

"Yeah, sure. We can use towels and blocks for positions you're having trouble with. My mom's a yoga instructor, so I've been doing it all my life."

"So, Yogi," Dirk called out. "You want to come out to dinner tonight? It's Friday, so we can celebrate the end of Tony's torture sessions."

"I'm in." Sure beat a salad in a room with only a white cat for company.

Reeds nodded. "Yeah, my wife's gone on a girls' weekend. So I don't want to go home and have to cook."

"I prefer to eat clean though," I said.

Dirk shook his head. "Oh man, you're as bad as Tony. Is this all part of the yoga lifestyle?"

Bomber interrupted. "Stop hassling the new guy. We can eat at one place, and then go out drinking after. But this means we should probably shower."

We started getting undressed. Dirk was still bitching though.

"You do drink, right?" he asked me.

"Actually, not if I'm driving."

"Well, sure, that makes sense. Not even one beer? You're not going to fit in on the Vice, I'll tell you that right now."

A flush ran up the back of my neck. "I've had a DUI. My truck is rigged so that it won't start if I've had a drink." Honesty was the best policy when it came to my past. All it took was a couple of Google searches to find the shitty things I'd done.

Dirk whistled. "Guess you will fit in on the Vice."

3

THE X FACTOR

AFTER DINNER, Reeds led us to a downtown pub that wasn't too far from his place. It was busy and had a friendly neighbourhood vibe to it. We got a table with a clear view of the football game on the big-screen TV. The Lions were getting whumped by the Roughriders, which made Dirk happy because his parents were from Saskatchewan.

"I'm gonna get a round. Sure you're not drinking tonight?" Bomber asked me.

I shook my head. Of course, I wished I could, but I had less than two months until I was free from supervision, and I wasn't going to mess that up.

"I don't know how you do it," Dirk said. "Alcohol is a diet staple for me."

"Paying my dues." I sipped on my mineral water. When the beers arrived, they looked tempting. The first sip was always so good. But the first sip was never the problem.

Reeds laughed. "Dirk needs beer goggles for the chicks he scores. I saw that lady you left with last Saturday." He started barking and howling.

"Oh, fuck off. Like you could do better?"

"I'm a married man. Don't have to do that shit to get laid."

"Sure. Excuses, excuses. You've got no game."

"I had tons of game—in my day." Reeds was a few years older than the rest of us.

"Prove it," Dirk said.

"The hell. I'm not cheating on Carly just to prove something to you." Reeds sounded virtuous, but he had hinted earlier that he still got around.

"Okay. Alls you have to do is get a phone number then." Dirk started looking around the room.

Bomber laughed. "And make sure it doesn't start with 555."

"Her." Dirk motioned with his head to a woman who was sitting at the bar with a friend. She had long blonde hair and was wearing a blue dress and high heels. She looked good.

Reeds swallowed. Even though he played in the NHL, it was one thing to pick up women after a game when they knew exactly who you were, and another thing to have to approach someone ice cold.

"I'm willing to put a hundred bucks on this," Dirk said with a snort. "'Cause it ain't going to happen."

Reeds eyed her and drank the beer that Bomber had just put on the table.

"Bock, bock, bock," taunted Dirk while flapping his arms. He glanced at me. "I bet Yogi here could have her panties off in ten seconds."

"Leave me out of this," I said.

"Yeah, right. You know that physio chick has the hots for you, right? She was checking you out today, even when she was supposed to be working on me."

Bomber snorted. "She's only trying not to look at your scrawny body." Dirk was on the skinny side and trying to bulk up. His size was probably why he hadn't gotten a good look at the NHL level.

Reeds cleared his throat and stood up. "Here I go, boys. Watch and learn."

He walked over to the bar and started talking to the two women. They didn't shoot him down right away, which was a good sign. As I was watching him, a waitress moved away from the bar and revealed a woman sitting there. She was looking right at me. I got the feeling she had been watching us the whole time. When our eyes met, her expression didn't change at all. She looked amused, like she knew what we were up to.

It was weird that I hadn't noticed her before, because she really stood out in this place. She was tall and slim. She wore beat-up jeans, a short white jacket, and a tight t-shirt with a faded logo. Her black hair was shorter than mine and had streaks of gold in it. I'd never seen anyone like her before. But what really drew me to her was how comfortable she looked—she was as relaxed sitting alone in a bar as she would have been in her own living room.

I was so busy watching this woman that I didn't even notice Reeds was back at the table.

"This close," he said, pinching two fingers together. "Then she asked about my wedding ring."

We all laughed at him. "Rookie move," Bomber said.

"Pay up," Dirk said, laying out his hand.

"Well, fuck. I don't have the cash on me. I'll give it to you tomorrow."

"You guys are my witnesses, right?" Dirk said.

"I'm going to the can," I said. I got up and moved towards the bar. The seat beside the woman was open, so I sat there.

"Hey, beautiful."

She turned and looked at me. She began at the bottom

and her eyes moved up slowly and deliberately—lingering around belt level before finally resting on my face.

"Hey, handsome."

She turned back to her drink and took a sip. Now that I was close, I could see her a lot better. She had dark eyes, thick eyelashes, and pale lips. She wore a lot of jewellery too —a bunch of thick bracelets, spiky rings, and a fancy belt that sat on top of her hips. I checked out her body. There was no bra under that thin t-shirt, and I could see her little nipples poking out. That was hot. Again I was struck by the idea that I'd never seen anyone like her before.

"So, you come here often?" That was corny, but since she was already interested I figured the small talk didn't matter. Not having a drink to hold, I needed something to do with my hands—other than putting them all over her, which was what I really wanted. I pulled over a bowl of peanuts and started shelling one.

She didn't answer me. She seemed to be people-watching through the mirror behind the bar.

"Why so quiet? I thought we were getting along well."

She turned back at me. "Nope. We were only stating facts. You *are* handsome, and I think you know that."

I leaned in and smiled. "And you are beautiful...."

She lifted one shoulder in dismissal. "How much money will you make if I leave with you?"

Why would she think that? I turned around and all the guys were watching us. Dirk leered and gave me a big thumbs-up. Fuck that noise.

"None. I wanted to come over and talk to you. That's all."

"Just talk?"

I nodded. Her eyes were like her hair—dark with flecks of gold. Her skin was golden and looked perfectly smooth even under the harsh artificial light of the bar.

Her lips curled into a smile. "So, if I asked if we could go back to your place and fuck our brains out—you'd say no?"

I spilled the bowl of peanuts onto the floor. "What?"

She blinked at me, as calm as if she'd asked for the time.

I swallowed. "Jesus. I mean, if that's what you want—then okay, sure. I'm Eric, by the way."

She ignored this and signalled the bartender. She handed him a twenty, left a tip from the change, and stood up. She was tall with long, long legs. Fuck, she was as hot as she was weird.

I scrambled up. Peanut shells fell from my lap and crunched under my feet. "Are we going now? Just like that? Shouldn't we talk first?"

"So you can throw more food around? Talking is going to spoil the mood. I can find better things to do with that mouth." She raised a finger to my lips to silence me, but I caught it gently in my teeth, pulled it deeper into my mouth and sucked hard. Her finger tasted like salt and whiskey. And lust.

Her eyes widened and then she laughed—a low, hearty laugh. She pulled her finger slowly out of my mouth, then deliberately ran it down her neck and into the V of her T-shirt—leaving a trail of my saliva on her. Fuck. Now all I could think of was running my tongue down the exact same path, but ending up on one of those hard little nipples. My cock had gone from aroused to so hard that I was afraid my zipper would bust.

"Let's go." She led the way, and her ass was amazing. It was high and round, and I could not wait to get my hands on it. If I drove fast, we'd be back at my place in ten minutes.

As we exited, the guys were watching our every move. Well, hers anyway. Bomber was playing it cool, but Reeds and Dirk were snickering. Dirk called out, "And that's how it's done, boys. That dog's going downward tonight."

She heard him, stopped, and leaned both hands on the

table. "Does Eric here win any bets for leaving with me?"

The guys stared at her open-mouthed. Bomber shook his head.

She looked back at me. "You're not a bullshitter. That's good."

Then she strode out of the bar, and I hurried after her.

IT WAS dark outside once we left the pub. "Which way are we going?" she asked.

"Uh, my truck's over there." I pointed. "But wait."

She swirled around and looked at me. She was so tall that I could almost look her in the eye. Her face was unreadable. I still had this feeling that she was pranking me somehow. Nobody leaves a bar with a stranger this fast, especially someone this good-looking.

"What?"

"Uh, I don't even know your name...."

"You can call me X."

"X?"

"Yeah, like in X-ray." She smiled.

"That's not your real name though."

"Look, Einstein, if you're getting cold feet, that's fine. See ya."

"No! It's not that. It's only—I don't know—I feel like we should get to know each other."

"Awesome. Of all the dudes in the bar, I get the romantic."

She came right up to me, so close that I could feel the heat of her breath and body next to mine. I could see the pulse in her throat and hear the jangle of her ridiculous bracelets. She pressed her body against mine and pulled on the collar of my shirt, bringing my face up to hers. Then she kissed me. Her lips were soft but her mouth was demanding

—opening up and sucking all the breath out of me. She kissed me even harder, and I opened my eyes to see her eyelashes fluttering against her cheeks, her skin tanned and glowing. I wrapped my arms around her and pulled her closer to me. I could feel those rigid little nipples against my chest, and I got even harder. She felt my erection too and rotated her body against mine. I let my hand move down to her ass and squeezed hard. Firm and bouncy. She lifted one leg and wrapped it around me. Man, she was so hot. It was like she was ready to fuck me right here in the street.

She stopped kissing me. She opened her eyes, and they were dark and liquid. "Wanna go now?"

"Oh yeah." I took her hand and led her over to the truck. I unlocked it, and we both got in.

My cock was aching, and all I could think about was getting inside her. Automatically, I grabbed the interlock and blew into it.

"What the fuck?" she said.

"Uh, I'm, I have to do this—it's an interlock system. You know, it locks the ignition unless I—"

"I know what it is. I'm out." She opened the door.

"Wait! Why are you leaving?"

"Duh, Eric. I'm not riding with a drunk driver."

Oh c'mon, she came on to me so hard, and now this was the deal breaker? "Please, um, 'X.' It's totally safe. See this?" I showed her the pass message on the reader.

"You don't get one of those things unless you've messed up big time. I like living intact."

"Well, at least give me your number. We can meet up another time."

She laughed. "What's the point? It was only going to be tonight."

She slammed the door. Mouth-breathing, I watched her take a few long strides and disappear out of my life.

4
_____

SOLVE FOR X

DIRK COULD NOT STOP LAUGHING at training the next day. "You're shitting me, Fairburn. Here I was thinking that you were the luckiest fucker in the world, and you went home alone?"

It was Saturday. There were no scheduled sessions, but none of us wanted to take two days off in a row. Today I'd done a light workout with Dirk and Bomber. Reeds was apparently hungover at home.

"She took one look at the interlock in my car and said she wasn't going anywhere with a drunk driver." I sighed.

"You poor fuck," Bomber said. "Why didn't you take a taxi or something?"

"Well, I wasn't exactly thinking straight." Taxis, or her doing the driving had occurred to me later. In the moment, I had been distracted by her tight body and all the things I wanted to do to it.

Dirk nodded. "No kidding. She was so hot. She looked like the kinky type too." We all imagined the possibilities. Fuck. "Well, maybe you can call her and invite her over. No driving needed then."

"I don't have her number. I don't even know her name."

"Go back to that pub," Bomber suggested. "Maybe she's a regular."

That wasn't a bad idea. I was having trouble getting her off my mind. I kept imagining the night that might have been. I went back to the pub that night. Being a Saturday, it was even busier. I sat on the same stool as the previous night, but she never showed up.

Finally, I asked the bartender. He looked familiar, and I was pretty sure that he was the same guy she had tipped.

"Hey, do you remember the woman that sat here last night?" I pointed to her place.

He squinted at me. "Uh, no. We get lots of people in here."

"She was special though. Tall, short black hair with streaks in it. Really pretty."

"Oh, her. Bourbon, rocks."

"What?"

"That's how I remember people—by their drink orders."

"Okay. Do you know her name?"

He laughed. "That's not how things work in a bar, buddy. People don't introduce themselves to me. I hear more if there's two people talking, but she was alone."

He left to make some drinks. Maybe I'd have to give up on finding her. But at least the guy knew who I meant. When he came back, I ordered another mineral water and then asked him more questions.

"Does she come here all the time?"

He shook his head.

"Well, do you remember anything at all about her? Anything she said or did?"

"What is this, *Law and Order*? Look, I'm not telling you anything." He went to the other side of the bar.

Should I have offered him money like they did in the

movies? But I had no clue what the right amount would be.

One of the waitresses came up to the bar and ordered drinks. While she was waiting, she smiled at me.

"I heard what you asked Don. Why are you looking for her?"

I shrugged. "This is going to sound dumb, but we left together and then she took off. I don't know, I felt like we had a real connection. Stupid, right?"

She blinked at me. "No, I think it's romantic. And you don't strike me as a stalker." She motioned her head towards Don the bartender. "Guys don't get other guys. You probably have women chasing you."

"Well...." They didn't exactly chase me, but I never usually had problems. Maybe that's why X was so intriguing for me—her elusiveness.

She giggled and smoothed her long curly hair. "No need to brag."

"So, do you know her name?"

"No. But I know something." The waitress leaned closer to me, her breast nudging my arm. "I was talking to her earlier in the evening. She had a big bruise down the back of her arm and I asked her about it. She said she got it at work —she does stunt work. You know, for the movies."

That was certainly something to go on. "That's great. Thank you so much."

The waitress was still standing there watching me, so I wondered, "Can I give you a tip or something?"

She shook her head. "Don't worry, blondie. Just go out there, find her, and make a happy ending. That'd be so romantic."

I wanted a happy ending all right. But maybe not as romantic as she was thinking.

SUNDAY WAS MY DAY OFF, but it was also the day that Joe wanted me to work on his kitchen installation. I woke up to the sounds of hammering and drilling. I checked my clock. Shit, it was only 8:00am. But it sounded like I wasn't going to get to sleep in. I pulled on some old jeans, a t-shirt, and running shoes. I hadn't brought my work boots since I never expected to need them in Vancouver.

"Morning, Eric. There's some coffee if you want."

"Thanks, Joe." I looked around and saw he'd already stripped the kitchen.

"Everything's roughed in. I've got the rest of the cabinets in the garage, so we'll put those in today. If we can get to the countertop too, that would be good. That's the part I really need help with."

"Just tell me what you want done."

Joe kept a close eye on me in the beginning, but once he realized I knew which end of the hammer was up, he left me alone. I had worked summers at my dad's construction business, so I was pretty handy.

This work was manual labour, which was good since I wasn't really awake yet. And my brain was full of X. I kept seeing her face—those lush lips and her brown eyes. The way she looked straight at me with absolute confidence. And kissing her had made me want her so badly. What was wrong with me, if one kiss was knocking me onto my ass like some hormonal teenager?

We worked in silence for a while. Joe had the radio on to his favourite hard rock oldies station, so that music filled the empty kitchen. Suddenly I realized that he was the perfect person to ask about X.

"Hey, Joe. I met this woman the other night, but I didn't get her phone number. I know she works as a stuntwoman though. So, maybe you know how to get in touch with her?"

"Well, I wouldn't know her personally, but I could ask the

stunt coordinator. He'd know pretty much everyone. What's her name?"

"Ahhh, that's the tricky part. I don't actually know her name. But she's very distinctive. She's tall—like close to six feet. She has really short dark hair with streaks, and she's beautiful."

Joe winced a little. "I don't know how to break this to you, but if a girl doesn't give you her name or her number—she ain't interested."

"I know that's what it sounds like, but we were so close to hooking up. She is into me, and I just want to get another chance."

Joe shook his head. "I take my work serious, Eric. I'm not going to play Match.com for you to get your rocks off. Besides...."

"Besides, what?"

"Dino told me that this your last big chance. You know, not just to make the Vice, but maybe beyond that."

"I know. The training's going great. Tony's the best." I had already been in good shape, but now I was going to be next level.

Joe put down his drill, leaned on the counter, and frowned at me. "You want to focus on one thing only. Cinch your position on the team first."

"I am focused."

He snorted. "Women are great. I love women. But they need attention, you know what I'm saying?"

"Kind of."

"If you go for the quickies, you spend a lot of time on the chase. Well, a guy like you, maybe it's easier. But a relationship takes time for sure." He motioned around the room. "Maybe the kitchen needed an update, but if it was up to me, it could wait. Margie put her foot down, and here we are. And once I finish this, I'm on to the suite reno."

Margie was reminding me of my high school girlfriend, Sunny: someone who always had plans for both of us. Joe started drilling again, but in between he continued his advice.

"I'm not really complaining, Margie's a great gal. But for a young guy like you, get your priorities straight. You could make some pretty good money if you make it to the NHL."

"If I was driven by money, I'd be back in Switzerland. I'd probably make more money there."

"Yeah, but long term you're not going to make millions in Switzerland."

"It's not about the money," I told him.

"That's nuts. It's always about the money." Joe continued his lecture. "In the movie industry, I've seen more than a few good guys get side-tracked from the main chance. So, I tell everyone that they need to pursue their dreams hard." He picked up the drill again.

"I agree with you, Joe, but I can't play hockey 24 hours a day."

Joe pointed the drill at me. "Women are complicated. They take time and energy—which is exactly what you need for hockey."

I shrugged. That was a matter of opinion. When it came to women, you had to steer clear of the head cases, for sure. But sex was good for your game. It was like the ultimate way to relax.

I walked out to the garage to get another load of cupboard doors. When I closed my eyes, I could see X again. She pulled me towards her, our lips met, and the heat of that kiss melted off our clothes. Her naked body was taut and tanned. I reached out to squeeze those pointy little nipples and felt a sharp pain. Like an idiot, I'd been caressing Joe's workbench. Fuck, now I had a splinter and a boner. Maybe Joe was right. I was getting too obsessed.

5

SILK STALKING

AS THE DAYS PASSED, I got used to Tony's training program, and my initial exhaustion cleared. I was still pushing my body to new limits, but my stamina was building up and I could recover faster. Tony was a real stickler for details. He watched me doing deadlifts and then pointed out exactly how I needed to position my wrists as I was lifting and what position my feet should be in. He believed that tiny changes in technique made huge differences.

"You have to train exactly right to maximize strength and prevent injury. You're lucky, Eric. Your yoga background has increased your flexibility. But I've never met one player who couldn't improve his core strength."

He was the first person to call anything about my hockey career "lucky." The fact that I was still getting to play pro was a good sign. And my fitness level and diet were at a better level than most. That was something I could thank my mom for. Guys used to laugh at my "healthy crap" diet, but now everyone was doing it.

As usual, there was bitching about the wholesome choices at lunch, but it was mainly the younger guys. The older you got, the more you realized that your body was in a delicate balance and needed proper fuel to function at peak performance.

I loved the food here. But my favourite part of lunch was when Tony weighed in with his opinions on game psychology. In fact, all the guys seemed to enjoy discussing the mental part of the game. Maybe the intensity of the program attracted guys who liked this kind of debate.

Dirk started today's conversation off. "You know what I don't get? Yogi here is so into meditation and keeping calm. Isn't that the opposite of what you want for hockey?"

Reeds snorted. "Don't worry about Yogi. He's all zen off the ice, but put a puck in front of him and he's a fucking menace."

"Still bitching about that hit on Tuesday?" I asked.

"You don't hit people in a fucking training scrimmage," he replied, rubbing his shoulder. He was right though: I was in another zone on the ice. But that only made me feel more confident—like all the parts of my game were coming back.

Tony said, "Intensity is important. Meditation is a form of concentration that can help your mind focus."

"'Focus' is a word that's overused," Bomber said. "Everyone wants to be more focused, but what is that exactly?"

"That's a great question," Tony said. "I like to think of it as stopping time."

"Stopping time?" Dirk asked. "Like in sci-fi movies?"

"Yeah, like *The Matrix*. If you could operate out of time, imagine what an incredible player you would be. So by honing your hockey skills with repetition, you can attain a certain amount of extra time. You can pull the right shot or pass out of your muscle memory. But more than that, you have to be able to factor in the physics and human factors of the situation to determine where the puck will go next. That's the key: how well you can predict the future."

Bomber nodded. "Like Gretzky said, 'I skate to where the puck is going, and not where it's been.'"

Tony nodded. "Everyone aims to do that, but half the time they do end up skating right at the guy with the puck."

"That's because consciousness disrupts your focus," I said.

"How so?" Bomber asked.

"You don't have time to think about what you should do. You need to do it without consciously realizing it. For me, the best shifts are when I get off the ice and I can hardly remember what happened. But all my synapses were firing and I feel great."

"You're so weird," Dirk said, shaking his head. "If you can't remember how you scored a goal, how can you do it again?"

But you could never score the same goal again. Each time, the variables would shift. Maybe the next time, the ice would be fresher, or the d-man would be out of position, or the pass would be the right play. You could never predict the future, but you could prepare.

Once Tony took off to do some paperwork, the conversation got more personal.

"So, did you get a line on Cinderella yet?" Reeds asked me. He was the most interested in my pursuit of X.

"Yeah. I'm not going to make a detective anytime soon. I found out that she works as a stuntman, or woman, I should say. But I asked the only guy I know in the film business, and he won't help me."

"Did you look online?" Reeds asked.

"For what?"

"I don't know. Maybe there's a directory or something."

I pulled out my phone and checked. One quick search and

a site called Stuntlist came up. Another click on Canada West, then Women, and I was scrolling through headshots.

"Shit. Why did I not think of this?" I muttered.

"Because you're just a pretty face." Reeds laughed.

"Here she is."

Her name was Josie Ray. Ha, ha, like X-Ray. She looked different in the photo because her hair was long, but she had the same deep eyes and ripe lips. Even looking at that mouth was making mine water. She was looking at the camera without smiling, hand on her hip, wearing a tank top so you could see the muscles of her arm. You could also see the outline of her tits, although this time she was wearing a bra. As an added bonus, her vital stats were listed: 5'10", 140 pounds.

Dirk was looking over my shoulder. "Soo-ey. When you nail her, I want all the details. A stuntwoman. Shit, maybe she'll throw you around or something."

"Maybe. Now I've got her name. But unless I'm a stunt coordinator, I'm not getting her contact info."

"Do I have to do everything for you?" Reeds asked. "Now you've got her name, search Facebook or Twitter. Or maybe that Internet movie database. Something'll come up."

Bomber groaned. "I am disturbed that you know all this, Reeds."

"Okay, I'll search her out tonight." It would give me something to do in the evening.

Josie Ray turned out to be a ghost. I found her credited on a few movies, but she wasn't on any social media at all. Another fucking dead end. This was beyond frustrating—at least my sex life had been the one place where I had total control. But now that was turning into another failure.

―――――

JOE'S GIRLFRIEND, Margie, felt sorry for me. She had kids on their own in Toronto, so she worried about motherless me. If she saw my light was on, she'd pop down and invite me up for dinner. Joe didn't seem to mind. I was burning a ton of calories every day, so I didn't mind either.

Margie worked in the film business like Joe, except she was in the costume department. Her current job was a television series about some superhero. She was a talker, and she was telling me about her day while Joe was out barbecuing. I was only half-listening until a familiar name popped up.

"Sorry, did you say Josie?"

"Yeah."

"Josie Ray?"

Margie nodded. "How do you know her?"

"I met her at a pub last week. But we keep getting our wires crossed, so I haven't been able to connect with her."

"Oh." She gave me a skeptical look.

"Do you have her number by any chance?"

She started slicing tomatoes. "Nope. We're not friends or anything."

"Hey, maybe I could drop by the set. Where is it?"

"East Van. There's a big property off Hastings Street, but it's a closed set."

"What time do you finish shooting?"

Margie laughed. "Gee whiz, Eric. This is the most excited I've seen you about anything other than food. Have you got a crush on her?"

"No way." It was more like an obsession. "Uh, what's she like?"

Margie was watching me with a big grin on her face. "She's nice. Kind of a loner, but she's a professional. Comes in and does her job. Gets it right the first time. The crew all appreciate that. I don't think she gets that much work because she's so tall. Not many actresses that tall."

She continued as she poured dressing over the salad. Ranch, and way too much of it. "I was fitting her yesterday in this evening gown. She sure looked good in it. You know, I might have a photo on my phone. I was proud of that one."

Joe walked back into the kitchen and laid a platter on the counter. "Steaks are done."

"Did you know Eric here has a little crush on this woman I work with?" Margie asked.

He frowned. "Who would that be?"

"Josie Ray. Do you know her?"

Joe shook his head. "Does she do stunts?"

"You *do* know her," Margie said.

He scowled at me. "How did you find out her name?"

I blushed. "Uh, I finally remembered it."

"I don't like it. Sounds like trouble to me. I told you, you should be concentrating on hockey and not women."

"Oh, for heaven's sake, Joe. Josie's all right, why shouldn't he see her?"

Joe took the platter to the dining room. "Let's eat."

Margie followed with the salad, and I brought in the bread and corn. We talked about other things through dinner. Afterwards, I helped Margie with the dishes while Joe watched the Whitecaps game.

"Okay, thanks for dinner," I said. "I'm off."

At the top of the stairs, Margie pulled me aside. "Give me your number," she whispered. "I'll text you the next time she's on set. If you wait by the main gate at the end of the day, you'll see her."

"Wow. Thanks, Margie."

"No problem. Don't mind Joe, he's a grouch tonight. You and Josie would be cute together."

When I got back to my suite, I lay down on the couch and wondered what was the best way to handle my second chance with Josie. Maybe Joe was right. She was becoming a distraction. Sometimes stuff like this took on its own momentum, and I ended up pursuing a goal for no other reason than it was challenging. That wasn't right when it came to people. I wouldn't go, and I'd tell Margie I had to focus on training.

My phone vibrated, and I found a message from Margie. She had sent me the photo. Josie had on a fancy wig, glittery make-up, and a gold evening gown. She looked incredibly beautiful. I wanted her so bad that I could taste it. But staring at her polished image on the phone, she seemed even more unattainable.

6

THE OUTLAW JOSIE RAY

A FEW DAYS LATER, I finished training and went to my locker. When I pulled out my phone, there was a message from Margie.

Josie's working. Did you want to know when we're wrapping up for the day?

Yes!!!

Shit. Three exclamation marks reeked of desperation. Then Margie sent me back a text full of heart and smiley emojis, and I had officially crossed into chick world. Maybe I should just wear pink tonight.

"What are you doing, Yogi?" Dirk asked me. "You just got dressed and now you're getting undressed."

"I'm taking a shower."

Reeds laughed. "Hmmm. He checks his phone and now he's taking a shower. Sounds like someone's getting laid tonight."

That was the plan anyway. I took off for the shower. When I came back, the guys were hanging around.

"Why are you still here?"

Dirk grinned. "We want to see her. Where you guys meeting up?"

"You've seen her already."

"Is it that girl from the catering place?" Reeds guessed.

"Stella? No."

His forehead creased. "Is it that physio chick, Brooke? Oh wait, I know—"

Bomber interrupted Reeder's next guess. "If we go through every chick who has a crush on him, we'll be here all night. Who is it?"

"Josie Ray."

That name didn't register with anyone except Reeds. "Oh, that long, tall drink from the pub. The one who turned you down." He laughed. "How did you get her to change her mind?"

I combed my hair. "I haven't yet. I'm going to accidentally bump into her, and we'll take things from there."

Bomber shook his head. "Like that's not borderline creepy."

"Yogi can get away with it," Reeds said. "Who wouldn't trust that angelic face?"

Dirk snickered. "Who cares if she trusts it, as long as she sits on it."

MARGIE'S INSTRUCTIONS were very specific, right down to a photo of the main gate, so I wouldn't get lost. It was a huge fenced-off compound that covered a couple of city blocks. I was standing outside, leaning against a car, when Josie finally showed.

She walked out in a red leather motorcycle jacket, ripped jeans, and another one of those faded t-shirts. I couldn't tell from here if she had no bra on. My cock rose a little just at the sight of her.

"Hey, Josie." I waved and tried to sound casual, but considering how much time and effort I had put into finding her, this felt like a big deal.

She didn't look surprised to see me and crossed the quiet street.

"Hey, if it isn't The Fast and the Fucked-Up."

"Uh, yeah. So, I was wondering if we could pick up where we left off the other night." She liked direct, so I was going for it.

"Where was that?"

"Something about fucking our brains out at my place...."

"Nope."

"Why not? This time we can take a taxi," I said. I had cabbed it here.

"Where's the blow-mobile?"

"The blo—? Oh, I left my truck at home."

"Aren't you the boy scout? Bet you have a pocket full of condoms too." She threw her head back and laughed. Her laugh was low, throaty, and contagious. I laughed too. We were getting along.

Then she started walking away, and I followed quickly.

"Josie, wait. Do you know how hard I had to work to find you? You didn't even give me your name." I fell into step beside her.

"I know. 'A' for effort. I'll let your professors at Stalker School know. Are you that desperate and dateless?"

"No. It's you. I can't stop thinking about you."

She rolled her eyes. "You need to start watching better movies, Ricky. See ya."

"It's Eric. Okay, how about dinner instead? There's an Italian place near here." Dinner would be better anyway, that was the way things normally went.

"If you're ESL, I can say 'no' in a whole bunch of languages."

"I don't get this, last week you're willing to fuck me and now you won't even eat pizza with me." And that kiss. She couldn't have forgotten how hot that was.

Josie whirled to face me. "I was willing to fuck you because I wouldn't have to see you again. But I don't want to date you—especially now that I know what a creep you are."

I reached out and put my hand on her shoulder. I felt her warm body underneath the smooth leather, and Josie softened a little at my touch. "I can do that. I can be your fuck buddy."

I leaned my head down and kissed her on the neck, up the curving line exposed by her short hair. And then the strong line of her jaw, up to her mouth. I felt desperate. When my lips met hers, everything I felt surged up. Her mouth was so soft and yielding—unlike her attitude. The attraction hit me like a tsunami. Surely I couldn't be the only one feeling this all this. I could barely pull my body away from hers.

I watched for her reaction. Josie's nostrils flared slightly, and she looked up at me. Her eyes were as dark and unreadable as ever. I was aching for her—I wanted to strip her down and kiss every inch of her hot skin. I wanted to fuck her and see her sweating and squirming under me. I wanted to make her lose control.

"Is that it? One kiss and I'm supposed to swoon?"

"Admit it, Josie. You felt something."

She took a deep breath in and I watched the rise and fall of her tits. No bra again.

She smiled. "You're right. I think I felt my stomach rumble."

"So, you're hungry. Dinner, then?"

"Man, you're persistent. Do you sell timeshares too?"

"No, I'm a Tantric sex master."

Josie laughed. "Whatever that is."

I caught her hand and lifted up to my mouth—kissing the

palm. I intertwined my fingers with hers and caressed her forefinger with my thumb. Her eyes widened like they did when I sucked her finger. I explained in a low voice, "It's when we have sex for extended periods of time—like an hour or more—to achieve sexual connection on a whole new level. It's all about prolonged orgasm for both of us."

Growing up with a yoga teacher meant there had been lots of instructional books around. Of course, I had never actually been able to hold out for an hour, but I was more than willing to try with Josie.

She shook her head and pulled her hand away. "Sounds like a crock."

I raised my hand. "Scout's honour. I always tell the truth."

Her face lost all expression. "Nobody does that, Ricky."

"This is the truth: I think you're totally unique. I'm sorry if it seems like I'm stalking you, but I haven't been able to stop thinking about you since we met. Sure, you're beautiful and I want to have sex with you, but you're also smart and funny. I'd like to talk to you and get to know you."

She gave a skeptical half-shake of the head. "You're crazy."

I waited.

"Okay. I have to eat. So, where's this Italian place?"

This huge grin from spread across my face. Finally, yes.

"So, do you see anything you like?" I asked.

We had walked to Campagnolo Roma, this Italian restaurant that Bomber recommended. I had also looked up Mexican, Vietnamese, and vegetarian places in the neighbourhood —just in case. I felt as nervous as if this were my first date. Except I wasn't nervous on my first date. It was a movie when I was thirteen, her name was Aggie, and we made out in the theatre.

But Josie was so hard to predict. She could get up and leave the restaurant on a whim, and I'd never see her again.

"Mmm, I think I'll have the pizza. It looks good." She looked over at the dinner on the table beside us. The guy eating the pizza offered her a taste, which Josie declined. I resisted an urge to insert myself between them and declare that she was mine and nobody else should look at her. What the fuck was wrong with me?

"Yeah, I might have that too."

I ordered mineral water and so did Josie. Then salads and our main courses. There was a short silence afterwards.

"So, how did you get into the stunt business?"

"I was doing stupid mountain bike tricks on Mount Seymour. This guy from a movie was hiring extras for an extreme sports scene, and I got picked. I met a stunt coordinator on the set, and he asked if I'd be interested."

She started eating a breadstick and looked around the restaurant.

"I guess it takes a lot of training."

"Yeah, for sure. Depends on the movie."

"What kind of training have you done?"

Josie blinked at me. "Do you think we could skip this whole what-I-do-what-you-do crap? And talk about something real instead."

The pizza guy at the next table had a slight smirk on his face. He probably figured he'd move in on her once this date went down the drain, which looked like it might be happening in the next five minutes. I desperately tried to think of something different to say.

"Okay, let's talk about what your spirit animal would be."

"My what?"

The pizza guy actually snorted out loud. Fuck you, buddy.

"Your spirit animal. We all have animal guides who

47

appear to help with the problems or opportunities in our lives."

"How do we find them?" Josie leaned forward and looked interested for the first time all night.

"Well, the best way would be for you to do some kind of physical journey, like a long meditation or a vision quest. An animal might appear to you in a dream." She looked dubious about this.

"But the most important thing is being conscious of what's around you—like animals reappearing in your life. Take a lion, for example. You might see a lion photo on the side of the bus, or when you turn on the TV an African nature show might be on."

"I don't have a TV," she said.

"On your laptop. Whatever. Notice what's around you and be sensitive to the signs."

Josie cracked a new breadstick in two. "There is one thing that keeps appearing in my life repeatedly and unexpectedly."

"Really, what?"

She pointed the breadstick at me. I laughed, and Josie smiled.

"If I had to guess, I would say your spirit animal is an owl," I told her.

"An owl? I think I'm more the lion type."

"A spirit animal doesn't mean an animal you identify with. It's your guide animal."

"What does an owl say about me—that I stay up all night?"

"No, it says that you're smart and knowledgeable, but you're watchful. You like to look around and take stock of things before you act. Maybe a little detached."

She closed one eye. "Hmmm."

"Is that a good 'hmmm?'"

"Yeah. You may be on to something." Then she added,

"Hey, you know what? One morning last week, I was out biking near Lost Lagoon, and these tourists had been attacked by baby owls. This woman said that the owls had actually torn out some of her hair and her scalp was bleeding."

"Did you see the owls?"

"Yeah, they were sitting up in a tree. They looked so cute I couldn't believe they were bloodthirsty killers. I read up on them and found out that they just have crappy vision so when it gets light out, they can't tell prey from the top of someone's head."

"I rest my case. Your spirit animal is an owl."

"Two killer owls do not make a case. Anyway, what's your spirit animal?"

"A butterfly."

Josie laughed loudly. I joined her, even though I suspected she was laughing at me.

"Why is that so funny?" I asked her.

"I don't know. You're this huge guy, and butterflies seem so dainty and feminine. It's the typical first girl tattoo."

I winced. Was she psychic? Maybe she was talking about herself. No tattoo on any visible body parts, but I was willing to do a full body inspection to make sure.

She had seen me checking her out. "I have no tattoos. I hate needles or anything medical at all."

Our pizzas and salads arrived. Josie dug in and began to eat. The way she ate was hot—she attacked her pizza with enthusiasm and then licked her fingers.

"Mmmm, I was hungry," Josie said after three pieces of pizza.

"I guess putting your body in danger does that. Fear makes you hungry."

Josie's dark eyes crinkled at the corners. "Actually, they

say fear is a powerful aphrodisiac. But maybe you're different."

I swallowed. Was this evening going to end up in my bed? Because I would be A-OK with that. The guys next to us got up and left. Pizza guy cast one sad glance back at Josie, but she didn't even notice. Clearly, our date was getting better all the time.

"Tell me more about your butterfly buddy."

"Well, a butterfly means change and transformation. Which makes sense since I'm going through a lot of life shifts now."

"You sound like a personal coach or guru."

I got that a lot. "I spent some time in the desert studying with a shaman."

Josie smiled. "You know, you're not at all like I expected you'd be."

"And that's good, right?"

"Yeah, I had you pegged as a jock."

"Well—I do play hockey."

"For a living?"

I nodded.

She visibly recoiled. "So, you're like some gazillionaire hockey player?"

"No. I'm not in the NHL. There are other levels, you know."

"I didn't know." She didn't ask me any more questions, and I wondered if going on about hockey was more "what-you-do" crap. But most women found hockey a turn-on.

"I played in Switzerland last year. But I'm hoping to play here at home this year."

"How was Switzerland?"

The first word that came to my mind was "lonely," but that sounded wussy. "Great. Mountains. Cowbells. Fresh air."

"All the stereotypes. How was the chocolate?"

"Okay, I guess. I only had it a couple of times. I eat pretty clean and avoid refined sugars."

"Did you want dessert or coffee?" Our server showed up exactly at that moment with little menu cards.

Josie took one and glanced at it. "I'll have the chocolate cake and an espresso. He wants to know if you have anything tofu-based."

The server began to stammer, and I ordered an herbal tea. I had this weird feeling that Josie only ordered dessert because I said I ate healthy.

Once the chocolate cake came, she ate it slowly and deliberately. "This is soooo good." She inserted a forkful of cake in her mouth, chewed, swallowed, and then stuck the tip of her tongue out to lick the fork and even her lips. Fuck. She must know what watching that tongue was doing to me. If not, she would find out once this boner raised my side of the table.

She lowered her voice to a throaty purr. "Did you know that chocolate is supposed to be an aphrodisiac too?"

Oh yeah, she knew exactly what she was doing. "Uh, no. Can I have some?"

"Eric. Of course not. That would not be healthy for you."

"Are you making fun of me? Just because I didn't eat my weight in Swiss chocolate while I lived there?"

"Well, it's my experience that people who are uptight about food aren't much fun."

"I am fun." But insisting I was fun sounded pretty lame.

When the waitress came back, Josie paid for herself despite my protests.

"I pay my own way, Ricky." The date seemed to have taken a wrong turn somewhere between hockey and chocolate. I sighed.

"So, would you like to do something else now?" I asked hopefully as we left the restaurant. My erection had eased up enough that I could walk normally, but it was still a pretty visible bulge in my jeans. Maybe she hadn't noticed though.

Josie yawned. "No, thanks. I'm tired tonight."

"Well, we can get a cab. You could come back to my place for, um, coffee."

She raised a skeptical eyebrow.

"You can trust me, I'm a gentleman."

"Then why go home with you?"

She was completely mystifying, and I let out a grunt of frustration. She walked quickly down the street, and I followed her. "Where are we going?"

"*I'm* going back to get my bike and go home. I have no idea where you're going."

"See, if you would only ride in my truck, I could have put your bike in it, and you wouldn't have had to cycle home in the dark."

She laughed. "Shame, that."

"Why wouldn't you come home with me the other night? Was it just the interlock or something else?"

"You're kind of tedious, Ricky."

"I wanted to know—for future dates."

"Aren't you optimistic? I think that if there's a sign that says sharks in the water, and you go swimming anyway, whatever happens is your own fault."

"Okay." That meant she wouldn't ride with me while the interlock was in the truck. "I'm graduating from the driver supervision program soon."

"Congratulations. I'll send a gift. Probably not champagne though."

We were almost at the gate where I'd met her. A security guard in a turban smiled at Josie and unchained the gate as she approached.

"So, when can I see you again?"

"I don't know. I'll call you." She slipped inside, and he slid the gate closed behind her.

"But Josie, you don't have my number," I called out.

"Yeah, I know." She laughed and then disappeared.

Fuck.

I stood by the gate, wondering what to do next. I'd have to catch the bus or a cab now. All that planning for nothing. But first, I could stop her when she came out and at least give her my number. Or better still, get hers.

I waited on the sidewalk. The guard slid the chain link fence back, and there was the loud roar of an engine. In the fading twilight, Josie rode out on a motorcycle as red as her jacket. She leaned expertly to one side and accelerated onto the side street, and then disappeared onto Hastings Street like a modern day action hero.

Could she be any more fucking cool?

7

FATE AND KARMA

I OPENED up my locker before lunch and checked my phone. Messages, but none from Josie. I threw the cell back in and slammed it shut. How exactly did I think she was getting my number anyway? Just because she looked like a superhero didn't mean she was one. I was holding out the hope that Margie might be involved somehow. Too bad I hadn't seen Margie lately, but both she and Joe had been working long hours.

"Something wrong?" Bomber asked.

Dirk snickered. "It's his big crush, he's waiting for a call from her."

I shook my head. "This is brutal. I hate feeling helpless."

"I'm sure Yogi is familiar with the concept of karma. How many girls did you say you'd call and then never did?" Reeds wondered.

"That's not the same." I considered this. "Okay, maybe it is. But what are you supposed to say afterwards if she asks if you're going to call? No? That would be way harsh." But the Josie situation wasn't the same because we hadn't had sex yet. Maybe this was worse—I was getting rejected on the basis of my personality.

Bomber shook his head. "This chick is messing with you, buddy. It's not going to end well. Women who play games are the worst."

Dirk laughed. "Yeah, but the ride can be fun."

I had to leave training early that day. My agent was in town, and we were meeting for coffee in the afternoon. You could always tell how important you were to your agent based on the kind of meeting you got. Meals were big; when Lance wanted to sign me, he took me and my parents out for dinner. But I wasn't complaining, I'd been phone-calls-only for years now so coffee was a step up. Besides, I got how important I was in the universe of a big sports agent.

I had to drive downtown since we were meeting at Lance's hotel. I parked on the street, fed the meter, and walked the three blocks to the Hotel Georgia. It was a great sunny day, and there were lots of people out. I was almost at the hotel when I heard a familiar low throaty laugh. I spun around and saw a bunch of couriers sitting in the sunshine on a marble building ledge.

And Josie was in the middle of them. She was wearing black shorts and colourful spandex layers on top. She was leaning against a pillar, completely relaxed—the only woman among a crew that looked like the cast from a Max Mad movie with body armour and layered clothing.

"Hey, Josie," I called out.

She looked up at me and lifted her sunglasses. "Oh hey, butterfly."

All the guys turned to check me out. Her casual greeting made me angry. Here I had been mooning over her, while she clearly hadn't given me another thought since our dinner. Still, I wasn't going to call her out in front of her tribe. I swallowed my irrational anger.

"Can I talk to you for a sec?"

"Sure."

She straightened up lazily, brushed herself off, and walked over. She faced me, but her mirrored metallic lenses weren't giving me any hint of her thoughts. Again, I was struck by her absolute confidence. I'd found her again in completely different circumstances, but she offered no explanation or apology.

I opened my mouth to complain that she hadn't called me, but then shut it. She was wearing a vest that had pens clipped to it, so I reached over and pulled one out. I grabbed her wrist in its black fingerless glove, extended her arm, and then wrote my phone number on her bare skin.

I put the pen back in her vest. That was a little trickier, and the sides of my fingers lingered against her breast. Josie's lips parted slightly as she breathed in. I leaned over until my cheek was brushing against her soft hair and my mouth touched the warm skin of her perfectly-shaped ear.

"You and me," I whispered. "It will be incredible."

Then I walked away. I could hear the voices of the guys and Josie's sarcastic tones, but I didn't turn around. If she was into playing games, I was into winning games.

"ERIC, YOU'RE LOOKING GOOD," Lance told me. He meant fitness-wise, of course. If he wasn't making tons of dough as an agent, he could have been one of those guys at the fair who guess your weight... and your body fat percentage and conditioning level. There was no fooling Lance if you were getting out of shape.

"You were right about Tony. It's not only fitness; the guy is into every aspect of playing. I'm so ready for this season."

"Yeah, I'm glad you took my advice. Tony's kept me

apprised of how you're doing. He thinks you're a very hard worker."

That was a huge compliment and not one I'd ever heard from Tony himself. I grinned.

"I wanted to tell you, I have been making a few phone calls—trying to get you into a better situation than the Vice. I might have a team back East, but you burned a few bridges."

I nodded. I was well aware that I screwed up badly enough that many GMs wouldn't consider having me on the team, even after a good season in Europe.

"Of course, there are pros and cons to every situation. With the Vice, they're crappy and you won't get great coaching, but you could still work out with Tony. And you'll get more minutes. There won't be any playoffs though."

"You make it sound like I've made the team already."

"From what Tony says, your game is back and your attitude has done a 180-degree turn. Look, you sacrificed some money to do this thing, so I'm sure you want it too. So, let me lay out what can happen."

Lance leaned forward. He loved this stuff—scenarios. He played high stakes poker because he believed he was good at assessing situations.

"One option: you do good. You have a great season, show people your scoring touch is back and you're keeping your nose clean. Then, at the end of the season, we've got tons of choices. A better AHL team or even an NHL tryout. That's what we're aiming for. Hell, we might even see some interest in January or February when some injury-ridden team is looking for help." Then he scowled. "Of course, it's not a sure thing. I don't want to get your hopes up. You might only get a good AHL career out of this, but it'd be similar money to Europe."

He held up two fingers. "Next option: you have a so-so season. Good, but not really turning any heads. Less options, maybe another AHL team if you stay clean, but probably back to Europe. You rolled the dice, but let's face, it you're getting too old to be a rookie anymore."

I sat back. Yeah, anywhere else in the world, 23 would be young—but not in hockey. Even though I had taken a half-season off and my body had less wear and tear on it, I was still competing with guys two or three years younger. Who had better reputations.

"I don't have to tell you what option three is. Don't go there."

Option three was me screwing up again. Boozing and fucking around. Crapping the bed on my last chance to make the NHL. And possibly even fucking up so badly that I couldn't go back to Europe. But I wasn't going there again, I'd learned to tame that side of myself. As long as I could keep it under control when I was under real pressure.

Lance frowned at me. "Is this going to be an issue for you? Especially playing for a party-hearty team like the Vice. I told you—there's one team in New York State that might give you a tryout."

I shook my head. "No. I really want to stay here."

"I get it. Family support and all that."

Yeah. That was part of it.

THE OTHER PART of it was no longer leaning against a polished marble wall when I got out. Josie and her buddies had taken off, and the only sign they had ever been there was a crumpled Starbucks takeout cup. Would she even call me? Or would she wash my number off her arm when she went home with one of those skinny bike jockeys?

After talking to Lance, the importance of this season loomed even larger. He might think I was a shoo-in to make the Vice, but I wasn't as confident. I decided to head back to the gym and do some more work.

Tony was still there, of course. He gave me a head nod when I walked in, and I wondered if this had been a test too. Seeing whether I would make up the two hours I had missed. Tony was such a master of psychology that was impossible to stay ahead of him.

As I got changed, I wondered what would have happened if I had hooked up with Josie instead of coming back. Maybe women were trouble. But when I closed my eyes, I imagined her half-naked, pressed up against the smooth marble wall with my cock pounding into her. Her head would be back and she'd be a screamer for sure, because she didn't give a shit about what other people thought. When I imagined us together, it wasn't about how good it would feel to fuck her—that was a given—but how good it would be to make her feel something. I wanted to rock her world and shatter that chill exterior.

I did a light workout, and then focused on my stretching. Tony came in to see me after he was done with his other clients.

"How did your meeting with Lance go?"

"Fine. He told me how great you think I am," I joked.

Tony grimaced. "He shouldn't have done that."

"Why not? Isn't a little encouragement a good thing?"

"I think players work harder in an atmosphere of uncertainty. Being too comfortable leads to complacency." Suddenly he smiled. Tony's smile was a little crooked, like it was rusty from disuse. "You know, Eric. I don't think I've discussed my philosophies of sport so much with anyone before."

I smiled back.

"One thing I encourage all my players to do is to consider their careers after hockey. Is that something you've done?"

I shook my head. "I guess it's taken me so long to climb back up the mountain that I can't see beyond the peak."

"You should think about it. Most guys get a pro career that's only a few years tops at any level. That's not going to set them up for life. It's not uncommon for players to become depressed once their career is over, because they've done no preparation. It's good to have something else to look forward to—in your case, it may alleviate your fears."

I nodded, but I was surprised that he had identified fear as one of my issues. I tried to be fearless out on the ice, but maybe he was right. I never thought beyond making the NHL. Suddenly, an idea occurred to me. "What would it take to work with you?"

Tony's eyes widened. He didn't reply right away, and he seemed to be actually considering this. "Well, your yoga background is intriguing...and you've read a lot about sports psychology. But to be honest, most guys in my business have some kind of degree in the field." He lifted his shoulders. "If not with me, personal training might be a good fit for you. I'll put together some information for you. But like most things, having been successful in hockey will ease whatever you do afterwards."

That's what everything hinged on—how successful I was this time. At least he wasn't saying I had to make the NHL, only that it would be easier.

"Tony, do you think that under pressure, we all revert to our true selves? I've worked so hard not to let my anger rule me. I think of it as the red side, but it's like that rage is always there. It's one thing to train and scrimmage—but in a real game, when things matter, it's different. And Lance underlined how important this season will be for me. So when everything is on the line, how will I keep my emotions in check?"

He stared at me, deep in thought. Then he answered.

"You can't. And you shouldn't. The best players have rage and unpredictability. And they do cross the line sometimes, because they want it so much."

"But, once I cross that line—" Wouldn't everything fall apart then? One lapse and I could be back at the bottom.

"It's wrong to injure someone deliberately. But in hockey, a little fear will keep your opponents a bit unsettled, maybe they'll give you that extra space you need to make a play. Our game has violence in it. That's inherent. Sure, it's going to be in direct contradiction to some of the philosophies you've studied, but that's hockey."

I didn't have trouble hitting guys, and I wasn't above a little stick work. And I had fought too. But Switzerland had been different—the bigger ice meant less crashing in the corners and a passing game that had suited me. Was I ready for the hard-driving North American style again?

"Besides, Eric, what is your true self? You played hockey for years without crossing any boundaries. Then after your accident, you began to have control problems—that's what you need to examine." He was right. But I hated going there. It was over, and the farther away it got, the less I had to remember.

8

A VERY PARTICULAR SET OF SKILLS

I WAS ALMOST asleep when my phone dinged. I cursed myself for forgetting to mute it and reached over to the bedside table to shut it down. It was 11:30. I squinted at the screen.

Unknown caller. *You still up?*

I answered, *Who is this?*

Hoot.

I sat up in bed. *Josie?*

The one and only.

I'm up. Everything was up, including my hopes.

Want company?

Yes. God, yes. Fuck, yes. Yes! I did a fist pump.

I sent her my address and told her to come around to the back door. Joe was home, but he went to bed early and I didn't want to disturb him. She didn't answer. She must have been getting ready.

I sprung into action. First I took a quick shower, then I gathered up my clothes and threw them into the hamper. I didn't have clean sheets, so I tried to smooth out the ones on the bed. The room wasn't that messy, but it smelled a little like hockey gear, so I opened the back door. The night was warm, so I went up on the deck. I'd be able to hear Josie's motorcycle better that way.

The moon was nearly full, and it glowed hazily through some clouds. I remembered when I had done my first night exploration in the desert. The moon had been so bright that it was like daylight. Although the desert was full of creatures, I had felt at one with them all. The spirituality in my soul was still so strong when I was out in nature, but it always became submerged when I was inside. It was that constant battle inside me—between the person I wanted to be and the person I was.

I felt a softness brushing against my arm. It was Misty. She wasn't really supposed to be outside, but Joe let her onto the deck if he was there. I stroked her back, and she arched into my hand.

"That's sickeningly adorable."

I looked up. Josie was standing there.

I had this rush of satisfaction that she even showed up. She was wearing her usual outfit, but instead of a leather jacket she wore a short jacket with metal studs all over it.

"Hey, where did you come from? I didn't hear your bike or anything."

"That's one of my superpowers, I appear and disappear at will."

"I've seen the disappearing part enough times."

She laughed. "So, did you set up that scene with the cat? As a panty-melter?"

I stood up and walked over to Josie. I lifted her chin and planted a hard kiss on her lips. "I don't need props to melt underwear."

"You're a big talker."

"Let me back it up." I held her hand and led her down the stairs into my room. Misty followed us, and I shooed her back upstairs. Josie was looking around, but she didn't say a word.

"No insults?" I wondered.

"Not really. It looks generic here. Nothing personal, except the health food." She motioned towards the protein powder, fruit, and the blender.

"I got here less than a month ago, and I don't know how much long—"

Josie planted a quick kiss on my mouth. "Let's not talk. Let's just be."

I wanted to know so much about her, but she was here, and I wasn't going to push for more.

Josie started to take her jacket off, but I stopped her.

"No. Let me. I've wanted to undress you so much." I went behind her and slowly pulled her jacket off. Then I kissed the back of her neck, that bare place between where her short hair ended and her collar began. I stuck out my tongue and tasted her, the warm salty taste of her skin. I ran my hands down her shoulders and along her bare forearms. She felt tense.

I took the bottom of her t-shirt and pulled it up. Her back was bared to me and her skin was golden and perfect. I put my hands back on her shoulders, dug my thumbs into her trapezoids, and massaged the tension out. Josie began to soften and relax, swaying slightly as she stood there. Then I leaned down and kissed my way down her spine, resting between her shoulder blades to inhale her scent. She wore no perfume and smelled spicy and primal. I kept kissing down to the place where her hips flared out and her jeans began. I laid my mouth hungrily along her exposed skin until she let out a little gasp.

"I want to kiss every part of you," I whispered as I stood up.

I rested my chin on her shoulder and looked down. Her dark nipples were already puckered with excitement, and her breasts sat high on her chest. I put my hands on her waist and let them move up her ribs one by one, and finally I stroked the undersides of her breasts with my fingers and watched her nipples harden even more. I took one breast in in each hand, cupping their soft weight in my palms. Josie leaned her head back against me and arched her back. I squeezed gently, relishing the feeling of her naked flesh.

She pressed her ass against my cock, but I was determined to take it slow. A quick fuck wasn't going to impress Josie. I squeezed the hard points of her nipples, and she groaned out loud.

I reached down and caressed her flat stomach, feeling the muscles flexing under my touch. I put my finger in the tiny indentation of her navel, and she squirmed and giggled. She was ticklish, a fact I put away in my tiny store of Josie-knowledge.

I undid her heavy belt buckle and then her jeans. I bent down to peel them off and was rewarded by the sight of the red thread of a thong between two round ass cheeks.

"Your ass is incredible," I told her, bouncing her cheeks in my hands.

Josie stepped out of her jeans and sandals and turned around.

"It's my turn now." Her voice was hoarse. She pushed me onto the bed, then straddled me and yanked off my t-shirt, tearing it in the process.

"Hope that wasn't your favourite," she said as she tossed it onto the floor. She ran her hands over my shoulders and then down the slope of my pecs.

"Oh, very nice."

She was looking down at my body with a slight smile. But my view was equally good—Josie, naked except for her tiny red thong, her skin glowing in the lamplight. She bent her head down and sucked on my nipple, causing a spiral of vibrations through my body. She moved to the side of me for better access. Then she kissed a trail down to my stomach, and then ran a finger down the line of hair. My cock twitched in anticipation as her hand moved closer.

Josie pulled off my shorts and then my boxer briefs.

"Mmmhmm," she purred, and I grinned. I raised my head and put my hands behind it for a better view. Josie had her hands on my thighs, and was staring at my erect cock. All this waiting meant I was rock hard already.

"You like?" I asked her.

"Yeah, sure. Don't worry, Eric. Size isn't everything."

"Are you fucking kidding me?"

Josie threw her head back and laughed. "Your ego needs the occasional deflating."

"Not about that," I grumbled.

"Awww, are you mad? I'll kiss and make it better." Josie bent her head down, and I felt the soft touch of her lips on the side of my erection. Then the exquisite feeling of her tongue licking up and down the length of it. And finally she closed her mouth over the head of my cock and bathed it in warm wetness.

I watched Josie taking my cock in and out of her mouth, her cheek bulging when I was deep inside and her lips stretching around it as she pulled away. This was something I had been fantasizing about for weeks, but real life was even better. How could I have imagined that almost blissful expression on her face like this was the best thing she'd ever tasted? Or the gentle way she stroked my balls with her slightly calloused fingers? Her eyes opened and met mine. She knew exactly how much I was enjoying this blow job.

Too much, in fact. "Josie, stop, okay? Or I'll come...."

But she didn't stop; instead she increased the speed and pressure. I closed my eyes and let my mind fly to that perfect state of not thinking. All my consciousness was centred in my cock and the sensations of what Josie was doing to me. I could see colours swirling and feel a dizzying whirl around me. I groaned and arched my back, then I came in a waterfall burst.

After a minute, I opened my eyes and stared at the ceiling fan. Josie was lying beside me. Her tits pointed up, there was a pretty valley made by her flat abs, and she was still wearing that thong. I needed to fix that. I pulled her towards me and kissed her.

"You're so fucking sexy," I told her. I moved my mouth down to one perfect breast and took it between my lips. Her nipple was already erect, but it got even harder as I sucked. Josie began moving her hips and moaning a little, and I cupped her mound with one hand. I tweaked her nipple with my other hand and continued the hard suction that was clearly turning her on. Her thong was wet right through, and I poked my finger through the fabric.

I paused from sucking to yank her underwear off. She was completely bald down there, which was exactly what I had imagined. I fastened my mouth to her other nipple and began sucking on that. Judging from the sounds she was making, Josie's tits were very sensitive, and I wanted to get her all worked up.

"Oh yeah," she breathed. I kissed between her breasts and then moved down the middle of her until I reached her belly button. I swirled my tongue in there, and she giggled some more. Then I made it down to the Promised Land. Her folds were deep—keeping her treasures hidden. I moved down between her legs and pushed her thighs wide apart.

This moment was one of my favourites with a new

woman. They were all so different and beautiful. And Josie was extra special. Her skin down there was dark and purply. I ran a finger up and down her crinkly folds, and she trembled all over. Her clit was tiny and hidden away under its protective hood. When I probed it with my finger, she arced up like I had electrified her.

I kissed the insides of her thighs as I spread her legs wider. And then I moved down slowly, and licked along her pussy lips—tracing them in a lazy circle. I went up and down, and then pushed my tongue inside her, and Josie wriggled around. Then I started on her clit, using my tongue on the tip and circling it and sucking the whole thing. Josie stayed absolutely still, and all I could hear was her hoarse breathing and sighing. I continued to work her, but she barely made a sound. It was kind of weird, but I kept going.

Man, Josie was taking a long time to come. My tongue needed a break, so I backed off and started using my fingers instead.

Josie raised her head, and called out, "Fuck me now."

"But you haven't come yet," I protested. She had given me such an amazing blow job, and I wanted to return the favour.

"It's okay, I will when we're doing it."

"Okay." I got up and got a condom from the dresser. I slid it on. My cock was aching to get inside all the sweetness that I'd been tasting. I looked down at her lying on my bed—naked, sexy, and accessible to me. All the time, I'd spent worrying whether I'd ever get to do this and now here she was. I got up between her legs and pushed inside.

Oh fuck. She felt amazing. Hot and slick, even through the condom. I stroked my cock deep and watched her arching up.

"Yeah. Fuck me hard. Feels great."

I pulled out and then plunged back inside. Her whole body jerked with the impact, and she cried out, "Oh yes.

Yes!" Every stroke was bliss for me, and for Josie too. Instead of the tensed silence as I ate her out, now she was reacting to everything.

"Oh God, I'm coming," she moaned. I looked down at her. Her eyes were closed, and she was touching herself. Her body looked different, and I realized her nipples were soft now. Something seemed wrong. I sensed it, rather than knowing exactly what it was.

Then it hit me. Josie was faking it. This incredibly sexy woman wasn't even getting off when I fucked her.

I pulled out. She opened her eyes. "What are you doing?" she gasped. "I was so close."

"Bullshit." I yanked her legs apart and held her knees up. I went down on her again, this time gently teasing that tiny clit until it began to swell and blossom under my tongue. Josie began to twist and squirm, but I kept her pinned to the bed and went at her determinedly. I kissed, sucked, and tapped that little button over and over. I ignored her moans and protests, instead watching her body's reactions. Her little nipples began to harden up again and then her whole body tensed and she pushed her pussy right up into my mouth. I worked her even harder, taking her whole clit in my mouth and trying to suck it right off her. I pushed a finger into her and felt her clamping down on it and then flexing and spasming. I could feel an extra flow of moisture inside her too. She was really coming now.

Josie moaned incoherently, her whole body flopping around as she recovered. I rubbed my hands all over her body, feeling the flexing of her stomach muscles and then pinching those tell-tale nipples. She opened her eyes, and they were unfocused.

I cradled her in my arms. I thought everything about her was straightforward, but she was complicated in ways I couldn't understand. To find out that she was vulnerable when it came to sex only made me want her more.

"Oh my God, Eric," she whispered.

"Don't lie to me when we have sex," I told her.

"Okay." Her voice was gentler than I'd ever heard it.

9

HARDER, BETTER, FASTER, STRONGER

MY COCK HAD SOFTENED a little in the time it took me to make Josie come, so I stripped off the old condom and tossed it in the trash. I kissed Josie and began feeling her up. Her tits, her firm thighs, and best of all—that luscious ass. She was into it too, running her hands all over my chest and squeezing my ass too.

"Your body is so hard—like you're made of titanium." She laughed. My cock got titanium-hard again, and I pushed it against her flat tummy.

I kissed her again. "You want to fuck now? Or should we try some other fun stuff?" I nudged her clit with my finger.

Her eyes widened. "Uh, no. I think I'm good for now."

But I was determined to make her come again—this time on my cock. I pulled on another condom. I moved her around to a hands-and-knees position and knelt behind her. Josie's ass was sticking up in the air, and I kissed each cheek. She turned her head and watched me, wordless.

I opened her up and slid my cock into her pussy once more. She felt even better this time—slicker and softened up. I plunged deep into her, enjoying every sensation from this angle including her spectacular ass pushing up against my abs. Once I got a rhythm going, I reached down and grabbed her hanging tits. They felt good bouncing back and forth in my hands as I thrust my cock in and out.

Josie began to grunt rhythmically whenever I went deepest into her. She was working hard to meet my every motion, pushing her hips and thighs up. In the dim light of my bedroom, I could see the beads of sweat forming on her smooth skin. I bent down and licked the sweat off her neck. She turned her head and looked back at me, and her face was contorted with desire. Her nipples were hard against my palms and I moved my fingers down until I was pinching them. I squeezed them up against her chest, relishing the feel of her soft flesh. Josie put her head back and moaned.

"Do you like that, baby?" I whispered into her ear, and she only grunted. "Do you like it a little rough?"

It seemed like she did. Sex between us seemed almost like a battle, with our bodies slamming hard into each other. But she turned to me, her dark liquid eyes met mine, and she shook her head.

I let go of her nipples instantly. I held her hips instead and didn't miss one in-and-out stroke. Then I ran one hand down towards her pussy. In the smooth folds, I found that tiny clit again and used her juiciness to coat my finger before I began a gentle friction.

Josie began to pant. The noises coming out of her were completely authentic this time. She made these low animal sounds that were a total turn-on. It was like she was finally letting herself relax into everything between us. My cock was enjoying every stroke, but my head was more into making her let down her guard. She couldn't enjoy sex without giving up the tight control she held over every part of herself.

The slick noise of my finger rubbing her clit got increased, along with her moans. My cock felt her spasms as the walls of her pussy tightened around me, and I fucked her faster.

"Unnnh, ohhhh," Josie's incoherent moans were almost as hot as knowing I was making her come again.

She collapsed a little, resting her head and arms on the pillow, but keeping her ass high. I pulled out, and she lay down completely. Since I had come once, I could hold out longer. I turned her over onto her back and she looked up with blank eyes.

"God. More?" she asked, as I raised one of her legs high. I liked seeing her pussy spread like that, reddened from all the sex, but still shiny with need. I eased my cock back inside, and she whimpered softly.

"This time, I want to watch your face as you come. As I make you come."

"Ohhh," she exhaled, and her eyelids fluttered.

I bent my head down and sucked on her nipple pulling it up into hardness. The sucking seemed to set off a vibration going straight to her pussy, which twitched and trembled and felt incredible. I sat up and maneuvered my hips until my pelvic bone was contacting her clit with every thrust. Josie's face tensed, and she moaned aloud again.

"Let go," I urged her. "Be in the moment."

The lines in her forehead smoothed out, and she visibly relaxed. I pulled both her legs into the air and spread them, then gently rocked my pelvis against hers. The slight, steady motion felt so good for me—in, out, in, out—our bodies joined and united. And it felt good for Josie too. Instead of fighting every sensation, her body was accepting and enjoying every movement. She made her sexy little grunts, and I answered her with noises of my own. It felt so good that I knew I was going to come soon.

But I held back. I watched her, and when she lifted her chin and her lips parted, I knew she was close. She began pushing her body into mine, tiny movements but every one of them electrifying our nerve endings.

"Oh, yes. Yes." She inhaled one huge breath and a flush came over her face. I bent down and kissed her. Her mouth was as soft and yielding as she felt inside. I lifted my head and thrust into her one last time and then came in a huge explosion. Then I collapsed on top of her.

When I opened my eyes, Josie was staring at me. I kissed her nose.

"You look cute when you come," I told her.

"You look scary," she replied. "I thought you were going to explode. There's this vein." She put her hand up and circled my temple.

"Ungrateful," I told her. I rolled off her and cradled her in my arms.

"As promised, that was incredible." She chuckled. "No lie."

I wanted to ask her why she had faked it before. But why spoil the moment? I kissed her instead. It felt so good to finally have her here beside me. I nuzzled her neck, and she squirmed. I wasn't letting go though. We lay there in silence for a long, sweet moment.

I got up and went to the bathroom to get rid of the condom. When I came back, she had picked up her clothes. She yanked her jeans on, bare-assed, and then stuffed her thong into her pocket. Then she pulled her t-shirt on.

"Why are you getting dressed? Why don't you stay over?"

She did up her belt. "I like to sleep in my own bed."

"But I want you to stay over." I sat down on the bed. Then I hooked one of her belt loops and pulled her over. "We can fool around in the morning too."

Not to brag, but it seemed pretty clear that I was giving her something that other guys hadn't. The least she could do was to stay. I wanted to sleep with her and feel her next to me all night.

She bent down and kissed me, then patted me on the head. "Don't worry, after sex like that, I'll be back. Same time tonight?"

That was more like it. "Fuck, yeah!"

"That's the idea, Ricky."

She walked out without saying goodbye. If not for the completely drained feeling in my body, she could have been a dream. I collapsed back on the pillows and shut my eyes.

"WHAT'S DIFFERENT TODAY?" Tony asked after our morning ice session.

"Nothing," I told him. Well, there was one thing, but it had nothing to do with hockey. I was trying really hard not to think about Josie and to focus. But everything that happened last night, and the fact that I was going to see her again tonight—I felt great.

He shook his head. "You're playing really well today. There's a smoothness and a confidence about you. You're in the zone. Why?"

"It's a girl," I muttered. Was I turning red?

Tony raised his eyebrows. "Really? That's interesting. I never considered that side of the equation."

I was hoping we were going to drop the discussion there, but he motioned me into his office.

"So, you're in a new relationship? You haven't been here that long."

I looked at the floor. I was happy to call it a relationship, but I was pretty sure that she wouldn't. "Well, I don't know exactly what I'm in...."

Tony continued, as casually as if he were talking about the weather. "Have you not been having sex recently?"

"Jesus, Tony. Do I really have to talk about this stuff?"

"Well, normally no. Usually the only sex talk I'd have with a player would be if he were partying too hard and sucking on the ice. But since this seems to be impacting your performance positively, I'm interested in why."

He waited, but I really didn't know how to phrase things.

He cleared his throat. "If this discussion makes you uncomfortable, then I'd urge you to think about this on your own. Try to figure out why things have changed and how to achieve that confidence on your own."

I tried to express my thoughts. "Having sex is not a problem for me. I can have sex when I want." I paused. "But Josie's totally different. She's special. I can't really explain it."

Being with Josie did make me happy, but I wasn't sure exactly why. I mean, she was beautiful and sexy, but it was more than that. Was it because I had to work so hard to get anywhere with her? Or was it something special about Josie? I envied her confidence, which was off the charts. I liked the fact that she didn't give a shit about hockey and didn't add to the pressure on me.

This whole deal was so confusing. But Shaman Felix would probably wonder why I needed to tear apart something good. *Relax and enjoy, Eric. Don't feel you have to analyze life.*

Tony was wrong. What Josie made me feel was something I would never be able to replicate on my own.

10

JOSIE AND THE PUSSYCAT

"YOUR CAT'S A PERV," Josie said as she and Misty walked out of the bathroom. I was a perv too, because I'd been lying in bed and waiting to see Josie to come out. Naked, she moved as naturally as when she was fully dressed—like a panther or cougar. We'd been seeing each other for a few weeks now, and I still couldn't tear my eyes away when she was in the room.

"Did Misty watch when you flushed the toilet?"

Josie nodded. "And she stared at me the whole time I was sitting there." She patted Misty anyway, and when Josie bent down, the view was awesome. The cat did one circuit of the room and then disappeared through the cat door Joe had installed when we both got sick of letting her in and out.

Josie stretched and then started looking around. "Where are my clothes?" She knelt down and peeked under the bed.

"Maybe it's a sign."

"What's a sign?"

"Not finding your clothes is a sign that you should stay over."

Josie jumped on top of me in bed. "Did you hide my clothes?"

"Maybe...."

"Eric! How old are you? Where did you put my stuff?"

I pulled her down on top of me. "C'mon, X-Ray. You said you don't have to work tomorrow. And it's Saturday, so I can set my own time at the gym. Please stay over?"

"X-Ray? Is that my hockey player nickname?"

Did she forget that was what she had called herself when we met? I remembered every single thing that had happened between us.

Josie rolled off me, but I kept an arm wrapped around her. "If you stay, I'll go to that bakery you like and get you cinnamon buns in the morning."

"Why is this such a big deal for you? We just spent hours together: we ate dinner, walked through Stanley Park, and had sex. I think that's enough."

"I want to sleep with you, feel you next to me all night, and then wake up with you. Besides it's our anniversary."

She gave me a blank stare. "What?"

"It's exactly a month ago that we went out on our first date. You know, dinner at that Italian place?"

"Is there a fourteen year-old girl hidden in that jacked body? *'Dear Diary, tonight we had our first date. Swoon.'* Then you wrote *'I'm Josie's guy!'* fifty times down the opposite page." She dissolved into giggles.

"A fourteen year-old girl?" I huffed. "That's sexist."

"Nawww. It's how I used to be at fourteen." She laughed again, but I found it pretty hard to imagine Josie as a lovesick teenager. No way.

But me as a lovesick guy? Unfortunately that was more the truth. It had been an incredible month. At first, Josie came over only at night—like a sex vampire. Once I got her to let down her guard and relax, sex got better and better.

Her early difficulties in having orgasms weren't anything we'd ever discussed, but now it was way easier. Our bodies responded to each other. It made me sweat to think that if I'd just fucked her the first time and she didn't come, she might never have come back. At least all the time I'd spent having sex with random women had paid off when it mattered.

And eventually we had moved into regular dating. It was still tough to pin her down, and she always insisted on meeting me, so I hadn't even seen her place yet. Still, it was great to go out with someone who was a lifelong Vancouverite. She knew all these cool places and things to do. We both liked to do outdoor stuff like hiking, swimming, or running. She wanted to do some hard-core mountain biking, but I wasn't going to do anything that might get me injured so close to camp.

"Okay." Josie got under the covers.

"Okay, what?"

"I'll stay over. Consider it my anniversary gift to you. But I think one month is normally the chewing gum anniversary."

I pulled her in close, so her ass was against my cock. "I think it's the latex anniversary."

"Every night is the latex anniversary for you."

"Hey, I've got an idea. Maybe we can stop using condoms. You're on birth control, right?"

She rolled over to face me. "Yeah. Hey, I have an idea too. Since I'm staying over already, maybe you could relax for one minute."

"Okay, sorry. I just wanted to let you know that I'm not, you know, having sex with anyone else."

"Considering how much we have sex, it would be a miracle if you were."

I waited but she didn't give me the same reassurance

back. Unless what she had just said meant she couldn't be having sex too. "So, does that mean—"

Josie shushed me. "Eric. Let's go to sleep now. We can hold each other and quietly appreciate how nice it all feels."

I nodded and kissed her. It was weird. For so long I had avoided saying what I knew women wanted to hear, because I didn't want to get tied down. And now that I wanted commitment, those scripted lines weren't working.

But Josie was right; I was worrying too much about the future and not appreciating the now. Her warm body next to mine felt fantastic, and she snuggled even closer.

IN THE MORNING, I woke up early. Josie was lying beside me, and I got up on one elbow to stare at her. She looked beautiful. It was like she was this talisman for me—I could relax when she was around.

Everyone thought that I was pretty laid back. But I had this constant low-grade worry about the future, specifically my hockey future. Right now, things were great because I was training hard and the only pressure was to get into better shape. But in a couple of weeks, I'd be at the Vice training camp. The pressure would be amped up then. Even the idea was starting to twist up my stomach.

I slipped out of bed and pulled on sweats and a t-shirt. I grabbed my flip-flops and wallet, then went out into the backyard. I stretched slowly, and then moved into a sun salutation. This was the best time of day, when the sun was rising and the neighbourhood was quiet. It was getting colder though, and the leaves were turning golden shades and falling. Then I sat down to meditate. Time to quiet my worries. I closed my eyes and concentrated on my breathing, on the sunlight on my eyelids, and on the peace I was still feeling. Calm.

Once I was finished my meditation, I put on my sandals and tucked my wallet in my pocket. I walked briskly to this nearby bakery. We had found it one evening when Josie got sugar cravings after I made her dinner.

When I got back inside with a paper bag of pastries, the bed was empty and the drawer where I'd stashed her stuff was slightly ajar. Shoot. How like her to take off. I had been looking forward to spending the morning with her.

Then I heard a voice in the bathroom. "Cat, you are weird." The bathroom door opened. Misty exited first and then Josie. She was dressed, and towelling her hair dry. She smiled at me, and I grinned back.

"Misty watched me shower too," Josie said.

Sounded like something I'd like to do myself. "Really? She's never done that to me."

"Maybe she's a lesbian cat, and your body is not turning her crank."

I pulled her in for hug. "As long as my body turns your crank."

Josie kissed me. "Oh, definitely. I borrowed your toothbrush."

"No problem. I'll get you one of your own for next time."

She shook her head. "Oh, Eric. Is your middle name Commitment?"

"No, it's Sky."

Her eyes widened, and she laughed.

I frowned at her. "What? That's normal where I come from."

"Yes, mythical, mystical Nelson, B.C."

"I want to take you there, you'll like it. It's a beautiful place—spiritual and welcoming."

"One sleepover and I have to meet the parents." Josie was smiling though, she didn't seem to mind my scheming.

"My mom will love you," I said.

"Apparently not your dad," she observed.

Shit. Nothing escaped her. "Well, my dad wants me to concentrate on hockey all the time. He keeps telling me it's my last chance to make it. So, he doesn't approve of any extracurricular activities."

"Ahh, like me? Awesome, I'm the sexual equivalent of taking jazz band. Let's see what you got at the bakery." She moved into the kitchen area, and I followed. I put the kettle on and put the pastries onto a plate. Then I got out the makings of my breakfast bowl.

Josie frowned. "Are you going to eat hamster food while I'm gorging on cinnamon buns? I could feel guilty."

"Are you kidding me? You have less conscience than a super-villain."

"Ya, you're right. But maybe I'll try a little of your breakfast too. Then I can have dessert. Although, it looks like you stole this stuff from a bird feeder."

She ate the oatmeal with flax, chia and pumpkin seeds that I made but passed on the boiled eggs and wholegrain toast. She looked far happier when she tore off a piece of cinnamon bun and popped it in her mouth. Then she frowned and returned to the subject of my family.

"I don't understand what more your dad could ask from you. You work out harder and eat cleaner than anyone I've ever met. And I've met some extreme people."

I exhaled. "None of it means anything unless I make the team. There will always be something I didn't do or should have done."

Josie nodded and patted my arm.

"Parents are never happy." She sounded calm, but she began tearing her cinnamon bun into smaller and smaller pieces. "Bike courier isn't exactly my dad's career of choice for me."

That was the first time she'd ever mentioned her family. I waited, but she didn't continue.

"Besides, Ricky, hockey is the Canadian dream, right? At least you're getting paid to do it."

"Yeah, but it's never enough. Europe isn't the AHL, and the AHL isn't the NHL."

"Seems like he needs to back off. Is he paying for your training stuff?"

"No, I'm using the money I saved up from last season."

"Then who cares?"

"It's not that simple, Josie. I love my parents, and I want to succeed for myself and for them too."

"Okay." That was something else I'd noticed about Josie. When she gave her opinion, she only said it once and then never argued. It was like she thought you were an idiot if you didn't agree, but she couldn't be bothered to convince you. She moved onto my lap. "You want to fool around before I go?"

I grinned. There were some things we could always agree on.

11

EASY RIDER

"BOMBER, HEADS UP," I yelled out as this big centre headed towards him behind the net. Some of these guys from junior had size, but no sense of timing, and they made out like wrecking balls out there. Bomber made a neat deke that left the kid slamming himself into the boards. A few strides and Bomber had the puck in the neutral zone.

I mirrored him on the other side of the ice, our skates gliding across the blue line at exactly the same time. Bomber went wide, and I headed straight for the net. I knew Dirk was trailing, so all I needed to do was take one defenceman out of the play, and he'd have a clear shot. I took one look over my shoulder and realized that Reeds was hustling to backcheck, and he was going to take Dirk out of the play. The d-man coming at me was slow though, and maybe I could use his indecisiveness to create a little room. I faked a move to the left and behind the net, and he started to follow me. I cut back sharply. Then, *swish*. The puck arrived on my stick, and I roofed it.

Cellies during scrimmage were for kids. I pointed at Bomber and he grinned. We skated back to the bench.

Dirk smacked me on the back. "You're on fiyah, Yogi. What's your secret?"

"Healthy living. Shit like that."

"Ugh. I'm not going to start eating your sprouted crap and doing yoga. I was hoping it was some magic pill."

Bomber shook his head. "There are no magic pills. And if there were, the League would be testing for them."

A few minutes later, we finished up and headed for the dressing room.

"I can't believe that this is the end," Dirk said sadly. "It's been great working out with you guys." Our training together was coming to an end. Reeds and Bomber were both leaving on the weekend. NHL training camps started a couple of weeks before the AHL ones. Dirk and I would still be working out, and then it would be our turn to leave. The whole place was starting to turn over as hockey season geared up.

"Nothing like the beginning of hockey season," said Bomber happily. I knew what he meant. Training was fun and stress-free, but I was starting to long for meaningful games— if I got through the tryout. Bomber was the guy I felt closest to. He had given me lots of advice and encouragement. I felt sure we'd all keep in touch.

"Don't forget about the barbeque at my place tonight," Reeds said.

"What barbeque?" I asked.

"What is wrong with your brain, Yogi? I told you a week ago. It's our goodbye bash."

"I've got plans to meet Josie. But maybe we can drop by later."

Reeds groaned. "Ever since you started dating her, it's like you're in a fog."

"All his mental energies are being drained down here." Dirk rubbed his crotch. "He's achieved nirvana."

"Actually, nirvana is a state of enlightenment beyond desire," I corrected him. Dirk threw a sweaty hockey sock at me.

But they were right. Ever since I'd started seeing Josie, I'd been in a bit of a daze. For a while, I was worried that staying up late and having strenuous sex was going to cut into my training regimen, but I'd been playing better than ever. It felt like my mind was clear and I could really focus. But I had added a pre-dinner nap into my day. You couldn't fake sleep, and as Reeds said, I'd been a little absentminded.

And I really liked hanging out with her, but I couldn't pin her down much, which was both frustrating and freeing. Reeds would say it was karma for all the women I'd brushed off when they wanted a relationship.

Today, Josie was working at some location in the valley, but we going to meet afterwards for dinner. I checked my phone but there was no message from her.

When I got out of the shower, the room was strangely empty. Usually, the guys hung around and shot the shit a little. But it looked like everyone had taken off.

Then it hit me that the guys might be planning some kind of prank, especially since I wasn't going out with them tonight. I opened the dressing room door carefully. No bucket of anything fell on my head. I peeked down the corridor, but it sounded completely empty.

I headed out to my truck. A bunch of the guys were gathered beside it, and I sped up. What the hell was up? If they were attaching dildos to the truck like I'd seen once in the A, I'd kill them.

"This is one nice ride," said Mars, one of the younger players.

"Sweetest motorcycle I've seen," Dirk chimed in.

"Dude. This is not just a motorcycle! It's a fucking Ducati Panigale. This baby could smoke any car on the road."

Bomber was as excited as I'd ever heard him. "How fast can she accelerate?"

"Zero to 100 clicks in three seconds." I could hear Josie's calm voice although I couldn't yet see her amongst the crowd. Then someone moved, and I saw her. She was leaning against her bike in a leather jacket, jeans, and aviators. The breeze spiked up her hair.

"Oooh, man. It's a beauty." Bomber was practically jizzing out there. "How did you get this bike anyway?"'

"I bought it from a little old lady who only used it to go to church on Sundays."

"No, seriously, Josie."

"I had to learn to race motorcycles for a movie, and I really liked it. Mario, the guy who taught me to ride, knew someone who wanted to sell the Ducati. So, we made a deal, and now I—" She looked up and saw me. "Oh hey, Ricky."

I pushed my way through the crowd, put my arm around her, and kissed her. It was probably the equivalent of an animal marking his territory. "You getting into trouble again?"

She leaned against me. "Always."

"Eric! You didn't tell me your girlfriend rode a Ducati." Bomber sounded shocked at my lapse. I didn't even know what kind of motorcycle it was. He kept running his hands over the leather seat and the chrome handlebars.

Reeds laughed. "If he talks about Josie, it's not going to be about her bike. But we all remember you from the pub."

"And from all the time that Fairburn spent stalk—" I jammed my elbow into Dirk's side to shut him up. "Er, I mean, *talking* about you," he finished.

Josie laughed. Not only had she heard his word slip, but she knew I had been obsessed with her anyway. How else could I have shown up outside her work site?

"Gentleman, Josie and I have plans. So, maybe you can clear out."

Dirk spoke directly to her. "Hey, Josie, we're all going out to a bbq at Reeds' place. It's a goodbye party because Reeds and Bomber are leaving. Yogi here can't come because he's too whipped. So, why don't both of you come? Please, please?"

"Yogi? Is that what you call him?" Josie laughed. "And you think I've got him whipped?"

"Hey, did I say it was a bad thing?" Dirk was eyeing her, and in her leather jacket and studded belt, she did look like a dominatrix.

She turned to me. "It's up to Eric."

I was worried that she wouldn't want to hang out with the guys, but it would be great to go. "Okay, we'll meet you there."

"Awesome," said Bomber. He was probably going to spend the evening caressing her motorcycle.

Everyone headed back to his car. I lifted Josie's face and kissed her properly this time. I could hear some rude remarks in the background, but I ignored them.

I kept her face cradled in my hand. "You came to see me. That's sweet."

"Ugh. Don't call me sweet, or I'll never do this again. I was on my way back and I figured this might save time."

"It will. You are so smart. And cute. And sweet."

She fake-punched me in the stomach. "Maybe I'll hop back on my bike and leave."

"Zero to 100 kilometres in three seconds. I could never catch up with that. How come I never get to ride your motorcycle?"

"I wouldn't let you drive it."

"Because of my driving restrictions?"

"No. Because you don't know how to handle this much

power between your legs." She rubbed my thigh as she said that, and I smiled down at her. If he had a face, my cock would have been smiling too, but instead he settled for getting hard.

I pulled her close to me. "I think I do. And I think I showed you that on Wednesday night."

Josie tried to hide her smile. I kissed her forehead and kept talking. "I don't mind if you drive. I could ride behind you." I rubbed my hand over her ass. "Right behind you."

She shook her head. "You wanna be my bitch, Ricky? Too bad, but it's not that kind of bike. It only seats one."

"Why did you get it? Other than it was fun."

"I like to do road trips. To clear out the cobwebs in my brain and be alone."

Josie made it very clear that she needed time alone, and again I worried that I was pushing her too much. But I enjoyed being with her—even beyond the sex.

"Are you sure it's okay if we go to Reeds' place? I mean, there'll probably be a lot of hockey talk, and it's mainly guys."

"I like guys."

"I don't know if I like that statement."

Josie laughed. "It beats 'I like girls.'"

"True."

She shook her head. "Seriously, if you want to do something—just say so. I'm not big on self-sacrifice. And you know I'll tell you if I don't want to do it."

"I guess. I want our times together to be fun for you."

"I'm not a princess, and I don't want you to feel whipped."

"Because if there's any whipping, I want to do it." I slapped her ass for emphasis.

"That's not going to happen," Josie said.

"Why not? I think it might be fun."

"I told you before—I'm not into pain. Not mine, anyway. Yours I can deal with."

"Why do you do stunt work then? There's so much potential for accidents and injury."

"That's why I'm good at my job. I do the maximum preparation to avoid risks. You always see those clips of fiery stunts gone wrong, but you never see the hundreds of times that things go right—except in the actual movie."

"All right. I guess I'm meeting you there, right?"

"Yup. Give me the address." I found it on my phone and showed it to her. She pulled on her helmet and fastened the straps.

"Aren't you ever going to ride with me?" Although who in their right minds would ride in a Toyota truck instead of the world's coolest motorcycle?

"Sure. When you get the training wheels off."

She roared off. Bomber was getting into his Porsche, but he watched her leave longingly. I knew that feeling well.

12

FEAR OF HEIGHTS

I SWALLOWED and looked down through the deep canyon to the river below. Way, way below. My sphincter clenched.

Josie was leaning over the side of the rope bridge and pointing. "Look! I think I can see a hawk soaring over there."

"Let's keep going," I suggested. There were more people coming and the suspension bridge was beginning to sway. It was a family and the kids were jumping and trying to rock the bridge.

She turned to stare and then giggled. "You know, for someone so big and strong—you sure seem to have a lot of fears."

I ignored that and walked swiftly to the other side. Once I was on solid ground I felt better.

"Lots of people don't like heights." No guy wanted his girlfriend to think he was a wimp. But Josie was so fearless, I was never going to play the hero in her life. She was still laughing at me.

"This is one of the secrets that Vancouverites know," Josie bragged. "Tourists pay tons to cross the Capilano Suspension Bridge, while this one is free."

"I do appreciate having my own tour guide." I grabbed her hand and kissed her on the top of her ball cap. Josie looked so cute in her hiking outfit: shirt, tank, shorts, daypack, and hiking boots. And miles of tanned leg showing.

"And I have more good news, I can route our hike so that we don't have to cross that bridge on the way back."

"I wasn't that scared," I protested. Truth be told, I was a little edgy already.

After hiking for an hour, we broke for lunch. We sat on a rock in the fall sunshine. I took out the sandwiches I had made, and Josie brought out drinks.

"Even your sprouted monstrosities taste good up here," Josie said. But she ate her whole sandwich. We ate most of our lunch in silence.

"Something bothering you?" Josie asked.

I nodded. "My tryout with the Vice starts tomorrow. I'm kind of nervous."

"Why? You're in great shape now, aren't you?"

"The best ever. Tony has been amazing." I'd thanked him yesterday, and we had one last talk about psychology and maintaining the right attitude during my tryout camp. And we'd agreed to stay in touch during the season—wherever I ended up.

"Then why sweat it?" Josie gave a casual shrug and then lay down, closing her eyes and basking in the sunlight.

Did she not get this? It was only going to be the most important two weeks of my life. If I made the Vice, I could still get a crack at the NHL. "It's a huge deal. I mean, everything I've done for the past two years—getting straight, playing in Switzerland, training with Tony—it's all been for this."

Josie opened her eyes. "It's not life or death, Ricky. What happens if you don't make the team?"

"I don't know. I try not to think about that possibility." I wanted to remain positive, and not even consider failure.

She sat up. "But imagining the worst can make you feel more relaxed. When I'm working, I spend a ton of time envisioning all the bad outcomes and how I would react to them. Then I put aside my nerves so I can relax and do things well. You can't overthink the physical."

"Jesus, Josie, don't you think I know that?" At Tony's I was the one who explained the whole subconscious performance thing.

For me, playing hockey was like driving. There were too many random factors to consciously consider at once. A defenceman coming at you from one side, where your linemates were going to be in ten seconds, what the goalie's tendencies were. If you thought about all that shit, you were screwed. Let your subconscious mind do all the work and your body would do the rest. And that was where it all started to go wrong for me, once I realized the importance of what I did on the ice. Conscious thought was death to my game.

She stood up and brushed off her shorts. "Let's keep going."

"Wait, I'm sorry. I didn't mean to snap at you."

Josie's gaze was level and honest. "I'm not mad. But I'm not enjoying this conversation." She began packing up the lunch stuff.

"You know, you could be more supportive." I packed up the garbage.

She rolled her eyes. "I am. But if you just want to bitch, get a real problem. You play hockey for a living. It's not brain surgery."

"Unlike the movies? That's really important stuff." Usually I liked Josie exactly the way she was, but right now I wished she were more like a regular girlfriend—sympathetic and caring. Sunny was the only other girl I'd dated seriously, and she would have been making a big fuss once she saw how I worried I was.

Josie didn't even answer. She put her pack back on and began walking away. Leaving was her answer to every problem. But seeing her disappear made me realize that I was being a huge idiot.

"Stop." I grabbed my pack and ran after her. She didn't turn around, so I had to catch up and spin her around. I held her in my arms. "I am so, so sorry. I'm stressed out and taking it out on you. And you're the best thing in my day."

She scowled at me. I tilted my head and kissed the straight line of her mouth. I gently nipped at her lips until I felt the stiffness in her body yielding to mine. Finally she put her arms around my neck, and kissed me back fully. This was more relaxing to me than any words.

Even after a long hike in the North Shore Mountains, I was still nervous and fidgety inside.

"You want to get dinner now?" Josie asked when we got to the trailhead.

"Naw, I want to go home, relax, and get prepped for tomorrow."

She squinted at me, shrugged, and then turned away. "No problem. See you later."

It wasn't like I was trying to hurt her or anything, but Josie's lack of a reaction really bugged me. I watched her as she fastened her helmet on, kicked her bike off the stand, and then mounted it and took off. She never even looked back at me.

If I could have caught her and changed my mind, I would have. Being with Josie would be more relaxing than being alone. But having been so irritable, I was now stuck with a long evening. I got in the truck and noticed that my dad had called. He would undoubtedly have a ton of advice for tomorrow.

THE CONTRAST between training with Tony and the Vice camp was like night and day. I shouldered my hockey bag and walked into an arena that looked like it was at least fifty years old. Not that it mattered, since some of the older arenas had the best ice, but I wondered if the management team would be old school as well. I certainly hadn't heard anything good yet.

I was nervous whenever I walked into a dressing room for the first time. From when I was a kid trying out for rep hockey, every year I would push open that heavy door and wonder what was waiting for me. A great bunch of guys who would be my new best friends? Assholes who would bully the younger guys? Coaches who were nice guys or screamers?

The vibe in this room was fear—sweaty, stressed-out fear. A lot of these guys were just like me, and the Vice was their only chance to make the AHL.

There were some confident guys in the room too. The guys who knew they were going to make the team. At the AHL level, there were guys on two-way NHL contracts who were getting developed. The NHL team paid their salaries, so they were on the Vice for sure. These same guys would get called up during the year. And I wanted to be one of them more than anything. But first, I had to make the team.

The morning was pretty standard. Paperwork, fitness testing, and then lunch. Again the contrasts were striking. Whereas Tony's fitness testing was exhaustive and input directly to a computer, here everything was clipboards and old-school measurements. We did Wingates again, but this time I managed not to barf. I was feeling really good and really strong after my hard training. And I could tell by the reactions of the assistant coach that my scores were very good.

Lunch was a bunch of carbohydrate crap that Tony would have kicked into the garbage. I managed to cobble together something half-healthy from the cafeteria options. I ended up sitting beside this young guy with wide eyes and a mess of brown hair.

"Hi, I'm Marcus Fox. My teammates call me Foxy."

"Hey. Eric Fairburn."

"You're in great shape," he told me. "You were killing those fitness evaluations."

"Thanks." Foxy was on the skinny side, but that could be deceiving. A lot of the leaner guys were speed demons on the ice. But size helped when you got hit or wanted to deliver hits.

Foxy told me he had played in the ECHL last year, but he was hoping to make the A this season. He was a couple of years younger than me, and this was his first tryout.

"You've done this before, right?"

I nodded. But it wasn't exactly the same. Before I was under contract to an NHL team. I was one of the confident, can't-miss guys. This time, I had a lot to prove. "I played a season and a half in the A before."

"So, you got any advice for me?"

I shook my head. This guy was so naïve that he was asking me straight up for help. I lowered my voice. "Well, first off—it's not like a regular team. Don't forget, you're in competition with everyone here. So you probably shouldn't be asking me for advice. What if I steered you wrong—just to get rid of you?"

His eyes widened. "Shoot. I never thought of that. But you wouldn't do that, would you?"

I laughed. "No, I wouldn't. My advice would be—no hot-dogging."

"What do you mean? We have to show how good we can be, don't we?"

I nodded. But if you were a big show-off, nobody wanted to play on a line with you. Everyone else wanted to look good too. So it was better to play well, but in a subtle way. The coaches would notice things like your work rate, how you made your line better, your defensive play, and your assists—so scoring pretty goals wasn't as big a deal. Of course, I had a rep as an offensive player, so I'd have to score the goals too. It was going to be a difficult balance, but I was looking forward to it. It was satisfying to play games that counted after all this training.

"You want to look good, but make the players around you look good too. That way they'll pay you back," I explained. Nobody would sabotage you in what was essentially a team game. But good players could do subtle things to make you look bad.

He looked worried now. I gave him a little shove.

"Forget it, Foxy. Just relax and you'll be fine."

Having someone around who was more nervous than me was calming. After lunch, we got dressed and went out on the ice. In the morning, we'd been divided into groups, but now I could see that there were about 40 guys here. Shit. That meant that almost half of us were getting cut. I hoped like hell that my invitation to camp hadn't been some big favour for my agent or my coach in Switzerland. But I wouldn't be able to tell until we began our drills and scrimmages.

The head coach had been around during the fitness testing, but he was mainly observing and not saying much. Now he was centre ice, and everyone's eyes were on him.

Robert Pankowski was a big beefy man with a red face.

Thanks to my new stalking skills, I'd looked him up online already. He had played two seasons in the NHL, as a forward for the Flyers. Since then, he'd been working his way up the coaching ladder—first in junior, then the AHL. This was his first AHL head coaching job, and he'd been here for two seasons already.

"Okay, boys. We're putting together a systems team. We're going to be looking for players that can play a two-way game, so keep that in mind. I want to see hustle at both ends of the rink.

"This is how it's going to go. We've got a big group, so we're doing some initial evaluations, and the first set of cuts will be on Wednesday or Thursday. Then another set next Monday. We have exhibition games the following weekend, and we'll decide our final roster after those games.

"Questions?"

Nobody had any. The coach was pretty intimidating. He had been a tough guy when he played.

The assistant coaches, Ian Lee and J.P. Tellier, ran us through a series of increasingly complex drills. I felt fit, and my confidence kept growing. There were a few guys here who were no-hopers, but most of the guys were decent players. Foxy turned out to be speedy with soft hands, and since he played right wing, I got to do a few line rushes with him. We worked pretty well together.

Just like in training, I could distinguish the NHL guys right away. Of course, unlike Bomber or Reeds, these were guys who had just gotten cut, so they weren't quite as good. But they were the best players in camp.

I felt good though. I was right up with them, and my conditioning was excellent. Now that I could see everyone else, I had a better idea of where I stood, and things looked pretty positive.

We wrapped up after our afternoon session, and the

coaches were huddling already. I got changed and headed home. I looked in the fridge, which was fully loaded. I'd done a big grocery shop, figuring I'd be exhausted this week. I wasn't tired tonight though. I'd put in a full day's work, and it had gone pretty well. But something was missing.

I picked up my phone and sent a text.

Hey beautiful. How about if your stupid boyfriend makes you dinner tonight?

I waited a few minutes, and then heard back.

Which stupid boyfriend?

I laughed. Josie wasn't one to hold a grudge, but that didn't mean I should keep pushing her. *The one who acted like a brat when you took him on a great hike yesterday.*

Oh, you mean Eric. What's for dinner?

Chicken, brown rice, grilled veggies, quinoa salad.

And…?

Dessert?

I'll be over in an hour.

I'd have to go out and buy some dessert, but I had time. Time enough to change my bed sheets too. Now that I was over my initial nerves, I wanted to relax in the best way— with Josie.

13

ISLAND OF THE MISFIT TOYS

TWEEEEEEET!

"Okay, ladies. Once more—but this time, give it some goddamn effort."

Coach Panner turned out to be an old-school coach who yelled and insulted us all day long. Although I liked him at the beginning, he turned out to be every bad thing that Dirk had said. Coach Panner reminded me of my first rep hockey coach, a guy who was always on the brink of a heart attack because he screamed his way through every game.

"Fairburn! Harder. Pretend you care."

It was weird that he was calling me out. Thanks to my work with Tony, I was skating well, maybe the best I'd ever skated. And having that extra fraction of a second to reach the puck was allowing me to see the ice better. Honestly, I seemed to be in better shape than pretty much everyone in camp. Coach Panner liked to skate us hard all morning and then see what we had left in the afternoon. I had plenty in the tank, but I could tell he wasn't impressed.

The assistant coach working with the forwards was Ian Lee. He, on the other hand, really liked coaching me. He liked to dream up fairly complicated plays that had half the guys crashing into each other, but I enjoyed trying something creative.

"Man, you're good." Foxy skated up beside me on the boards. "Have you ever played up in the show?"

I shook my head. I'd never even come close.

We finished our drills and then went to change for dryland work. Afterwards we were milling around in the hall, waiting for the head trainer.

"Eric! Over here." A big dark-haired guy called me over. He was a skilled centreman, but I hadn't played on his line yet.

"I'm Daniel Ramsey," he told me, holding out his hand for a firm shake. He had a friendly smile and a relaxed way about him. But if he was the captain, Dirk had warned me about him. "You're looking good out there. It's nice to get some fresh blood into camp."

The guys around him nodded and introduced themselves. Everyone seemed to have played for the Vice last season. They had a confidence that new tryouts like me were lacking.

"Where'd you play last year?" Daniel asked me.

"Swiss A League," I said, and he nodded.

"You got some skills. We could use a finisher around here. Your last name's Fairburn, right?"

"Yeah."

"The way you skate, we should call you Burner. Short for Fairburn, get it?"

And thus, I got yet another nickname. Some guys kept the same names throughout their careers, but I seemed to get a new one every time I changed teams, which was pretty frequently. Daniel's was the more predictable "Rams." He was really friendly, and I wondered if Dirk had been mistaken.

The first few days in camp, I'd been acutely aware of a

sense of competition and mistrust—like what you'd expect if you threw one piece of meat into a den of lions. Every player was pitted against each other. I missed the friendly team atmosphere of normal hockey.

Once Rams took me under his wing, things seemed to go a lot more smoothly. He tipped me off about a few of Coach Panner's pet peeves, and I felt accepted into the gang of last year's players. I relaxed and felt better out on the ice.

Good thing too, because as the finale to each day, Coach Panner went around the room and basically tore into every single guy in the room.

"One thing you better learn from day one is that we play a system here. That system is defence first. If you want to show off your fancy-ass moves like Fairburn here, you should look for a new fucking place to play. We play as team here, and everyone better buy into the two-way game!"

That was kind of confusing. When I looked at last year's stats, it was clear that the Vice needed more scoring. It was great to be defensive, but you weren't going to win games with zero goals. I had good hands, and I was hoping that was what I could bring to the team. Coach Panner wanted me to think defence, but Coach Lee wanted me to stay high.

The huge guy sitting beside me in the dressing room seemed unaffected by the coach's outburst.

"Did you play here last year?" I asked him, and he nodded.

"I'm Devo—Marty Devonshire." We shook, and his ham-sized hand enveloped mine. I introduced myself.

"Are things always like this?" I asked in a low voice. This was the quietest room I'd ever been in. Outside of Rams bragging about some chick he had bagged last night, everyone was silently getting changed. That undertone of nervous tension remained.

Devo smiled. "You got plans now?"

I shook my head. I wasn't exactly sure when we'd finish up today, so I hadn't arranged to see Josie.

"Let's grab dinner. I'll fill you in."

I expected a big guy like Devo to suggest a burger joint or steakhouse, but instead we went to a little Vietnamese restaurant. He ordered a lot of food though. I had salad rolls and a big bowl of pho.

"You're a pretty good player," Devo told me. "So, what's your issue?"

"My issue? Well, I guess it's that I already had a go-round in the A, and I messed it up."

He nodded. "In case you haven't noticed, Vice camps don't exactly draw the cream of the cream." He bit into a spring roll. "Yum. I love Asian food. Anyway, all the teams in AHL have an affiliation with an NHL team, right?"

"Yeah. Don't the Vice have one with the Millionaires?" But come to think of it, nobody from the local NHL team had shown up around our facility.

"Well, kinda. Everything went great until two years ago, when Vince Richardson died. The Richardson family owns the team, so his brother, Thomas, took over. Tom Richardson is a greedy guy, and he wanted a better deal. He played chicken with the wrong guys and ended up with nothing."

"But the Millionaires own the rights to some players?" My agent had mentioned that.

"Yeah. A few. But there's been so much bad blood that they've started loaning players to other teams. It's not ideal for them, and I wouldn't be surprised if they switch their AHL affiliation soon. The biggest problem for us is that our team can't compete when we don't have an NHL team covering part of our salary pool."

Devo was a smart guy. He was so big and quiet it was easy to underestimate him.

"So, the Vice gets stuck with players that nobody else wants?" I asked. That was certainly true for me.

He nodded. "Anyone who won't complain about his salary. Take our starting goalie for example. Bloc's a good player, but he's got off-ice issues. He's going through a court case right now. If it gets resolved, maybe he can focus on his game, but meantime, he's all over the place."

"What did he do?"

Devo frowned. "Domestic dispute. He's pushed his wife out of the house and locked her out."

"Is that a crime?" It seemed stupidly cruel, but unless it was in freezing weather how was that a crime?

"She was naked at the time."

I made a face, and Devo nodded. "Yeah, sometimes it's tough to go to war for these guys. They're your teammates, but man, I'd rather play with guys I respected—even if they were crappy players."

"How did you end up here?"

"Got traded here last February. I'm on a cheap AHL contract, and they needed someone big with a few skills. We'll see how long it lasts."

I nodded. Teams in the A were mandated to develop players, so your time in the league had an end date—usually after three seasons of pro hockey. If you were really good, they might keep you after that, but most guys were pretty young. I was already one of the older rookies at camp. If I even was a rookie, since I'd played over two seasons of pro. This really was my last chance.

"What about the coach? Is he always like that?"

Devo nodded. "Yeah, he's pretty tough. But he's fair, he hates everyone equally." He laughed, and our main courses arrived.

After a few minutes of concentrated eating, we started talking about more pleasant stuff. He was from

Saskatchewan, and he reminded me of a lot of straightforward prairie guys I'd played with. He was a huge guy and he obviously played an enforcer role on the team. But like a lot of those guys, he was gentle and thoughtful. To me, one of the ironies of the games was that the smallest guys were usually the biggest S.O.B.s, because they'd had to fight for every moment of playing time. Whereas the biggest guys were often the smart, strategic guys who only fought as a last resort.

"So, what's it like playing for the Vice? I've heard some bad stuff."

He shrugged. "I only got here late last season. The room's kinda divided. I stay out of team politics and do my own thing." He paused and seemed to be on the verge of saying more, but then shook his head. "I don't want to prejudice you, you might find things different."

I waited, but Devo kept eating. "Well, I guess we still get to play hockey and keep the dream alive."

He nodded. "People don't get how hard it is even to make the AHL."

The next day, camp went a lot better. Coach Panner was still yelling at me, but I liked feeling that a few guys were backing me up. Rams was nice, and Devo was a guy I could see hanging out with off the ice too. Foxy liked to hang around me, but he was more like a little brother. I was happy to help him out. He was on the small side, so if he worked harder in the gym that could make a big difference on the ice. Foxy started joining me for light workouts at the end of each day.

Coach Panner saw us in there one evening.

"Am I not working you hard enough?" he demanded. But I sensed that he wasn't unhappy to see that we were putting extra effort in. I still wasn't sure where I stood, but it felt like my chances were good.

14

ATHLETIC SUPPORTERS

"Hi, Eric. I have some forms for you to fill out."

A lady from HR had found me during lunch in the crowded players' lounge.

"Okay, sure. You want me to do them now, or bring them by later?"

"Why don't you do them now? We can go out in the hall, since there's no room here."

A couple of the guys started nudging each other and whispering. I took a better look at the woman—she was a short, busty brunette. But a lot of the guys at the camp were total pigs when it came to women of any kind. We had a female physio, and a few guys had been claiming groin pulls to get a massage from her. Idiots.

I went out in the hall and started filling out the forms against the wall, since there was no table or anything.

"I'm Brenda, by the way."

"You know, I'm pretty sure I did this already. All the questions seem familiar." We ran a gauntlet on the first day, doing personnel forms, medical forms, and releases.

She blushed. "Oh, really? Your paperwork must have been misplaced then, because it's not in the proper file now."

"Okay." I finished and handed the papers back to her. "Sorry you had to chase all this way after me."

"Oh, no. I apologize if you had to do this twice." She produced a business card. "If you ever have any questions about the human resources end of the team, please give me a call." I looked at her card. It was a blank one with the Vice logo, but her name and number hand-printed on it.

"I better make the team first."

She giggled. "I hear it's not a problem. You're one of the stars of camp."

"Too bad you're not a coach, Brenda."

Now, she giggled even louder. I excused myself and went back to lunch.

"Oh Burner, you're one of the stars of camp," Smitty trilled.

"Fuck off. You guys were listening?"

"She's hot and she wants you," Rams said. "Give it to her."

I shrugged them off. After Josie, nobody else looked good to me.

TOO BAD BRENDA wasn't a coach because the real coach didn't think I was one of the stars of the camp. Yesterday he had been complaining that I was taking too many of the shots myself, so I made a real effort to set up my linemates today.

After one line rush, he called me over.

"What the hell was that, Fairburn?"

"What, Coach?"

"That pass at the end. You put Marky in a bad place there. He couldn't shoot and he could have lost the puck."

"So what should I have done?"

"You should have shot the fucking puck. That's why we brought you into the camp, you're supposed to be able to finish. You're certainly not a defensive asset, so what else have you got?"

Was he fucking kidding me? He spent yesterday telling me to pass more and now he was complaining that I was wasn't taking enough shots. I skated away, but it suddenly struck me that he wasn't an equal opportunity hater.

"Hey, Rams." I skated up to him along the boards where he was waiting for the next rush.

"S'up, Burner?"

"Do you think Coach Panner has it in for me?"

Even through a visor, his expression was clear—he did think so. "Naw, don't worry. He picks someone every game to fuck with."

That was hardly comforting. I wasn't oversensitive when it came to hockey, but I hadn't noticed the coach singling anyone else out. Sure, he yelled at all of us, but he really seemed to be doing a number on me.

At the end of the day, Foxy and Devo both asked if I wanted to go out for dinner, but I turned them down. I got into my truck and sat there without starting it. Reality sucked. The Vice were going to be crappy team with a coach who hated me. So even if I made the team, I wasn't going to look good. No NHL scout was ever going to see some player who got buried on the fourth line and never played any special teams. My numbers were going to tank. I should have just gone back to Switzerland. Maybe after another excellent season there, I could have gone straight to an NHL tryout camp.

I put my arms on the steering wheel and looked at the interlock system. It symbolized all the ways I was a failure. I was a drunk driver. I had fucked up Gary's life. Then I screwed up my chance at a hockey career. And my girlfriend wouldn't even ride in the truck with me.

I rotated my head around and sighed. The essential shittiness of life struck me. I flexed my wrists and there was a familiar ache in my joints. That low-grade pain that would keep growing until I obliterated it by escaping everything in my head. I was so sure I was over all this shit, but right now I felt like getting wasted.

15

RAY OF LIGHT

By the time I got home and ate dinner, it was late. I went out and sat on the back patio, but I felt too twitchy to relax. Probably too late to call Josie, but I kept pulling my phone out and then shoving it back in my pocket.

Finally, I found myself punching up her number.

"Hey, Ricky." Josie sounded tired.

"Oh hey, I was wondering if we could get together tonight."

I heard her exhale loudly. "Look, I had a pretty long day. I'm not really up to it." She had been doing stunt work today, which was always exhausting for her.

"Oh, okay. Well, how about just coffee or something?" I felt guilty pressuring her, but I couldn't stop.

"You know, tomorrow I'm not working at all. Tomorrow would work."

"We don't need to have sex or anything. I'd just like to see you."

There was a long pause.

"Please, Josie," I said into the silence.

"Uh, okay. Why don't you come over here?"

I felt a rush of relief. "Great. I won't stay long either, I know you're tired."

Josie gave me her address and hung up. I grabbed my jean jacket and headed out right away. I was oddly excited at the prospect of finally going to her place. Since she never rode in my truck, I never had to pick her up like a normal date. Our relationship was so weird, but I had never felt closer to anyone in my life. Maybe Josie was right; it was better because we talked about different things instead of the normal crap.

Josie's building turned out to be a really nice modern one. I wasn't quite sure what I had expected, but it looked pretty expensive. She buzzed me in. The lobby was all polished marble and furnished with square leather chairs and a giant metallic disc on the wall. I took the elevator up to the four-teenth floor and found her apartment.

The door swung open as soon as I knocked once. Josie stood there. She was wearing jeans and a t-shirt with the sleeves cut off. Her feet were bare.

I put my arms around her and pulled her to me. The comfort of seeing her and feeling her body next to mine was enormous.

"Um, did you want to actually come in?" Josie finally asked.

I released her and looked around me. I was in a hallway that led in two directions. One way went towards her bedroom where I could see a low bed and not much else. We walked the other way, passed the entrance to a silvery kitchen, and entered a wide-open living room. It was furnished with only a large sectional and a slab-like coffee table. The couch faced a wide set of windows where the city and the mountain background were laid out in front of us. Her home gave me a feeling of light and space.

"Your place is really nice," I told her. We sat down on the

couch side-by-side and faced the view. "It's pretty much the opposite of my home in Nelson."

"How so?"

"My mom has a lot of stuff—fabrics, nature stuff, souvenirs, art. And crystals, she's really into crystals."

Josie was naturally quiet, and I sometimes found myself blabbing away to fill the silence. I longed to be as serene as her—the whole point of meditation was to achieve a state of calm relaxation, but too often I found my mind wandering. Ironically, while I was the yoga and meditation expert, Josie was the more zen of the two of us.

"Did you want something to drink?" Josie's glass of white wine was sitting on the coffee table. Her whole life looked like a page ripped out of a lifestyle magazine.

"Have you got mineral water?"

She nodded and padded off to get it. Josie moved with the fluid grace that was even more noticeable here at home. I looked around the room. The wood floors were polished and stained dark. Even though she didn't have a ton of furniture, everything looked expensive and special. I thought that coming here would tell me more about her, but I understood less. How could Josie afford a place like this working two part-time jobs? Stunt work might pay a lot, but she didn't even work full-time at it. Maybe she came from money, but in all the time I'd known her, she'd never bragged about her family. She'd barely mentioned them.

Still, I knew better than to ask her a million questions. With Josie, I took whatever she was willing to give me and accepted that. Because she didn't ask me questions either, unlike everyone else in my life who wanted to tell me what I should be doing, thinking, and saying.

But tonight, I needed to be with someone and Josie was that person. She handed me a glass of sparkling water and sat down on the other corner of the couch.

"So, what's up, Ricky?"

"I don't know. Camp isn't going that great."

She took a sip of wine and waited.

"I mean, I think I'm doing the right thing, but at the end of day, the coach rips into me. But then, the next day I try to do what he says and then he rips into me for something else."

"Sounds like he's doing something psychological. It's not personal, the guy's probably a jerk."

"That's the weird part, it *is* personal. He really seems to hate me." It felt good to be able to admit that to someone. Like putting the truth out there would lessen it.

"That's weird. Did you know him before?"

I shook my head. "No. There are a lot of reasons for people to hate me, but I've never done anything to him personally."

Josie smiled. "You? You're a guy who catches and releases spiders. Why would people hate you?"

I couldn't meet the clear gaze of her brown eyes. "I've done bad shit. I'm fixed now, but that doesn't change everything I did before."

She didn't say a word, but she reached out and held my hand.

"My best friend got injured—badly—that night when I got my DUI."

"Details. I knew you had done something like that the night I met you."

"Oh, when you saw my truck." Did I think that if I never told her stuff, she didn't know? Josie was too smart for that. "But that didn't stop me from drinking. It only stopped me from drinking and driving."

"A fine distinction that M.A.D.D. would be happy to hear," she replied.

"Look, Josie, could you stop joking around? I'm trying to tell you stuff that's important here."

"Why do you want to tell me everything bad about yourself? We know each other on an essential level—to me that's better." She let go of my hand. "Besides, I know exactly what happens next. You're going to expect me to share all my shit too."

"No, I won't. I know you better than that. I came here because I felt shitty and I needed to be with you. But now that I see how nice your apartment is, I feel like—I don't know—I don't have anything to offer you." She would be the perfect girlfriend for a guy in the NHL. A guy with money, fame, and a future. Like Bomber: he loved her motorcycle, and he would be a way better match for her.

She took a sip of wine and frowned. "You don't have to offer me anything other than what we have now."

"You could do way better than me."

Josie exhaled in frustration. "You are all over the place tonight. Where is this pity party coming from?"

She was right, I was throwing up all my defences. What was the real problem? Maybe I had been overconfident, but I was sure I was going to make the Vice. They were a crappy team, and I was one of the best players at camp.

"It's just... I feel like I'm not going to make the team—not because I'm not good enough—but because Panner doesn't like me.

"Again, why does he not like you?"

"I don't really know. I mean, he's in a negative space generally, so I thought he was that way to everyone. But I started noticing that he was calling me out for stuff way more. And if I did what he told me, he'd switch it up to something new."

"Sometimes people are harder on you if you're really good. Are you?"

I shook my head. "Nobody ever admits that, it's not the hockey way. You're supposed to be humble."

She faked a look around the room. "Don't worry, there's nobody here to tell the God of Hockey. And I don't really care if you suck—at hockey, anyway."

I laughed. I knew Josie would make me feel better. "I am really good—at least at the levels I've been playing at."

"Whatever that means."

"It means that I was really good in Switzerland. But the AHL will be harder. From what I've seen in camp, I'm still pretty good. That's why this situation is so frustrating."

"Can you still go back to Switzerland?"

"Yeah, maybe." It wasn't a sure thing, but pretty likely.

"So, then you'll still be playing hockey. Sounds like you can't lose."

Did it not bother Josie that if I didn't make the Vice, we wouldn't see each other anymore? I searched her face for clues, but she only looked a little tired. Besides, going back meant I would have failed.

"It's my last chance to make the NHL." Although I thought this constantly, I never said the words aloud. They sounded naked and desperate.

"You need to make the AHL first?"

I nodded. "It's a chance for NHL scouts to see me, to see if I've changed from my first go-round."

Josie sipped her wine. She waited.

"I was in the AHL before, and I fucked it up royally. It's taken me years to straighten up and get back in shape." I slid closer to Josie, and put my arm around her. Feeling her body next to mine was comforting, but not in a sexual way for once. "So many people have helped me—even when I didn't deserve it—and I don't want to let them down."

"What people?"

"My mom and my dad. Well, really my dad. I'm an only

child and he's always expected so much from me. The guy calls me every other day to make sure I'm working hard enough. You know how hard I work, right?"

She nodded. She didn't offer any reassurance, but she was listening.

"And there's other people—Lance, Tony, Mike Guildford, all my coaches ever, and tons of people back in Nelson. I used to be this sure thing. This is how I can prove they weren't wrong."

Josie was frowning. "Is it what you want?"

"Yeah, of course. It's what every hockey player wants. And I've made it back this far."

"Why, though? If you can play in Switzerland and be a star, why wouldn't that be enough? Is it about money?"

I shook my head. "It's not the money. Everyone wants to measure themselves against the best. Even if you only play a few games, you made it." But I knew that a few games wouldn't be enough for me. What would be? One season or two? Winning the Cup? I had never allowed myself to think that far ahead.

"If you make the Vice, how good are your chances to make the NHL?"

"Honestly—not good at all. But this process is a stairway —one step at a time." Because if I didn't make the next step, my chances went to zero.

"That sounds more like Zen Master Fairburn."

I put both arms around her and squeezed. "Thank you, Josie, for letting me unload on you."

"It's okay. I could tell on the phone that you were upset."

That kindness was unexpected. I kissed Josie and tasted the alcohol on her lips. She opened up her mouth, and I pressed mine harder against hers. Kissing her was like this gateway into ecstasy and escape. But I had promised not to stay too long. I pulled away.

"I'm sorry. I'll go now."

Josie looked up at me. "You don't have to. Why don't you stay?"

"But aren't you tired?"

"Yup. I'm just going to lie there while you do all the work."

I chuckled. "Isn't that what you do normally?"

She whacked me with a cushion. Then she got up and headed straight for the bedroom.

She didn't lie there, of course. Josie met my every move with one of her own, and the sex between us was intense. But she did fall asleep immediately afterwards.

I lay there with Josie's head on my chest and enjoyed the moment. We had finally achieved a new level of trust and caring. That Josie had finally let me into her life was huge. But she had done it because she sensed it was what I needed, and that was the important part.

Her bedroom was as minimal as the rest of the apartment. There was this large photograph on the wall: a black and white aerial view of fields and lakes. Sliding closet doors took up a side wall. We were lying in a large bed with soft white sheets and a duvet. The bed was luxurious and comfortable. It reminded me of my bed in Switzerland.

Josie was so self-contained. Her apartment was exactly like her—sleek and beautiful. I realized that I'd never had a place of my own; I had lived in furnished rentals, sublets, and at home. I didn't even have a vision of my dream home.

And maybe that was the key to overcoming my anxieties, knowing that life could be good outside hockey or after hockey. If I had a place like this to come home to, would I be less stressed about the end? Well, a home like this was perfect with Josie in it. She made me realize there was a life beyond hockey. I spent so much time with people who thought about hockey 24/7.

That's where my dad and Joe were wrong. Women weren't a distraction—they helped you put hockey in perspective. Sure, it had been a challenge to get to this point, but stuff that got handed to me wasn't worth having.

Still, that meant I had to make the team. Lying here and feeling so good only showed me how important Josie already was in my life. And if I left Vancouver, we'd never get to see how good things could be.

16

EXCESS

THURSDAY WAS the last day of the training camp. I had survived two rounds of cuts, and next we had a couple of preseason games. Rams guessed that they would keep the rest of the guys until after those games and then cut the team down to the final roster for the last preseason game.

We were all in the room getting changed at the end of the day when Coach Lee walked in. Instead of his usual smile, his expression was tense. The room got quiet fast.

"Brown, Jablonski, Lirenman, Stazio. When you're dressed, please come to Coach Panner's office."

Shit. The four players named finished changing, grabbed their gear, and headed out—all without a word. After they left, a little ripple went through the room.

"Do you think they're getting cut?" I asked Rams. Lirenman wasn't a surprise, but the other guys seemed pretty good to me. This round of cuts was unexpected.

He nodded. "It's tough, but that's pro hockey."

"What are we down to now?"

"Five more cuts to the opening day roster."

I looked around the room. There were five natural left

wingers remaining, but that didn't mean much. Coaches were constantly switching up wingers and even centres. And the AHL had rules about the numbers of veterans on a team too. It would take a pencil and paper to figure everything out. But there was one big left winger, Danny Ortiz, who I was most worried about. I was more skilled, but he was bigger. It depended on what the coaches wanted.

Rams stood up. "C'mon, boys. Why the glum faces? We've all survived three sets of cuts—now it's time to have some fun."

There were a few murmurs. Nobody wanted to be the one to screw up now by getting fucked up.

But Rams was just getting started. "Boys, it's our first night off in almost two weeks." We had all of tomorrow off due to some issues with ice time. "You know what they say— all work and no play...."

It was easy to see why Rams was captain, because he had charisma and enthusiasm. Soon he had everybody excited about going out to dinner and then on a bar crawl.

"You're coming, right, Burner?"

"I have to make a call first."

He squinted at me. "Don't let the old ball and chain stop you. Tell her it's a team bonding thing."

I didn't really have plans with Josie, but we tried to spend our free time together. She'd been doing stunt work on a movie shooting over in Victoria, so we hadn't seen each other much this week. While I wanted to see her, I also wanted to hang out with the guys. If this was going to be my new team, getting to know everyone off the ice was important.

I went outside to call her. "Hey, it's me. We didn't have specific plans for tonight, did we?"

"Not really," she replied. "Why?"

"Well, the team's going out, and I wanted to go too."

"Fine."

"Really?" Whenever Sunny used to say that things were "fine," I got in trouble the next day.

"Yeah. I told you, Eric. If you want to do something, just do it."

"I've got the whole day off tomorrow. So maybe we can spend it together?"

"Sounds good. I'll call you when I get up."

It sounded like she was ready to go, but I wanted to keep her on the line. "Sooooo, what are you going to do tonight?"

"Remember that bar we met at?"

"Yeah. That British pub place?"

"I think I'll go there alone and see if I can meet a hot hockey player."

"Josie! You are pissed off. I'll come see you instead."

"I'm kidding. Actually, a friend from high school called about dinner and I turned her down. I'll see if that offer's still open."

That was unexpected. Of course, Josie must have friends, but she never mentioned any before.

"How come I never meet your friends? Or your family?"

"Dude, chill. You're blowing me off this evening, you should be happy that I have plans."

I sighed. "Sorry. I am happy for you. And I know I'm being an idiot. I just want to do it all—see the guys and see you too. Maybe I can come by afterwards?"

"Oh, the old drunken booty call? Yeah, no."

"I'm not going to be drunk. You know that."

"Whatever, Ricky. Have fun."

Again, I wondered if she was mad at me. But she didn't sound upset, and Josie wasn't a bullshitter.

"All right. I'll see you tomorrow."

When I disconnected, I still felt unsettled. I was tempted to change my plans back and get together with Josie. But she was the one encouraging me to do my own thing. Then Rams draped his arm over my shoulder.

"All set?"

I nodded and off we went to dinner.

RAMS WANTED to do a bar crawl after dinner, so we could find this season's "official" Vice hangout. He had a whole list of requirements, and the third bar we hit seemed to meet them all. It had a dance floor, a live band, and a good crowd. The drinks were priced right too. But it had a slightly dive-y feel to me. It reminded me of the places we went to in junior when we were underage.

We were seated at a large round table. I was enjoying being part of a team again. Rams slammed a couple of pitchers on the table.

"My treat, boys. Congrats on surviving training camp!"

Everyone reached for glasses and beer started sloshing around the table. The sharp scent of the lager signalled something inside me. One bitter sip would take me back to the time when everything was easy. When all I had to do was go out on the ice and play hard.

I released the death grip I had on my glass of Coke and turned to watch the band. They were covering nineties rock songs.

Rams slid into the seat beside me. "You're not drinking, Burner?"

I turned back to the table. Someone had poured me a glass of beer. It sat beside my Coke. I looked at the golden colour, the weightless foam, and the glistening drops of condensation on the glass, and imagined lifting the glass to my lips. The cool rush of refreshment—all I wanted was one sip.

"No...I can't drink and drive."

"Oh yeah. You had a little trouble in that area, right? But you've been working your ass off this week, you need to relax." He leaned in towards me, so close I could smell the beer on his breath. "Tell you what, I'll stay off the juice and drive you home."

"But I've got my truck here."

"Leave it in the parking lot. They're not going to tow it. One of the boys will give you a ride back here tomorrow." I liked the way he talked, like I was one of the team already.

I hesitated. All the stress and pressure of the tryout was getting to me, and I wanted a little relaxation. And it wasn't like I was an alcoholic or anything. I could have one drink without getting drunk. Even Shaman Felix believed that alcohol in moderation was okay.

Rams slapped my shoulder. "I can see you need this, Burner. We're a team, we've got your back."

"Okay, maybe I'll have a beer."

"Attaboy." He raised his drink. "To the new season, boys! It's gonna be a good one!" Everyone clinked their glasses in the centre and drank. The taste of the draft wasn't quite as refreshing as I'd imagined. But what was good was the feeling of belonging. For once, I wasn't the odd man out. I was the same as everyone else.

I didn't want to get completely wasted, but the buzz felt good. All that pressure that Coach Panner had been putting on me was hard to take 24/7. I'd been dealing in all my usual ways—meditation, yoga, sex—but even Josie was adding to my stress. Even after that night she let me come over and complain, I still didn't feel confident about us. Alcohol was the easiest way to relax.

So, I had a few beers. It felt great to kick back and be myself. We were all laughing and joking around in that team way. It hadn't been like this in Switzerland; because of the cultural barriers I'd always felt isolated. Now, I was home—

almost on a team and back in Canada. Hell, it was as close as I could get to Nelson and still play hockey. I couldn't even remember why I'd been so worried earlier tonight.

Rams bought a round of shots. He was true to his word though: he stopped drinking and seemed to be everyone's designated driver. Dirk had been so wrong about Rams, and I resolved to straighten out the record when I saw him again.

After the shot, I started feeling a little weird. I didn't think I'd had that much to drink, but it was really hitting me hard. Maybe my tolerance for alcohol was declining.

Rams was staring at two girls across the room. They wore jeans, high-heeled boots, and skimpy tops. He poked me in the arm.

"Why don't you ask those chicks if they'd like to come back to my place for a party?"

"Me? Why don't you ask them yourself?"

"Oh, I could. But I think you might be more likely to get a yes."

I shook my head. "They look too young. You don't want to get mixed up with teenagers."

"Are you shitting me? Tight little pussies and they've never taken it up the ass. Nothing like an ass virgin. If they squeal a little, I get off on that too."

He was one sick puppy. I was already queasy, but he was making things worse. Now Ortiz was saying something about sloppy seconds. These guys were twisted. Shit like this had gone on since juniors, but it seemed worse now that the guys were older.

I exhaled loudly.

"You scared, pussy?" Blackie scoffed. He was a big asshat d-man. "We can send the A team then, right, Rams?" They both laughed.

"Okay, I'll ask them." I went over and slid into a chair at their table.

"Hey."

"Hey, hottie," the taller one said with a smile. Her friend looked nervous. Close-up they looked even younger. I wondered if they were even legal to drink.

"You know, I've got a younger sister your age."

They both looked surprised at this pick-up line. As an only child, I was surprised myself.

"Yeah, so I feel kind of protective of you two. The guys I'm with back there—" I motioned, and they both looked over my shoulder. "They want me to invite you over to a house party. But you know what? If you go somewhere with guys you don't know, bad things are going to happen. Really bad."

"Um, why are you telling us this?" They looked nervous now. They probably thought I was a psycho axe murderer.

"Because I really think you should leave this bar now and go home. Do you need money for a cab?"

The nervous one answered, "No, I've got a car."

"Have you been drinking?" I asked her.

"Just Coke."

"Okay. Shoo."

They both got up and left right away.

I returned to the table where all the guys were laughing.

"Fuck, Burner. Not only did you strike out, they ran out of the bar," said Rams. "What the hell did you say to them?"

I leaned back in my chair. "I guess I shouldn't have mentioned the ass-fucking."

"You moron. You didn't really?"

I laughed, and Foxy laughed along with me.

Rams drawled, "Well, it don't matter none. I've got a whole list of ladies who like to party." He held up his phone. "Why don't we go back to my house and invite a few of them over?"

Most of the guys nodded. This evening was turning into an epic party night.

He turned to me. "I'll give you my address and you can meet us there."

"I don't know." I was pretty sure that I was going to blow over the limit if I went out in the truck right now. But how was I going to get my truck home? Every problem seemed huge right now. "Maybe I better get a ride with you."

"Are you shitting me, man? You only had a couple of beers and a shot, right? You're fine to drive."

I shook my head. I didn't feel fine. "Really? You think so?"

"I do. And I'm an expert on booze." He laughed. "C'mon to my place, Burner. There'll be hot chicks and we'll have a great time. What did I tell you about being a team player? That's what they want in the Vice—guys that would lay it on the line for their teammates." He punched his address into my phone.

"Okay. I'm going to take a piss. I'll meet you guys there."

I went to the washroom. Once I was out of the noise of the bar, there was a ringing in my ears. The queasiness returned, and I lurched into a stall and leaned over the toilet. My stomach was knotted and my throat felt all choked up. If I could just puke, I'd feel better. Hunching over a toilet was reminding me of something, but I couldn't even pull a complete thought out of my memory banks.

I waited, but nothing happened. I took a piss instead and flushed the toilet. I stood there, leaning against the cold metal wall and not moving. I dizzily fixed my eyes on the words scratched into the paint—*I love kristy*. But did Kristy love him back? Poor lovesick bastard, I felt sorry for him. Fuck. What was wrong with me?

I went out to the sink and washed my hands. I peered into the cracked mirror. I looked like hell. My eyes were bloodshot, and my face was all slack. It was weird. I didn't even feel drunk. But everything was in slow motion—like an out of body experience. Hell, some people meditated for hours to reach the state I was in right now.

When I went back out in the bar, everyone was gone and this waitress with hennaed hair and a skull tattoo was cleaning up our table. She gave me a disgusted look, and I wondered what we had done to earn that. I grabbed my coat off the chair and headed towards the door.

Then an idea hit me. Maybe I had alcohol poisoning. This seemed both ridiculous and reasonable. My anxiety level was increasing, but I couldn't remember what to do about that.

I went out to the parking lot. The fresh air woke me up a little, and I unlocked the truck and slid into the driver's seat. I automatically reached for the interlock remote and lifted it to my lips.

Then I dropped it. Shit. Could I drive? Was I drunk or not? A vague memory was coming back to me—of me thinking I was fine to drive when I wasn't. And then something bad happened. Maybe I should take a cab to be safe. Yeah, that would be the right thing to do.

I pulled out my phone. But I didn't actually know the number of a cab company here. That seemed like a huge problem. Maybe I should just lie down and have a nap. I closed my eyes. Yeah, this was the easiest thing to do.

Shit. What about that alcohol poisoning thing? I still felt terrible and I didn't want fall asleep and then die here in the truck. Especially when I was so close to making the Vancouver Vice.

I held the phone up close to my face and poked the redial button.

"Hey. I'm kind of fucked up. Do you think you could help me out?"

17

RESCUE RANGER

"Wake up."

Josie's voice sounded like it was coming through several levels of cotton batting. My eyes wouldn't even open, so I gave up. Sleep. Her footsteps got softer and then louder.

Cold water poured over my face and went up my nose, in my ears, everywhere. Freezing cold water.

"What the—" I sat up, blew out water, and shook my head. "Okay. I'm up. I feel like crap though. Why didn't you let me sleep?"

"Look at this." She shoved my phone in front of my face. I blinked a little. My eyes were not really open or in focus, and the letters looked blurry.

On the locked screen was a new message from Coach Panner.

Extra ice time. Mandatory team practice at 10:00am.

"Fuck! What time is it?"

"You have 35 minutes to get ready and get to the rink." She was already pulling me up. I had been lying in a sleeping bag on the floor beside Josie's bed.

"You didn't even let me sleep in your bed?" For some reason that seemed important.

"Do you not remember throwing up out the truck window? I'm not into getting the mattress dry-cleaned. But we can relive our tender moments another time." She yanked off my t-shirt and pushed me into the bathroom. "Shower now. And start drinking water. I left aspirin on the counter, take two."

I took a piss and then did everything she told me to. Her shower was one of those rain shower ones and felt great. I was coming back to life slowly. Half of me was stressed, but the other half was moving sloooowly.

She banged on the door. "Get out now."

Josie's towels felt soft. Her place was so nice. What was in her bathroom cabinet? I was going to peek inside, when the door opened.

"Eric! You don't seem to be panicking sufficiently." She grabbed me and guided me back into the bedroom. "Okay, I found a clean t-shirt that will fit you, and your jeans and underwear are here. Get dressed."

I dropped the towel that was around my waist and noticed that Josie was still in the doorway watching me. "What is it?"

She smiled. "Sorry. I needed a little reward for everything I've done for you in the past ten hours."

I pulled on the grey t-shirt. It read *Team MBC* in black letters and was a little tight.

Five minutes later, we were in my truck.

"Why are you driving?" I wondered.

"Because you may still have an elevated blood alcohol level. And you need to eat everything in the bag."

I peeked inside. Besides a bottle of Gatorade, there was toast, a banana, and salted nuts. I felt queasy just looking at food, but I nibbled at the toast. Josie seemed to be on a mission.

I swallowed. "Um, I can't remember everything I said to you last night. I hope I didn't say anything stupid."

"You mean the wedding's off?"

"What? I didn't...."

Josie laughed. "This is too easy. You must have fried some brain cells last night.

"I feel pretty slow this morning."

"Okay, Eric. Let's get serious here. You know that guy—Ram, or whatever?"

"Rams. Yeah, he's the captain."

"He's an asshole. He set you up. He got you drunk, hoping that you'd miss the mandatory practice. Or even get hit with another DUI."

"How do you know this? I don't even know this."

"I don't have proof. But it makes sense. He's not your friend, and you're an idiot if you keep trusting him."

I started eating the banana. She might be right, but how would he even know we were having a surprise practice? "Why wouldn't he want me on the team? I can help the team."

"You go around in this love-peace-om daze. Wake up. People have a zillion different reasons to do shitty things."

"That's not good, Josie. You have to look for the best in people."

"Okay, forget it. Just listen and do what I say. You go into that hockey arena, and don't let anyone know you're hurting. Play your guts out, and be good. If anyone asks if you're hungover, deny it. You feel great. Got that?"

I nodded. "Yes. I feel great."

"What is wrong with you? Did he roofie you or something? It's like you're still totally out of it." She pulled right up to the door of the arena.

"I'm not a morning person. There's Rams now." He was

walking in from the parking lot. He peered into the truck at the two of us.

"Kiss me," Josie said. I leaned over and was surprised by how passionate she was getting. She ran her hands all over the back of my head and practically pushed me onto the seat. Abruptly, she let go. "Now get out."

I put my hand on the door handle. "Um, how will I get home?"

"Text me, and I'll pick you up."

I got out, and Rams was waiting there. "Hey, Burner. Are you hurting this morning?"

"Nope."

Josie rolled down the passenger window. "Eric baby, last night was incredible! I'll pick you up after practice for Round Two." Then she blew me a kiss and drove away.

"Wow. She sounds like a happy woman." Rams said. "So that's what you did instead of coming to my place. Dude!" He held out a hand for me to slap. I slapped it, but watched his face. Did he look disappointed? Maybe Josie was right.

COACH PANNER WAS USING the whistle a little too loudly at practice.

"Come on, guys. Wakey-wakey. Let's see who was out too late last night."

Obviously, this practice was his way of seeing who partied hard and who went to bed early. I was going through the motions during practice, but at least I was performing instead of barfing into a toilet or waking up in some random's bed.

Coach kept getting after me, but I had zero anxiety. It felt like a miracle that I was even here. I was more worried about upchucking on the ice. At least nobody was hitting. I realized that about half the guys looked as green as I felt.

I skated up beside Devo. "You feeling okay?"

He nodded. "I left early and went to bed. I was worried that Coach Panner might pull this stunt."

"Why? Has he done it before?"

"Sorry I didn't mention it. I overheard a couple of the vets saying something, but I wasn't 100% sure."

Fuck me. Josie was right.

One of the younger guys threw up onto the bench, and the stench was making everyone a little queasy, so Coach called the practice a few minutes early.

"Fairburn."

"Yes, Coach?"

"You up to your partying tricks again? You didn't have a very good practice."

"No, sir. I'm fine." I wasn't going to admit to anything—not even a bad practice. And I hadn't been that bad.

I texted Josie before I got changed. Rams came up to me in the room.

"A few of us are going out for lunch. You want to come? I've heard some stuff about team composition that might interest you."

"Thanks. But I have to meet someone."

"Oh yeah. That chick in your truck. She's hot. Needs a little more up here though." He motioned to his chest.

I shook my head. "She's perfect."

"Whatever. Later."

Yeah, when hell froze over.

I got outside the arena just as Josie was pulling up.

"Hey, good timing." I hopped inside. "Wow. It's nice and clean in here."

"Yeah. I had your truck washed and detailed. Had to get rid of your empty water bottle collection though."

"Wow. You didn't have to do that. Let me repay you."

"The receipt's on the dash. And I did have to. Driving the vomit comet wasn't good for my reputation."

"So, what happened last night?"

"You don't remember anything?"

"It all comes back eventually, but I was hoping you'd give me a little recap." I reached over and took her hand. "The most important thing is that I owe you huge for everything you've done for me."

She checked the side mirror and pulled out. "Be a shame to waste all your hard work now."

"Yeah. You called that setup thing right. Apparently, Coach Panner does this every camp—the unexpected practice. So, Rams was screwing me over, and a bunch of the other guys too. Man, you're smart."

"I'm normal. You're too trusting." She turned onto Hastings Street. "Did you want lunch?"

"Sure. But you know, in hockey, there's this huge trust between teammates. Even if your best friend was on the other team—" I swallowed. My throat was dry, and I took a swig of water. "Anyway, your friend would be the enemy and you'd always stick up for your team. Like war."

"Yeah, but in a tryout, everyone is your enemy. You're not a team yet."

I nodded. This was the exact advice I'd given Foxy, and I'd been too stupid to take it myself. "I wish I was as smart as you."

"I know nothing about hockey. I've been piecing things together from what you've said to me."

Feeling like I was an idiot wasn't good. A guy who'd been around should know better. "Owls are so good at sitting back and assessing the situation."

Josie hooted and parked in front of a crappy little diner. "Don't give me any of your food lectures. Everyone knows that burgers and fries are the best hangover food."

She was right again. I could almost sense the grease sliding down my digestive system, but I was feeling better and better. Little bits of the night were coming back. Me talking nonstop. *"Oh babe, you're so great to come and get me. You're so amazing. I've never felt like this about anyone."* And then, shit. Did I tell her I loved her?

"Uh, Josie... I seem to remember saying some, um, sentimental stuff last night."

Her eyes met mine, and she smiled. "You are correct."

"What did I say exactly?"

She laughed and ate a French fry. Then she didn't say another word.

"Aren't you going to tell me?"

"Why? You said you remember everything—eventually."

I tried hard to remember more. I especially wanted to know what she had said back to me. "It feels like you have the advantage on me."

"Always."

Suddenly, there was a click of clarity. *"Josie, I think I'm falling in love with you."* And her answer: *"Don't. People love me, and then they leave."* Could that be right? Josie—being vulnerable?

"It's not fair. You know so much about me, and I know nothing about you."

"That's me, international woman of mystery. Don't worry, I'm sure there'll be a time when I get completely trashed, call you to rescue me, and bare my soul."

I snorted. "Yeah, right. You're always in total control." That came out more insultingly than I'd intended, and I looked up at Josie to see if she was mad. She wasn't. She doled it out, but she could take it too.

"I like myself. So I don't need to alter my reality."

"Are you saying I don't like myself?"

She shrugged.

134

"No, really. Tell me."

Josie exhaled. "You spend a lot of time worrying about what people want you to be. That seems like a waste to me. But it's your life, do what you want."

"It's easy for you. You've got a great place to live and a job you love. I'm not in the same place yet, I'm still getting there."

I watched as she dragged her French fry through the ketchup on her plate. She drew an "X" over and over. When she finally spoke, her voice was hesitant—like every word was costing her. "Life is never easy. You should know that better than anyone."

"I'm sorry, Josie. I shouldn't be making assumptions about your choices."

"Enjoy today. Stop stressing about everything you've done and everything you still have to do."

Her philosophy sounded too simplistic to me. I had thought so much about flow and being in the moment, and achieving a higher level of consciousness. "That sounds too much like an unexamined life."

"No. You crave this state of nothingness—like not thinking. I would never want that. I like to turn ideas over in my head. And when we have sex, I like to be conscious of it all."

That was hot.

"Actually, that reminds me—there *is* one time when you lose control. I think it's between the third and fourth orgasm."

Josie flashed a smile and held up her hand. "Check, please."

18

WHIPPING BOY

I PLAYED the first preseason game on Saturday. The series was with the Manitoba Moose. They must have been tired from their trip here, because they were going through the motions in the first period. I was on a line with Rams and Foxy, and we scored on our second shift. It was a tic-tac-toe play with Foxy burying the puck over a sliding goalie.

Foxy was excited back on the bench. "That's a good thing, right, Burner? Coach'll like that I scored."

I slapped him on the shoulder. "You're the man, buddy. Nice mitts."

We had a two-goal lead going into the middle of the game, when Ortiz stuck a lazy leg out on his check and took a penalty. Then one of the d-men put the puck over the glass and suddenly we were defending a five-on-three.

"You're up, twelve," Panner called out. It took me a moment to even understand that he meant me. I was wearing the number twelve for the first time. And I wasn't exactly the star defensive player on the team, so it was weird that I'd be the only forward out there. I hopped over the boards.

The Moose were coming out of whatever funk they had

been in and gaining momentum on the power play. They were moving the puck around the perimeter and taking a few shots from the outside, but we never managed to get possession. The seconds were ticking off, and we were all getting tired. Suddenly I noticed that one of the points was about to make a pass across to the far boards. I darted out, and picked off the puck, and took off for their end.

The Moose defenders were trying to catch up, but I was already at top speed. The goalie was sizing me up, but neither of us knew each other's tendencies. I faked a move to the right, then cut back and let go a wrister that he deflected out. One of the defencemen picked it up and passed it hard into our zone, where our two d-men had barely managed to change. The Moose forward got a shot off, and Bloc managed to freeze the puck. Exhausted, I made it back to the bench, and Rams took my place on the P.K.

I was catching my breath, when suddenly, Coach Panner appeared beside me, and grabbed my shoulders.

"What the fuck's wrong with you, Fairburn?" he screamed in my ear. "It's a fucking 5-on-3, and you handed them their best scoring chance of the period."

"Sorry, Coach," I muttered. But I didn't agree with him. I had a chance to score, so I had gone for it. The goalie had barely stopped it, and I hadn't fired a slapshot because I understood the dangers of a big deflection.

"It's a fucking team game, and we play a fucking team defence! When we've got a lead, you need to think defence first."

Seriously? I was supposed to skate the puck into the fucking corner when I had a breakaway? I understood team defence, but that was insanity. I shook my head. Coach Panner walked away to yell at the penalty killers. Unfortunately, the Moose scored on the remaining power play, and Panner decided he needed to yell at me some more. That was really crazy, because I wasn't even on the ice for the goal and what I had done was thirty seconds earlier.

But I was Panner's whipping boy. He decided to bench me for a few shifts as a punishment. Since this was my chance to show my stuff in a real game, that was pretty discouraging. Coach Lee patted me on the shoulder during my grocery stick stint, but he didn't say anything. The head coach was the boss around here.

I played again in the third period, but instead of playing on the top line with Rams, I was demoted to the fourth line. Ortiz took my place on the first line.

"Don't worry," Devo told me. "Coach wouldn't be yelling at you if he didn't want you to improve."

"Thanks." But maybe Panner's real mission was to show that my defensive issues outweighed my offensive potential. The only break I got all night was the fact that we managed to keep the lead and won. If we lost, I would have been Exhibit A for selfish play. As it was, Coach Panner glared at me in the room, but at least he didn't say anything more. I didn't even have Josie to turn to for comfort because she was working out of town until Monday.

He read out the team for tomorrow night's game. All the guys who had sat out were in. And I was out. Tonight had been my one big chance to make an impression. One assist and one screw-up. Even if I still didn't agree that I had done the wrong thing.

AFTER THE SECOND GAME—A loss to Manitoba on Sunday night—Coach Panner told us that the coaches would be meeting that evening, and individual meetings were tomorrow. He would post a list of meeting times in the morning. This was typical of the Vice's half-assed way of operating. They should have just pulled the fucking bandage off all at once by posting the roster, instead of extending everyone's pain. And it also meant that we had to come in first thing to see our meeting times. These guys were sadists.

Since I was still in a suit, I didn't need to hang around the room. The mood was mixed. A few guys were happy, sure that they were making the team. Others were resigned, ready to go back to the ECHL, or wherever they had come from. A lot of the guys were young enough that this was good experience for them. They'd be back and be better next time.

I felt calm inside, even though I had no idea what my fate would be. I had had a good camp, maybe even a great one. Coach Lee was really high on me and wanted me. But after the big night out, I had fallen out with Rams. I wasn't rude, but I wasn't interested in his bullshit. Usually, what another player thought didn't matter, but he was the captain.

The real question mark was Coach Panner. For whatever reason, he had a grudge against me personally. Was my on-ice performance enough to overcome that? There was no question that my past was reason enough to cut me, but if that were true—why even invite me to camp?

Panner was the guy in charge of the roster. Unlike most teams, the GM didn't seem to get overly involved in the player selection process. Thomas Richardson had barely been seen at camp. According to Rams, the GM was busy assembling the best possible squad of Ice Girls, which was a stupid waste of time. But since the Richardson family owned the team as well, that wasn't going to change soon. The reasons for the team's problems were crystal clear once you spent a few days around here.

The next day, I headed back to the arena. Not surprisingly, I was the last guy on the meeting list. I decided to go to the gym to kill the time before my meeting. I could do a light workout and a long stretching session to get the kinks out.

I was halfway through my routine when Foxy interrupted me.

"Hey, Burner."

I untwisted myself. I couldn't tell from his neutral expression if he was in or out. "What's up?"

"I got cut." He tried to shrug like it didn't matter. "So I guess it's back to Wichita."

"That's a shame," I told him. It was dumb. The kid had potential, and all he needed was a chance. If I ran a losing team, I'd take guys with lots of upside over guys who would deliver a solid but average game. Panner seemed to prefer the sure thing, judging from last season's roster. But Foxy was on the small side, and some coaches liked the big, bruising players. "You're good though. I'm sure you'll get more chances, you just need to work on a few things."

"Yeah. Thanks for all your training advice. I will work on bulking up." He grinned. "Don't know about the yoga though."

"Flexibility. It's important."

He told me everyone he knew who had made the team. It seemed to be mainly the same guys from last season, although I was happy to hear that Wendell Black, the asshole defenceman, had been cut. The other good news was that Danny Ortiz had been cut. Less competition in my position was a good sign.

"You're gonna make it for sure," Foxy said.

"Nothing's for sure. Especially around here."

"Well, I guess you could go back to Europe then. I wish I could do that."

"You should look into it." But they had limits on import players, and I wasn't sure if Foxy was good enough.

We shook hands, and he took off. I finished up my workout and still had enough time before my meeting for a shower. As the water poured down on me, I thought about

Josie. Was she the reason I was feeling so calm? But getting cut would make things that much more difficult for us.

I got dressed and headed towards the coach's office. One of last year's Vice forwards walked out into the hall, looking pissed. He ignored me, and I assumed he had just been cut as well. Were they saving all the bad news for the end? I knocked on the door.

"Yeah," Coach Panner barked.

"It's me." I poked my head in. Coaches Panner, Tellier, and Lee were all crammed into the little office. There was one empty chair, and I took it.

Ian Lee began. He pulled out a sheet and pulled down his glasses. "Eric, you've had a good camp. You had the highest scores on the fitness testing. Your play throughout camp was also excellent. I was impressed by your ability to absorb direction and make the adjustments we requested."

Coach Panner interrupted. "Let's stop the love fest right here. We're all aware that Eric has the tools. Hell, he was a first round draft pick—but that was five years ago. But your biggest issue is between your ears. Once the season starts and the pressure ramps up—can you hack it? We don't need some fucking prima donna going all psycho and cheap-shotting everyone. Nobody wants that shit in the game."

I breathed deeply. He was trying to bait me, but he was right. You couldn't replicate the real stress of the season in a training camp or preseason games.

"I'm a different player now. I've cleaned up my lifestyle. You can look at last year's season for proof."

"Waltzing your way through a bunch of Euros is not the same as playing with the big boys in the A." That was the kind of stuff I heard from people who had never been out of North America, so I ignored his insult. Guys in the Swiss League were tough too.

"But we're not here to argue. We're going to offer you a

contract—but, and it's a big but—there's a morals clause inserted in it. If we think you're up to your old ways, like boozing, whoring it up, or being a distraction in the room— you are out of here. No second chances, because you've already had enough of them."

"Okay. Thank you. You don't have to worry about that stuff anymore, I'm in a better headspace now."

Panner rolled his eyes, but the other coaches smiled at me. Maybe they'd had to lobby for me to make the cut. Coach Lee stood up. "Since we're done here, I'll get you set up."

We both walked down the hallway. He clapped me on the shoulder. "Congratulations, Eric. I didn't tell you before, but Mike Guildford is a good buddy of mine. He was the one who convinced me we needed to give you a good look."

"Thanks a lot, Coach." His genuine enthusiasm was finally making me felt good. Panner's backhanded offer had dulled the fact that I was finally here. Not in the NHL, but a big step closer.

Or was I still worried about screwing up? I couldn't deny that Panner was right—what would I be like under real pressure? But I had handled last season's playoffs, and I managed to stay in control.

"Rob's bark is worse than his bite," he assured me. "The guy cares a lot about winning, and he understands that you can help us." The Vice had one of the lowest goals-for totals in the league last year, so scoring was something they'd be leaning on me for. A lot would depend on who my linemates were, but having Coach Lee in my corner was going to help that.

"Damn. You're the last player today, and I'm missing a handbook. I'll be right back." Coach Lee disappeared, and I sat on the edge of his desk. I pulled out my phone, and Lance had called twice. I called him back.

"Hey, Eric. Congratulations—you made it."

"Thanks. Feels good."

"Okay, my assistant looked over your contract. Everything is standard except two things. The money is league minimum and there's this wonky morals clause they've inserted. I'd like to negotiate on both these issues before you sign."

"It's okay, Lance. I'm ready to sign."

"Look, it's my job as your agent to get you the best possible deal."

"But I get to tell you when I'm good with a contract, right?" I knew a lot about the Vice organization now. There wasn't going to be any more money, and I wasn't going to screw up. I felt good about myself and happy about living in Vancouver and having Josie on my side.

Lance argued with me, and we finally agreed to him negotiating some performance bonuses. "I'd like to sign everything by tomorrow morning," I told him. I wanted everything in black and white before Panner changed his mind. And Josie was due back in town tomorrow night, so I wanted to celebrate with her.

"Done." He wasn't completely happy with me, but I figured he would be if I managed to make it to the next stage. Coach Lee had returned with the materials for me.

"Thanks, Coach. Just talking to my agent."

"Well, we'll get everything done up right. You've got two days off, and then we start the season for real. Practices and games are in the schedule. You've been here before, so I don't have to explain how things work, right?"

I nodded, and we shook hands.

THE NEXT MORNING, I went back to the facility and signed my contract. My good mood kept growing. Besides, I had another good thing happening today. I drove to the provincial insurance office where I met with Maude, who had been supervising my driving restrictions since I moved to Vancouver.

"Big day, today," she said when I got there.

"Huge," I agreed.

She went out to the truck to check the readings. "Looking good. Let's go back to my office, and I'll get the paperwork done."

She filled out a bunch of forms on her computer and began printing them out. Once I took them to the garage, I could get my interlock removed.

"Well, Eric, I spoke to you about responsible driving on the first day we met. Driving is a privilege and not a right. Your readings have been perfect, and I'm happy to see that you've been taking this so seriously. Are you drinking at all any more?"

"I only drink if I'm not driving. So, if I know it's going to be a night out, I arrange for a ride or take a cab." I shivered thinking about how close I'd come to blowing this accomplishment the night of the bar crawl. But still, I hadn't actually driven—something in my brain had stopped me.

"What about drugs?"

I shook my head. "My trainer warned me they're going to be cracking down in my sport."

"Which is hockey, right? Who do you play for?"

I grinned, as I replied for the first time. "The Vancouver Vice."

19

UPSIDE DOWN CAKE

I RAN my hand over the dashboard of my truck. Or rather I ran my hands over the place where the interlock system used to be. Nothing. Normal. Four long years later, I was finally free.

"Yes!" I leaned against the seat and extended my arms in victory. A businessman was walking by at that moment, and he gave me a pitying look. I only laughed. First I made the team, and now my driving supervision was over. The best way to celebrate this would be to take my woman out for dinner. And then sex—lots of incredible sex with Josie. For once, I didn't have practice, training, or anything tomorrow.

I started to send a text, but that wasn't personal enough, so I dialled her up instead.

"Eric?"

"Josie baby. My gorgeous, beautiful Josie!"

She laughed. "Someone's in a good mood."

"How can I not be in a good mood when I'm talking to you? When are you coming back from Victoria?"

"I'm back already. We wrapped early."

"Because you're such a professional, right?"

"What's gotten into you, Ricky? I've never heard you be so—I don't know—kid-at-Christmas excited."

"It's because I have a ton of good news. Can I come over now? Or should we go out for dinner?"

"Dude, chill. It's only four o'clock."

"Resistance is futile, as the aliens say. I'm coming right over."

"Eric, I literally just walked in. I need to shower and get all the crap off me. I think there's fake blood on my chest."

"This is why I need a key. You could be taking your shower, and I'd join you. I would scrub your back... and your front... and that little place between your legs...."

She laughed again—that rich throaty sound that I could listen to forever. "Give me thirty minutes. I'll see you then." And then hung up before I could bargain her down.

Still, this gave me time to get organized with snacks and stuff. And I stopped by the liquor store. As I went in, I felt guilty and elated. "Look at me! I'm buying booze and putting it in my vehicle." No alarms went off. I was going to have to get used to freedom.

I buzzed her condo from the lobby. The marble floor gleamed up at me and once again, I wondered how Josie afforded a place like this. Asking financial questions would be too nosy. Still, I was a million times further ahead than when we first started dating.

Josie opened the door at my first knock. She was wearing black leggings, a huge sweater, and a black top underneath. Her hair was still a little damp, but her eyes were already rimmed with dark liner and thick lashes. She smiled at me and my face flushed.

"Hey, beautiful." I put down the grocery bags and hugged her, lifting her into the air. She giggled and kissed me. Her mouth was warm and tasted like peppermint tooth-paste. She thrust her tongue into my mouth, and I sucked on it. Her body wriggled against mine, and I was already getting hard. Even a few days apart and I had missed her so much.

Finally, I put her down.

She smoothed out her hair. "You're probably the one guy in the world who can lift me up like that."

"That's why we're so good together." I picked up the bags.

"What's in there?"

"Snacks. Champagne. We're celebrating."

Josie tilted her head but asked no questions. She headed into her kitchen. I followed her, and she stretched up to pull two champagne flutes down from a high cupboard. I watched her excellent ass flexing in her tight leggings, and I couldn't resist copping a feel.

"Watch it, buddy. I almost dropped these." Josie plunked the flutes down on the counter.

"You can't flash an ass like that in front of me and expect nothing to happen."

She shook her head and laughed. Then she ran her hand over the bottle. "It's a little warm. Stick it in the freezer for a few minutes to chill down."

I bent down and opened the freezer drawer. Inside was a bottle of vodka, a package of frozen berries, and ice cubes. I opened her fridge next. Two lemons and a carton of soymilk.

"Jesus, Josie. What do you eat?"

"The beating hearts of guys who nag me," she said.

I got out two bowls and portioned out some carrot sticks and hummus. Josie snuck one and crunched on it.

"Wait, I have something else for you."

I reached into the bag and pulled out the box of expensive Swiss chocolate I had ordered online. A teammate from last year assured me they were the best.

Josie looked at the box and then began to laugh. "I guess I'll have to eat these by myself."

"No, I'm going to eat them too—just to show you how much fun I am."

"I was so mean to you. You must be a masochist."

She ripped off the wrappings and pulled out a dark truffle. I reached out for one, but she stopped me.

"Eat this one." She held it in her lips and raised her face to mine. I wrapped my arms around her and pressed my lips against hers. We kissed hard, our mouths a mess of melting chocolate. My tongue explored her mouth, and I felt her body pushing up against mine.

Josie's eyes were half-closed when we finally stopped. I licked a final bit of chocolate off her lower lip.

"Yummy."

"I told you you'd love chocolate."

"Not the chocolate." I put one arm around her and grabbed the carrot snacks with the other. We went out to the living room.

She sat down on the big sectional, tucking one leg underneath and leaning back. I sat right beside her and put my hand on her thigh. I couldn't stop touching her.

"I missed you," I said.

She smiled at me. "So, did you want to tell me your good news or wait for the champagne?"

"Wait." I pulled her onto my lap, positioning her ass over my expanding cock. Then I reached around and slid my hands down the V of her big sweater. I circled each breast, cupping and squeezing until I felt her nipples begin to harden and peak through the thin fabric. Then I pulled at those hard nibs until I heard Josie moan aloud. I kissed the back of her neck and licked the bumpy bones of her spine. Her short hair meant every delicious part of her was exposed. Josie leaned forward and took her neck out of my kissing range. That pushed her ass harder onto my cock, so I wasn't complaining.

I couldn't see what she was doing, but I heard the clicks of her phone.

"Jeez. Are you texting while I'm trying to seduce you?" I'd have to go next level. I moved my hands up the bottom of her sweater and went to get inside her leggings.

"No. I'm setting the timer. If we leave the champagne in the freezer too long it's going to explode." She sounded like she knew this from experience.

"So, how long do we have? And how come I can't find the top of these leggings?"

Josie laughed. She got off my lap, stood in front of me, and pulled her sweater over her head. "It's a bodysuit."

Whatever it was, it looked great. The black, stretchy fabric clung to her body everywhere—her small waist, her muscular legs, and her slim hips. I had messed with the top enough so that it barely covered her pointy nipples.

"Christ, you look hot. Do we have time to fuck?"

She looked over her shoulder. "Twelve minutes. Probably not."

"Strip," I commanded her. I was already taking off my jeans. Josie peeled the tiny straps off her shoulders, and I watched greedily as her tanned skin was revealed bit by bit. First her tits popped out, then her shallow navel, her thong, and her legs. As she bent over to pull the bodysuit off her legs, I yanked down her thong and enjoyed the view of her ass cheeks and her puckered anus. Josie had so many sweet places to put my cock.

I was naked before her, my clothes tossed over the other side of the couch.

"I have an idea," I said. "Can you do a headstand?"

She laughed. "Yeah, sure."

I pulled her down to sit beside me. "Put your head in my lap. No, facing me."

She did. I spread my legs and my hard cock bobbled up towards her face. She kissed it.

"Okay, headstand time." I picked her up by the waist, and positioned her head between my legs, and waited until she had her hands balanced on each side of my thighs. Her pussy was positioned in front of my face, her thighs resting on my shoulders. I breathed hot on her mound and then kissed it. I separated her legs until they were vee'd out and she was wide open to me.

Josie was strong, but this position was going to be hard for her to maintain. The blood rush to her head would intensify all her sensations, and I could make her come quickly. I put my hands on her ass cheeks and pulled her close to me. I could feel her tits pressing into my stomach, and the warm, wet suction of her mouth on my cock.

I began by licking along her pussy lips, and then traced the line between her clit and the entrance to her pussy. Back and forth until Josie's moans began to vibrate on my cock. Then I attacked her little clit, tapping it with the tip of my tongue until it emerged from its hooded hiding place. I could see all of Josie in the bright light. There were some secrets she couldn't keep hidden—like everything her body wanted. I alternated between sucking gently on her clit and tongue-fucking her, and I was rewarded by hearing her moan louder. The added vibrations on my rock-hard cock were only a bonus. Making her feel this way, making her lose her detachment and distance, breaking down her walls—that was what I really wanted.

For long moments, the only sounds in the room were sex: slurping, sucking, moaning, and wetness. Josie's body was trembling from the exertion of holding her position, while I could have sat back and enjoyed this for hours. She had already climaxed several times and now she was making a nonstop series of grunts and mews as I tongued her relentlessly.

"Unnnh, nnnnnuhhhh," Josie said from around my cock. Maybe she was asking me to stop, but she kept her legs tensed and spread wide, like her body wanted more. She tried to move her vulnerable pussy away from my mouth, but with her sweet ass cheeks firmly in my grip that was impossible.

So, her only option for rest was to suck my cock as hard as she could to make me come. I loved the sensation of her hot little mouth as she tongue-bathed my cock and sucked it deeper and deeper. I could have gotten release at any moment, but I concentrated on enjoying every fantastic feeling.

I moved one hand to insert a finger inside her. I explored until I found the bumpy raised surface of her g-spot. I tapped that while suctioning her clit and Josie began to scream. The sound was muffled by my cock in her mouth, and the vibrations were incredible. I kept going even as her body began trembling and jerking within its limited range. I was moaning now too. Everything felt so fucking good.

Despite all the noise we were making, we both heard the tinny ding of the timer. I finally let go and released the pent-up come of three days without sex into Josie's mouth. I released her body as well, moving her gently into a sideways position to allow the blood to return slowly to her body. She lay there, her head on my lap. Her face was still flushed with colour, her eyes were closed and my come was leaking from the corner of her reddened lips. I wiped it away with a finger. She sighed.

I let her rest a few minutes, then I untangled myself and went to get the champagne and the glasses. When I came back, she was still lying exactly where I left her. She opened her dark eyes and gave me a hazy stare.

"Do you buy endurance at the store? I thought you were never going to come."

I chuckled as I sat down beside her. "Mind over body."

Josie sat up. She shook her head at the complicated body-suit, and pulled on her thong and sweater instead. I didn't bother getting dressed—just in case.

She gave me a pouty glare. "I'm not going to be able to ride my bike if you keep abusing me this way."

"That's nothing. Wait till we actually fuck. Anyway, a little soreness is nothing, you get beaten up for a living."

She snuggled up against me. "Nobody touches me between the legs. Especially while I'm upside down."

"Glad to hear that."

"I didn't peg you for the jealous type." She watched as I twisted off the wire cage on the bottle top.

"Never was before." That was the truth. And it wasn't that I was jealous about Josie, more that I wanted some assurance from her that she felt as much as I did. If I knew that, I could relax. I pushed off the cork, and the champagne bubbled over and dripped onto my legs.

"Mmm, let me." Josie's pink tongue lapped at my thigh. At the sight of that, my cock stirred slightly. I stroked her hair and when she sat up, I kissed her firmly on the lips.

I poured out two glasses of champagne and handed one to her.

"Cheers." We clinked glasses, and she took a sip.

"Okay, what are we drinking to?"

"To me. I made the team."

A huge smile broke across her face. "Wow! That's fantastic news!" She kissed me enthusiastically and then sat back. "Tell me all about it."

I explained how Coach Panner had called me into his office and given me the news. I didn't mention how much of a prick he had been about it, but more about how great Coach Lee had been.

"Sooooo," I ran my hand up her bare thigh. "Looks like I'll be sticking around Vancouver."

Her face tensed briefly, then went to neutral. "Good thing too. I still haven't experienced the Tantric sex you promised me."

"Hey! You're not complaining about the sex we have, are you?"

Josie shook her head and ran her hand over my pecs. "No. I am strangely addicted to sex with you."

"What's so strange about it?" I found sex between us both amazing and exhilarating. I definitely played better afterwards because I was so loose and happy.

She smiled. "I don't know. But on the face of things— should we even be together? We're so different. Yet, I am very attracted to you."

"I don't think we're that different." Of course, it was easier for her to judge. My life was an open fucking book, while hers was full of unexplained mysteries. "Let's go out to dinner now. We can come back here afterwards and explore that attraction." I picked up my clothes.

"Okay. Let me get changed." She stood up, and picked up the glasses. "Hey, you hardly drank any champagne."

"That's the other surprise. I'm driving tonight."

20

WISH UPON A STAR

"Does anyone eat healthier than you?" Josie asked, eyeing my grilled chicken with three salads, as she dug a fork into her paella. She ate pretty healthy too, but she had a sweet tooth.

We were at a restaurant way out by U.B.C. that a team-mate had recommended. It was far away, but driving was a pleasure tonight.

"Eating clean is a way of life. You might like me better once the season starts though. I have to increase my calories, or I'll lose too much weight."

She looked down at my chest. "I like your body the way it is now."

"Wow. Was that a compliment? Either you're mellowing, or you're finally falling for me." It made me happy that Josie was more relaxed these days. Her toughness was how she kept people away, but I had broken those barriers down.

"I have a great fondness for that tongue." She watched my mouth as she said that.

"Just my tongue?"

"Hmm, maybe other parts too...."

"My brain? You like me for my brain, right?"

She laughed. "I have to admit, you're a lot smarter than I thought a hockey player would be. Prejudice, I guess."

"I've done a lot of reading. Mainly non-fiction. I like to read about psychology and philosophy." No need to mention that I did a lot of this reading when I was trying to sort out my own mental issues on the ice. Right now, everything was on straight.

"What did you learn from all this research?"

"One of my favourite theories is about flow. You'll like this—it's being one hundred percent in the moment. To consistently achieve maximum performance, you need to practice your skills, study game film, learn physics and physiology, memorize your opponents' tendencies, and a million other details. Then you forget all of it and just play. You become so absorbed in the actual playing that you're not conscious of the calculations or facts, your body and mind are fused in performance. You lose track of everything else because you're completely in the now."

Josie nodded. "I like that idea. Sometimes, when I'm on the set, I feel like everything I've done before has perfectly prepared me for what I'm about to do. That's a golden moment."

We smiled at each other. The server interrupted to offer us dessert and coffee. After Josie had a Pavlova and a green tea, we got the bill. As usual, she insisted on paying for her share.

I scowled at her. "I don't know why you have to do that all the time. I wanted to celebrate and take you out. I've got a decent contract now."

"I like to be independent."

"I know you do, I get it. So can't we move past that? We're going out now, so you need to relax sometimes."

She stared at me, her lips in a straight line. Fuck, had I

overstepped some line in her head? We saw each other a few times a week. I talked to her nearly every day. Maybe we never had that official relationship discussion, but we were going out. Weren't we?

Then she smiled, and I felt a rush of relief. "You can take me out to McDonald's sometime," she said.

"Okay. But I don't usually eat there."

"Me either. But it would be worth it to see Mr. Perfect breaking his dietary vows."

I goosed her as we walked away from the table, and she jumped.

"You think I'm perfect," I whispered in her ear. "You're crazy about me."

We were holding hands as we walked out to the car. "Look at the sky," I told her, pointing. It was darker here in the suburbs, and you could see more stars. I liked looking up at the sky and thinking that people you loved—no matter how far away—could see the same stars.

Josie looked up. Her neck was stretched out, and I bent closer and kissed it. Her short hair revealed this deep hollow on the back of her neck that I liked to kiss. I licked behind her ear, and she shivered.

"C'mere, you." I turned her around and squeezed her in my arms. She raised her face up for a kiss, and I obliged. I pressed my lips firmly against hers and opened up her mouth. Our shared breath was warm and intimate. Maybe because of our pre-dinner 69 session, our kisses felt gentler. It wasn't foreplay, but affection.

Her brown eyes were even more unreadable in the darkness, but her body wasn't. Her body was relaxed and yielding against mine. Everything was so good tonight, so right.

"I used to wish on a star every night when I was a kid," I said. I kept my arms wrapped around her warm body.

"For what?"

"To make the NHL, of course."

Josie watched my face. "Do you still?"

"To be honest, it's kind of automatic now. I guess I'll keep wishing until I make it, or…." I didn't finish that sentence, but making the NHL was never a given. Now I was one step closer, but I knew better how hard it really was.

She didn't say anything, but I knew she was listening. That was another of the things I liked about Josie—her silences.

"It's about fulfilling expectations. I went in the first round, and everyone always thought I would make it."

"The first round?"

"Yeah, the NHL draft goes seven rounds. If you're one of the top five picks—you're a shoo-in. You're going to play NHL hockey. Who knows for how long, but most guys will get a career. They'll get every opportunity to make it. I went twenty-first, so I had a good shot, but no guarantees. Still, I had it all: size, skills, desire."

"Until the car accident," Josie said. That bluntness was another quality of hers, but one I wasn't 100% sure I liked.

I sighed. "Yeah. Until I fucked up Gar's life. He was drafted to be in the NHL too, same year as me."

For some reason, sharing things with Josie didn't make me feel as guilty. She wasn't judgemental, and I felt that she understood me better. But thinking about Gar always made me sad.

I stayed silent, and Josie hugged me tightly. As I held her in my arms, I became conscious of a different sensation. Instead of worrying, I felt relaxed. All the nagging voices inside me were silent. In their place, I felt warmth and joy. I had searched so long for this feeling—contentment.

I was happy to be in this moment—right here, right now. Instead of always wishing for more, like the NHL, I was happy to be here with Josie and my new team. This realization bubbled up inside of me, and I felt my eyes tearing up.

"Butterfly," Josie asked in a wondering voice. "Are you crying?"

"I'm so happy. I've never been this happy—like ever."

Even when I got drafted, I was disappointed not to go higher. Everything was so easy in those days that I appreciated nothing I'd accomplished. But now I did. Now I knew how tough it was just to get to the second-best hockey league in the world.

And less than a week ago, I had screwed up, gotten drunk, and almost blown the whole thing. But Josie had been there for me. She saved me from myself. I wasn't going to keep fucking up though. Maybe I was finally maturing, but I felt as happy as a kid.

Josie didn't say anything. I kept on holding her. Maybe if I moved, the magic would disappear.

"Are you happy most of the time?" I wondered. She had said that thing about liking herself.

She nodded, her soft hair rubbing against my neck. "If something makes me unhappy, I change it."

"But is that realistic? There are crappy things in life that you can't avoid."

She laughed. "I can. I am a huge believer in *carpe diem*. So, I get rid of the things I don't like."

I kissed her. Her lips opened up to me, yielding in a way her mind never did. We made out until a car door slammed nearby. Then we walked to the truck, my arm wrapped around her.

"Hey, that philosophy means you like me," I pointed out.

"God, you're needy," she replied. But she was smiling.

Once we got inside the truck, I couldn't help running my hands over the dashboard again. Maybe I had underestimated how guilty the interlock system had made me feel.

Josie smiled. "Yes. Your generic truck now looks like every other generic truck. Happy?"

"Yeah. I don't have to start out every date explaining what the hell happened four years ago."

Josie's laugh was low and authentic. "I'm sure most girls don't mind at all."

"You know, I was totally stunned when you got out of the truck that first night."

"Ya. That kind of thing never happens to Goldilocks."

"I wonder if things would have turned out different if we had hooked up that first night?"

Her lips curled in that familiar way. "You spend too much time in the speculative past. We're here now."

The speculative past. Even the way she talked was like poetry. From the moment I saw her, I liked her. And when she blew me off, I had to work so hard to even find her again. But it wasn't like I had neglected my hockey, more like she gave me something else to think about. Something bigger. Hockey had been stressful for me for so long, but being with Josie had put everything in perspective.

And I was flying ever since the first night we had slept together. My game was so on point now. Being with Josie made me feel happy and confident. She was strong and smart. It felt like we were a partnership. Now I had made the team. Who knew what else I could do with her beside me?

What I felt for Josie was so different.

It was love. Real love that made anything I had felt before seem like dust. Of course, with Josie, I'd have to tell her at exactly the right time. Now that I'd be staying in Vancouver, she knew it was more than a temporary thing. And while I never knew exactly how she felt—I was sure that she cared about me too.

Josie slid across the seat towards me. "Did you forget how to start a truck without sucking on something? 'Cause maybe

I could arrange a substitution." She kissed me, then pushed my head down towards her chest. I sucked at her tit right through the thin fabric of her t-shirt and bra until she threw her head back and moaned. The noise of her desire filled the truck cab. I stopped and looked at the wet print of my mouth staining the grey fabric. Mine.

"Let's go to your place," I said. "This truck isn't big enough for everything I want to do to you."

She growled in response, but slid back to her seat and clicked her seatbelt.

We drove on without talking. A light rain had begun to fall, and the wipers were the only rhythmic sound.

I pulled up at a four-way stop, waited, and then started into the intersection. There was an explosion of glass, metal, and sound. Then nothing.

I could smell something awful and familiar. What was it? Oh yeah, the gases that inflate airbags. That smell took me right back.

21

THE FIRST ACCIDENT

"DUDE! THAT WAS A PARTY."

Gary and I walked through the woods together. Some of the other kids were camping for the night, but we both had our summer jobs the next day.

He punched me in the arm. "Who the fuck was that smoke show?"

"I dunno. Kara something. She came up from Hope." I had been making out with this brunette chick.

"Oh shit. Sunny's gonna have your balls if she finds out."

"I guess. But I didn't fuck her or anything." Sunny was scary. She had a sixth sense for any trouble I got into. She was hot and a great girlfriend, but she was sort of controlling.

"Where is she anyway?"

"Sunny? She went to Spokane with her mom."

"Which mom?" Sunny's moms had split, but they were still co-parenting.

"Jennifer."

"It doesn't seem fair. You get Sunny, and other chicks too."

"No biggie. Once we get to the show, we'll be fighting off pussy with a stick."

"I know. I can't wait." Gary had a big stupid grin on his face. Why was he even complaining? He'd had his share of pucks in junior.

"Rookie camp was sick."

Gary sighed. "Yeah, but only it showed me how far I've got to go. Not like you, Mr. First Round superstar. Sounded like you killed it."

Yeah, I'd had a good camp, but all the Detroit coaches had been pretty low key. They kept harping on everything it took to make the big team—and exactly what I needed to work on. The Wings had a rep for keeping guys in the minors longer than most teams, but I didn't mind. It was a great organization, and I was so proud when they selected me at the draft.

I scolded Gar. "Boo-freaking-hoo. We're both making it. And then when Detroit plays in Jersey, you and I are going out on the town in New York City. We'll be popping bottles."

"You can't drink in the States until you're 21."

"Jesus Christ, stop being such an old lady. This is going to happen. It's our dream and we're getting closer all the time." But he was right—I had always imagined I would make the NHL before I was legal.

"Yeah. You're right." Gary quieted down as he imagined all this. When we roomed together on road trips, he always wanted me to talk about the stuff we'd do someday. When we were older and had money—when we had made it.

The trail finally led to the lot where I had parked the Mustang. Gary ran his hand over the metallic blue hood.

"Your old man is sure good to you," he said.

"Yeah." The new car was my high school graduation present. But it was tied in with a bunch of emotional stuff. My parents had told me they were splitting up right after the draft in June. The car was my dad's way of making things up to me. Whatever. It still felt shitty, and I would rather have had my parents together than a car.

We got in and reversed out. It was warm out, so we rolled down the windows and cranked the music. Driving like this, when there wasn't anybody else on the road, was sweet. We headed towards the bridge.

Something ran out on the road. Was it a deer? I swerved to miss it and when the car hit the soft shoulder, I couldn't control it anymore. It was like the Mustang was flying and spinning. I saw the dark sky and then trees. There was an explosion of glass, metal, and sound.

Then nothing.

Maybe I lost consciousness for a moment. There was a terrible stench in the air. I opened my eyes, and the airbag was crushing my chest. There were tiny bits of glass everywhere, and all my slow-functioning brain noticed was that the glass sparkled like diamonds. The airbag began to deflate, and I could move around. I started flexing my hands and arms, then my feet and legs, and I stretched out my neck. I felt okay, and I almost started to laugh. How could the car flip over, land on its side and do no damage? Then I touched my face and my hand was wet with blood. But I wasn't in pain.

"Gar? You okay?" My ears were ringing, and I couldn't hear his answer anyway. I looked over and saw him strapped into his seat. He was moving a little from side to side. I reached over and touched his arm, and he turned towards me. His face was all twisted up and there were tears running down his cheeks. And he was one of the toughest guys I knew.

"Fuck. What's wrong?" I undid my seatbelt and tried to get closer without falling on him.

"Hurts."

"Where?" Why was I even asking? It wasn't like I was a

fucking doctor. I knew I wasn't supposed to move him though, that was one of the first things you learn on the ice. I noticed that there was blood all over him; it had soaked right through his jeans.

Nobody was going to drive by and find us. I had to call for help. My phone had been in the console, so I started searching for it. I finally dug it out from the back. The glass was smashed, but it was still working. I tried to hit the emergency key, but my hand was shaking too much. I had to breathe in and concentrate. Finally, I succeeded and heard the voice of the operator. I told her where we were and that we needed an ambulance. She stayed on the line with me, but I wasn't even listening to her voice. I kept talking to Gar, trying to keep him from passing out.

"It's okay. They're coming now—the ambulance. You're going to be fine."

The weird sound of his moaning was terrifying. I reached down and wiped off a thin line of blood off his forehead. "C'mon, bud. Don't forget, we're getting together and going out in New York City. The dream, right?" I cursed myself for saying something so stupid, but it was all I could think of.

I finally heard the sirens—faintly at first—across the water. They got louder as the ambulance drove across the bridge. It was the most beautiful sound I'd ever heard.

"They're almost here. Hang in there."

After a fucking eternity, the paramedics got Gary strapped into the stretcher. They loaded him into the back of the ambulance and told me to get in as well.

Gary lay there with an oxygen mask on his face. I couldn't hear his moaning any more. They had given him something for the pain, but he wasn't unconscious and his eyes kept fluttering open.

I got up and patted his shoulder. "You're gonna be okay,

Gar." I kept saying the same thing over and over, but it was all I could think of.

"Sit down," the paramedic commanded. "You can help your friend more by strapping in so we can get going." He had gone to my high school, but he was a few years older. His name was Buck or Brock or something.

"He's going to be okay, right?" I sat, but stretched to squeeze Gary's hand. I wasn't sure if it was to make him feel better or me.

Brock shrugged. He kept talking to the hospital, but I didn't understand what he was saying, it was all numbers and medical terms. Gary sighed and closed his eyes. His hand went limp and I let go of it.

I put the seatbelt on. I felt cold and wrapped my arms around myself. Once Brock got off the radio, he handed me a tissue and motioned towards my face. I realized I was crying. And from the dampness of the tissue, I had been crying for ages. A tear fell onto my jeans, but I couldn't feel my own tears. In fact, I could hardly feel anything at all.

When I unclenched my hand, I noticed my palm was a criss-cross map of bloody lines. But I felt fine—it was all Gary's blood. Fuck, fuck, fuck. He had to be all right.

By the time we got to the hospital, both Gary's parents and mine were already there. My mom grabbed me and hugged me tightly, even though I still had blood all over me.

"I'm sorry, Audrey. We're going to have to examine Eric first." The emergency nurse pulled us apart. It was Carol Ford, a neighbour of ours, and I wondered why she was being so harsh.

My dad was watching, his arms crossed and his face tense.

"Sorry, Dad. The car's totalled."

He nodded, and my mom answered for him. "That doesn't matter, dear. As long as you're okay."

"I feel fine." I could tell by the expression on her face that she didn't believe me. Was I still crying?

The nurse guided me through a doorway. "Eric, let's go in here."

"We'll be right here, son," my dad said.

It didn't take them long to clean up all the cuts on my face and arms. No stitches or anything. The doctor warned me that I was going to have some major bruising from the airbag. Then he and the nurse left, and two R.C.M.P. officers walked in.

I was still wiping tears away in this bizarre state of shock. I knew one of the officers. "Hey, Sergeant Burton."

He nodded but didn't smile. "Eric. This is Constable Schmidt."

"Hi," I said, but Constable Schmidt looked even more stern and didn't respond. "Do you guys know how Gary is?"

Sgt. Burton shook his head. "We're going to have to ask you a few questions about the accident."

"Sure."

He went through everything, step by step. How long we were at the party, our estimated speed on the highway, the deer, and how the accident happened.

"Eric, when there's a serious accident like this—late and after a party—we have to find out if you were driving impaired."

"I wasn't. I felt fine."

"Still, we have to test you." He brought out a squarish black box with a protruding tube. "Take a deep breath, and blow in here."

I did, and then he and Constable Schmidt looked at the reading. Sgt. Burton frowned at me.

"Did you smoke any marijuana tonight?"

I shook my head. "What's my reading?"

Nobody answered right away. Finally Constable Schmidt said, "It's .052."

"What's the limit?"

"It's .049."

"So, that's hardly over. I told you, I felt fine to drive."

"Son, we're testing you at least an hour after you got in the car. That means it was higher when you started driving. In addition, you're still in the graduated driving program. Since you don't have your full licence yet, the penalties will be stiffer."

I put my head in my hands. This night was so fucked.

I TOLD my parents what had happened with the police. My dad probably wanted to lecture me, but even he could see how exhausted I was. My eyes were aching, but the weird crying had finally stopped. I went home with my mom. Gary was in surgery, and the staff said to come back in the morning to visit him. They still wouldn't tell us anything about how he was.

In the morning, my mom dropped me off at the hospital on her way to work. Sgt. Burton said my driver's licence was suspended indefinitely. I finally found Gary's room; his parents were still there. Gary was asleep.

"How is he?"

Gary's mom turned and looked at me. She was a sweet lady, but now her face was drawn and unsmiling.

"Get out," she hissed.

I backed out and then leaned against the wall outside his room. How stupid was I not to realize that I was the one to blame for Gary being injured? I didn't think I was drunk, but legally I was. The fact that I wouldn't ever hurt my best friend didn't mean shit.

I sank down into a squat. I had done this to him. Whatever his injuries were—I still had no fucking clue how he was.

"Eric!"

I looked up, and Sunny was running towards me, her long blonde hair streaming behind her. She looked like an angel. I stood up, and she threw her arms around me.

"Are you okay? We came back as soon as I heard what happened." I felt a rush of relief at seeing her beautiful face again—like things could get back to normal somehow.

"I'm okay. But Gary's not."

She looked me over and squeezed my arms as if she was making sure I was still in one piece. "Are you sure you're okay? I heard your car flipped."

"Yeah. I'm fine. Cuts and bruises, that's it."

Sunny's mom caught up to us. She looked me over expertly as she was a nurse in this very hospital. "You're a lucky boy."

"I know. Jennifer, can you find out how Gary is? Nobody will tell me, and I'm going crazy not knowing."

She glanced at Sunny first, then nodded. "Why don't the two of you go down to the cafeteria—no, better yet, go to the coffee shop across the street. I'll ask around and meet you there. Sunny, you haven't eaten a thing today. Now that you can see that Eric is fine, have some breakfast."

She nodded and took me by the hand. Once we got outside, I wrapped my arms around her. I bent down and leaned my forehead against hers. I closed my eyes. My body trembled slightly and she reached up and wrapped her arms around my neck.

"God, Eric—when I heard you were in a car accident, I was so scared. If anything happened to you…."

"Shine, it's so good to have you here. I feel like I'm in some horrible nightmare and I can't wake up."

She tilted her mouth towards mine, and I kissed her. My

mouth was hungry for hers. I wanted her so bad. It was like all the stress, fear, and worry of the past twelve hours was churned up into this desperate need to fuck and to feel alive. I ground my erection into her body.

Finally, she pushed me away. "Eric, stop. My mom will be back anytime."

"Sorry. I need you real bad."

"Um, yeah. I can tell. But it's not the time or place."

"It's like you're the only real thing in my life now."

She smiled and led me across the street. The place was half-full, and as soon as we walked in, everyone went suddenly quiet. Before, people couldn't stop coming up and congratulating me on the draft or rookie camp, but now they turned away. We sat at a back table. Sunny had a muffin and coffee, but she only picked at her food.

"Do you want to tell me what happened?"

"Not really." I didn't want to relive this thing. "But there's one thing you should know. I'm going to get charged with a DUI."

"Oh no, are you sure?"

"Yeah. Fuck."

"What does that mean? Can you still drive?"

"I have no clue. I've been too worried about Gar to figure out all the shit I'm in."

Her mother walked in, ordered a coffee and an identical bran muffin, and sat with us. She had a sip of coffee and frowned at me. "Eric, were you driving drunk last night?"

"Mom, stop it." Sunny pulled on her mother's arm. "Eric already told me about this. He's been through enough without you starting in on him."

"Really? Because if my daughter is getting driven around by someone with judgement that poor, I think this is my business."

"Look, Jennifer, I blew a .052 last night, barely over the

limit. I did not feel drunk when I got behind the wheel, and my reflexes were fine. If a deer hadn't run across the road, none of this would have happened."

"We'll see what happens to you next, but this discussion is not over." She scowled at me a little longer, then her expression softened. "I'm telling you this in confidence, but Gary's condition is very serious. He has a punctured spleen and a broken leg."

"Oh man. What does that mean? How long is he going to be in the hospital?"

"A while. He fractured his femur." At my blank expression, she continued, "It's your thigh bone, the biggest bone in your body. It takes a lot to break that bone, and the recovery time is long and painful."

"Is he going to miss part of the season? We're supposed to be back in Kelowna at the end of August."

Jennifer shook her head at me. "Do you not get this, Eric? It's not a question of playing hockey. Gary is going to have trouble walking normally."

I closed my eyes. There was so much stuff to process, and I felt completely drained and tired. The essential unfairness of life struck me. How could I walk away unharmed and everything bad happen to Gary?

22

INVINCIBLE

THE AIRBAG BEGAN TO DEFLATE, the smell disappeared, and I stretched my neck. I felt sore, but otherwise okay. Disoriented, I looked around—Gary's face in the passenger seat dissolved into Josie's beautiful one. She was slumped against the seat, her eyes squeezed shut. For one moment, she looked almost peaceful, and I was elated that she was okay.

Then I saw that she was struggling to breathe—the sound of her deep, choked gasps filled the truck cab.

"Fuck—no!" I cried out. "Josie."

I undid my seatbelt, and then hers as well. Her side of the car was smashed in, and I tried to make sure nothing was pressing into her. Her hand was clutching her chest, and blood was seeping slowly between her fingers. Her lips were turning blue and I felt fucking useless. I yanked off my jacket and draped it over her to keep her warm. Then I started searching for my phone.

Please God, not Josie. Don't let Josie be seriously hurt. Not that she'd let me, but all I'd ever wanted to do was take care of her—and now I'd done the opposite. I'd messed up the most perfect person in my life. Her whole life would be so fucked if she couldn't do all the physical stuff she loved.

There was a tapping on my window. An older man was there and he opened my door carefully.

The man stuck his head in. "You okay?"

"I am. But my girlfriend needs help—right away!"

The older man reassured me. "Don't worry, I've already called 911. They're on their way."

I turned back to Josie. I stroked her arms, her hair and her face. It seemed like she was in another zone—concentrating on keeping her pain in check. Her whole body was trembling. I kissed her forehead and it was moist and clammy. "You're going to be okay," I whispered. But what the hell did I know? I was wrong last time.

Everything about this accident was the opposite of the last one. Instead of being alone, there were people all around. The noise of the crash had attracted everyone in this quiet neighbourhood. Through the side window, I could see a woman in the driver's seat of the other car. She looked terrified.

I could hear sirens in the distance getting louder. This time there were two ambulances. Josie was the priority, and the expressions on the paramedics' faces as they rushed her into the ambulance only confirmed how serious her injuries were.

Everything went so fast this time. Surely that was a sign that she would be all right. I insisted on coming with her, but I sat back and stayed out of the way as the paramedics went to work. They sliced open her t-shirt and I had a glimpse of the blood and swelling just below her chest. I shut my eyes for a moment, then forced myself to open them. I had to watch over her.

They had put a large bandage over her chest, and she had an oxygen mask on her face. I held Josie's limp hand the whole trip, but she never looked at me. It was an all too familiar ride. Once we got to Vancouver General Hospital, they ran Josie's stretcher through Emergency. I followed along until we came to a set of swinging doors.

A nurse held up her hand. "I'm sorry, sir. You're going to have to stay in Emergency until you've been examined."

"But I want to stay with Josie. I have to know she's going to be okay. Please." I knew the drill, once you got locked out, that was it.

She shook her head. "No. You're just holding things up by arguing." Then she let the doors swing shut, and I could only watch through the narrow windowpane as Josie disappeared around the corner. I closed my eyes and leaned my head against the door. For the second time tonight—my eyes teared up. But this time, the tears were out of anger, frustration, and worry. One ran down my cheek, and I brushed it away with the back of my hand.

I had to sit in a curtained-off room for ages—worrying and wondering. When I closed my eyes, all I could see was Josie lying there with blood on her chest. All I could hear was the terrible croaking sound as she had tried to breathe. Finally, a young doctor came in and examined me.

"You're lucky, Eric. Looks like you'll be fine except for bruising here." He motioned towards my chest and kept filling out his forms. "You'll need to watch for longer term effects like whiplash. I would recommend consulting a physiotherapist in the next few weeks."

Of course, I was fine. I was like one of those comic book characters who walks away from burning buildings or spewing volcanoes. Nothing ever happened to me—only to people I loved.

"Can I check on my girlfriend now?" The word girlfriend seemed so insignificant to what I felt for Josie. How weird was that? That one person could be in love and the other not be committed at all. Of course, whatever injuries I had inflicted on her weren't going to make her love me now.

"We're almost done here," the doctor replied. "But the R.C.M.P. want to talk to you."

I laughed hollowly. "Of course they do."

There was only one officer this time, a dark-haired woman who marched into the examination room with a black binder in one hand and a breathalyzer in the other.

"I need to take a reading from you, Eric." She hadn't introduced herself yet, but she knew exactly who I was. Once a drunk driver, always a drunk driver. I nodded and took the machine in my hand. Last time, it was the first time I'd ever used a breathalyzer, but now I took a deep breath in and blew out like the pro I was.

She looked at the reading and one eyebrow went up. "Point zero, zero, one."

"Surprised?" I asked.

"Well, let me put it this way. You wouldn't be the first person to celebrate getting rid of your driving supervision program by going out drinking. I'm Constable Lucy Vinci, by the way."

"Do you know how my girlfriend is?"

"No idea. Could you answer a few questions about the accident?" She asked me about the intersection, the visibility, and whether distracted driving might be involved.

I shook my head. "You probably know this already, but I was under supervision for over four years. I wasn't about to screw up now." I didn't mention how Josie wouldn't even get in the truck while I had the interlock system. It was the first night she'd ridden with me. And probably the last.

She asked more questions for the paperwork she was doing. Finally, we were done. "Can I see Josie now?" I asked.

"You've got a one-track mind. But sure, let's go together, I need to know the extent of her injuries for my report."

Thanks to Constable Vinci, we got answers right away. Josie had fractured ribs and a collapsed lung. A tube had been inserted into her lung to drain blood and fluids.

Fuck. Poor Josie. I had done that to her. What would that mean to her work? She couldn't do either job with a collapsed lung. Would there be long-term effects? And I remembered how much she hated hospitals. Guilt was swirling around my mind.

Josie had already been transferred to a room, and the nurse outside murmured something about immediate family only, but Cst. Vinci walked right in and I followed her.

Josie was lying in bed, asleep. With no make-up on and only the pale blue hospital gown, she looked completely different. She looked younger and more vulnerable. She was still beautiful, but in a completely different way. Her beauty was pure and clean under all those protective layers. My heart pounded in my chest as if it were trying to leap out and find its mate—her heart.

The nurse smoothed the sheet over Josie. "She's been through a lot tonight. She was awake through the insertion, but afterwards we gave her something for the pain. It may be a while until she wakes up."

Cst. Vinci asked the nurse a few more questions and then left.

"You should be leaving too," the nurse said.

"Please. I want to stay here until she wakes up."

She frowned. "Shouldn't you go home and get some sleep? You're not even supposed to be here."

"I'm her boyfriend. I was driving the truck she was in." I yanked at my hair, pushing it away from my face.

The nurse seemed to be deciding if I was a threat to hospital security. I smiled and tried to look friendly and safe. "Please? Nobody cares more about Josie than I do. I won't be able to sleep until I get to talk to her."

She must have had a romantic side, because she finally nodded. "Okay. But you might want to wash up. There's a bathroom down the hall."

I followed her and went into the washroom. I looked like hell. I washed my face and pulled off my t-shirt and tried to clean off the smears of blood and dirt. I had gotten my wallet and phone back from Cst. Vinci, and I debated whether I should call my parents. But it wasn't like anyone was going to phone them—this wasn't Nelson, and I was an adult. I could tell them in the morning.

I went back to Josie's room and watched her sleeping. The planes of her face were so right—her high cheekbones and the delicate square of her chin. I didn't know why she even wore false eyelashes, because her eyelashes were naturally long. I reached out and touched the smooth skin of her cheek. I ran my fingers down to her lips and felt their softness. I wanted to kiss her too, but Josie might not like that.

I pulled the chair right up beside her bed. I laid my cheek against her warm arm. She was alive, and she was going to be all right. The only question was whether she would forgive me for what had happened—and if things would be the same between us. I really didn't want to think about the alternative, because without Josie I would be fucked.

"WHO THE HELL ARE YOU?"

A woman's voice woke me up. I had fallen asleep with my head on Josie's bed. I blinked and sat up. There was sunlight coming in the blinds, so it was morning.

"I'm Eric," I replied stupidly. "Uh, Eric Fairburn."

She was tall with long dark hair and an angular face. She looked vaguely familiar. Her dress and jewellery looked expensive.

"What are you doing here?" she asked.

I stood up and walked closer so we wouldn't wake up Josie.

"I'm her boyfriend. Who are you?"

"I'm Josephine's sister. You're her boyfriend? You're hardly her type. Were you the one driving the truck?" She said "truck" like she meant "piece of shit."

"Yeah."

"Oh, well done. She rides that stupid motorcycle—which I've warned her is really a donor-cycle—but you're the one who lands her in the hospital. What do you do?"

I wasn't fully awake, so I just kept answering her questions. "I'm a hockey player."

"Okay, now I really don't believe you're her boyfriend. Josephine has as much interest in sports as I have in—" she paused, and just then a tall man walked in. He was dressed in a dark suit and looked like a successful businessman. "—legal matters."

"Cynthia, you're here already." He glanced at Josie, who was still asleep and then gave me a questioning look.

I introduced myself and offered my hand. He ignored it, but replied, "I'm Richard, Josephine's brother."

"He's the driver," Cynthia said. Again, it sounded like she meant "piece of shit." The two of them walked over to the bed and looked down at Josie.

Richard spoke in a low tone to his sister. "I spoke to the doctor. Apparently, the fractured ribs mean that she can't do anything strenuous for up to a month. There's also a possibility of infection in her lung. You're going to have to look after her."

"Thanks, Richard. If you knew what a pain it was to even get a babysitter so I could come here first thing in the morning. I don't mind doing it, but you know exactly what kind of patient she's going to be. She's so prickly. I would have loved to look after the old JoJo, but not this one."

"I'll do it," I offered. I stood at the foot of her bed and smiled at both of them. I was acutely aware that right now I didn't look like someone to whom you'd hand over someone you cared about. But frankly, it didn't sound like either of them cared that much. "I have hockey, but I can look after her when I don't have games or practice."

Cynthia looked like she was going to argue with me, but Richard held up a hand to shush her. "Eric, Josephine has a family who can look after her. I'm sure she'll contact you as soon as she's feeling better, but for now—I think the best thing would be to give her some space."

No way. I had been through this before with Gary. Once you were out, you never got back in. "No. I'm sorry. But I really want to stay until Josie—Josephine—wakes up and then talk to her. I have to know how she's feeling."

"Perhaps I'm being too polite. I'm a lawyer. When the hospital called in the middle of the night to let us know that Josephine had been admitted, I contacted a friend in the police department to find out what had happened. Apparently, this isn't your first accident, Eric. You're a drunk driver and a poor excuse for a human being. If I find out that my little sister is even breathing the same air as you, I will get a restraining order. And you can be sure that you'll be facing a lawsuit for the injuries you've inflicted upon her."

He stopped talking and watched my face carefully, to make sure that I had heard everything he said.

"But... I wasn't even drinking last night. It was an accident."

"Taking responsibility for your actions is the only way to grow up. You shouldn't even be on the road. Now, please— get out."

My fingers tightened on the rail at the bottom of the hospital bed. I looked at Josie, wishing that she'd wake up and tell everyone what she wanted. But she lay there, her body straight and arms at her side, in the same position as when the nurse had tucked her in. I could see the dent in the blankets where my head had been.

What struck me now was how little her family seemed to care about Josie herself. They saw her as an obligation and a victim, but nobody had even touched her yet.

I walked up the opposite side of the bed, then leaned down and kissed her on the forehead.

"Bye, Josie." I'd leave now, since there was no point in antagonizing this guy. But the only person who could tell me to stay away from her would be Josie herself.

23

MORE, MORE, MORE

I WAS SITTING DAZED in my suite when I got a text from Coach Panner that he wanted me to come to the rink and see him in the afternoon. So much had happened in the past 24 hours that I had almost forgotten about hockey. Usually hockey was all I could think about.

I showered on automatic. My chest felt tender where the airbag had expanded against it. I stretched my neck and that was a little sore too. I had a few cuts and scrapes, but that was nothing compared to Josie. That familiar sense of guilt was washing over me like the water pouring down. Why was I always the one who walked away? Why was I the golden boy? And if I was lucky, why did luck feel so shitty?

After I ate lunch, I forced myself to write a list of things to do. I needed to pick up a rental car. Cst. Vinci had said that the damage to my truck was repairable, and I needed to file a claim and get the truck to an auto body shop. Now that I was staying in Vancouver, I'd need to find a new place to live, although Joe seemed pretty happy to have an excuse not to start another set of renovations. A few guys had mentioned finding a place together, but nobody had wanted to jinx things by assuming he would make it. Of course, my ultimate fantasy would be moving in with Josie.

Josie. Seeing her lying in the hospital bed had been a huge shock. She had never looked so helpless. Josie used her clothes, her attitude, and her words to keep people away— even me. All I wanted was to penetrate that armour, but not like this. Now I saw that she was part of a complicated family, who were all as assertive as she was. Even though her brother and sister had been called in the middle of the night, they hadn't bothered coming until the morning. Did anyone actually care about her in the normal loving way? And where were her mom and dad? My dad might be full of criticism and expectation, but when I was in the accident, he was right there for me. The more I knew about Josie, the less I knew who she was. We knew each other so intimately, but we hardly knew the normal stuff because Josie had forbidden those conversations.

None of this made me feel any less for Josie. It only made me care about her more since she seemed to be so alone. But at the same time, I was struck by the short timeline between realizing I was in love with Josie and something bad happening to her. It was like my love was some kind of curse.

I hustled out to get a rental car and then headed up to the arena. Panner's office was hidden away down in a cement bunker between the arena and the small gym.

His door was shut, and I knocked on it.

"Yeah?"

I poked my head in. "Hey, Coach. You wanted to see me?"

"Yeah, Fairburn. Come in."

I sat down across the desk from him. He had an unfamiliar expression on his face and I tried to place it. He looked —happy. He usually looked completely pissed off. I smiled at him.

"I hear you've been a busy boy," he said.

"I have?" What was he talking about? Sure, I'd been in the accident, but there was no way he could know about that already.

"Yeah. So, tell me about your relationship with Josephine MacMillan."

"Who?"

He scowled at me. "Guys like you make me sick to my stomach."

Then he started clicking his computer mouse. He turned the screen to face me. It was a screenshot from the local newspaper. I scanned stories about declining fish stocks and a pending garbage strike.

"On the side." Panner pointed his finger.

Car accident injures two

Josephine MacMillan, daughter of prominent Vancouver lawyer Grant MacMillan, has been hospitalized with serious injuries following a late night car crash in Point Grey. Ms. MacMillan was in a vehicle driven by Eric Fairburn, who plays for the Vancouver Vice, an AHL team better known for its exploits off the ice. The team was involved in a bar fight last year which resulted in $900,000 in damages to The Backdoor Pub. There were also sexual assault charges filed against three members of the team, but later dropped.

The driver of the other vehicle has not been identified, and is also in hospital. According to a police source, charges will be laid in the incident.

Josephine MacMillan. I was in love with her, and I didn't even know her real name. C'mon, Josie, it was one thing to skip the conventional stuff, but not even to tell me who you really are? I rubbed my temples. It was like my brain was being assaulted by too many things at once.

I looked up at Panner. He was definitely smiling now. His spirit animal would have been the fox—the trickster, full of cunning and deceit. I braced myself for what was going to happen next.

"You okay, Fairburn? You look fine. Looking at you, I wouldn't have guessed what an eventful night you've had."

"I'm okay."

"You're not from around here, are you?"

"No. I'm from Nelson."

"So, you probably don't know that Grant MacMillan is head of the biggest law firm in the city: MacMillan, Brunswick, Carr."

I shook my head. Now Josie's expensive condo was making sense.

"Yeah, your little puck fuck's dad advises the mayor, among other important people. He's buddies with the Richardsons too." They were the team's owners.

"Excuse me, Coach. Josie is my girlfriend. She's not some girl I picked up."

"Don't give me that horseshit. You don't even know her name. You fuck girls and forget all about them. You're a dog without a sense of morals. I know guys like you." Panner's face was filled with loathing as he looked at me.

"Guys like me? What does that mean?"

"Guys like you make me sick. You're a first round draft pick. You've got all the tools. You've got the leadership and the 'media-friendly' looks. But all you do is piss it away. Do you know how many guys bust their asses to get even one of the opportunities you've been handed?"

He rose from his seat and leaned towards me with his hands planted on the edge of the desk. "When I made it to the show, I didn't unpack for three months. I kept thinking that I was going to get sent down. I took it one day at a time and I worked. I worked like someone who knows exactly how many guys would cut off their right ball to be in my shoes. One hundred and forty-eight games in the NHL, and I never took one of them for granted."

I watched him, wordless. I knew he disliked me, but I thought it was something we could work through.

"I didn't even want to sign you. I told Ian you were going to screw up. I can see how good you are, but I also know your track record. As soon as there's any kind of pressure, you crack." He pointed to his forehead. "You don't have the mental toughness to make it. I was sure you went out and got plastered during camp, but I had no proof. But even I couldn't have guessed that you'd fuck up before the season started."

"Coach, get serious. This accident was not my fault." I didn't know the exact circumstances yet, but I hadn't been drinking or speeding or disobeying any road rules.

"Not like the last time? See, the team dodged a bullet. If that lazy reporter had bothered to Google your name, this story would have been a whole lot juicier. *Eric Fairburn, drunk driver who already ended the career of an NHL prospect, has injured the daughter of a prominent Vancouver lawyer.* Must be those great reflexes. Do you steer the car at the last moment to ensure that the passenger side takes the full impact? Then you can walk away."

I felt the red heat of anger rising up, and I took calming breaths. Control that anger. Channel that anger.

"I'm not in that space now. I don't drink and drive anymore."

"I can see right through you and all this new age shaman shit that you spout. You're a fuck-up, and I don't want you on this team. You're out."

"How can you do that? I told you, it was an accident. I'm not at fault."

"I had that morals clause built into your contract, because I knew. Your car crash has triggered it. Anything that brings notoriety to the team, and a story in the local media like this is enough."

"All the notoriety in this story is due to things that happened before I even got here." Under your morals watch, I thought, but I didn't say that. He was blinded by his own prejudices. Anyone who took a different route from him wasn't good enough for his team. He was small-minded in ways I'd never be able to reach.

"You can bet that her daddy is going to sue your ass. This is a guy who sued his own brother. We need to get clear of that fallout. Leave your passcard here and clear out your locker. Since your contract doesn't go into effect until the first day of the season, we owe you nothing." He sat down and reached for the phone. "Send up someone from security. I need him to escort Eric Fairburn to his locker and then out of the building."

I WAS LOADING my gear into the back of the rental car when I saw Rams walking towards the rink. I nodded at him, but he ducked his head. I had a sudden flash of intuition.

"Hey," I called out and ran after him.

He turned slowly. "S'up, Burner?"

"I just got cut from the team."

He looked down and then raised his eyes to meet mine. "Really? That's too bad."

"You don't sound surprised."

He smiled slightly. "Well, I knew about your car crash. You okay?"

"Oh, I'm fine. Are you the one who told Panner?"

He shrugged. "I'm the captain, it's part of my job to keep the coach informed of what's going on with the team."

I thought back to what Josie had said about Rams, and how right she had been. "That's fucked. The captain's job is also to lead the team. Tell me—since I'm leaving anyway—why did you want me to get cut? I could have helped us win."

185

He shook his head. "It's nothing personal. You're good and you'll get on somewhere else, I'm sure. Just not here. This is my house." Then he walked away.

I watched him go through the doors and disappear. The guy was ten kinds of an asshole, but I couldn't blame him for anything that had happened.

Rams wanted to be the best player on the team. He wanted to make the NHL as much as I did, and having me showing him up was not going to help that. Getting a break meant making your own breaks—no matter what the human cost. That was what happened when you wanted something this badly.

Fuck this. My mind was ready to explode with all the crap getting thrown at me. I drove back to my suite and threw my hockey gear into the corner. Now what? Go home? Go to Switzerland? All I wanted to do was see Josie and hold her. But at the same time, I was angry at her. How could she not even tell me her real name?

I remembered all the time I had spent searching for her online. No wonder nothing had come up. I was searching for a ghost. Josie Ray must be her acting name. I punched Josephine MacMillan into Google search.

Bingo. A Facebook page, set on private but I could still see her photo. She looked a lot younger, with long hair and a shy smile. Very different from the confident woman of today. Another page where she won some science competition in high school. I knew Josie was smart, but she had mentioned she didn't have a university degree, and now I wondered why not. I looked further and only found random mentions like track events and school awards. There were a few people with the same name muddling the search.

Then something jumped out at me. An obituary. *Sara Ashrita Ray MacMillan. Mother to Richard, Cynthia (James), and Josephine. Grandmother to Zachary. Former wife of Grant MacMil-*

lan. Died in her 48th year of life. In lieu of flowers, donations may be made to the Canadian Cancer Society.

I could hear Josie's voice, "People love me, and then they leave."

There was a click in my brain as all the pieces came together. Her father loved her and left. Her mother loved her and died. And maybe a lousy boyfriend—who never even bothered to discover the secrets of Josie's incredible body.

Was this why she kept everyone at a distance? A family as dysfunctional as hers could screw anyone up. My anger burnt away, and all I could feel was sympathy.

I had tons of questions, and there was only one person who could answer them.

24

SHOWDOWN

I DROVE TO THE HOSPITAL. I didn't know exactly what I was going to say, but it was time we stopped playing games.

Luckily, Richard hadn't posted any security guards at her door, so I walked right in. Josie was sitting up in bed and staring out the window. She turned when I came in and looked at me. She didn't look happy to see me, or unhappy—only wary. That was her way: the owl, looking and watching first.

"Hey, Josie. How are you feeling?" I had brought some flowers, and I held them out to her. It was stupid and cliché, but women usually loved flowers.

"I feel like crap. Getting crunched in an car accident does that." She took the flowers and sniffed at them. Then she jammed them in the glass of water on her bedside table. "No scent. Store flowers are all show."

"Do you want different ones? I can get you roses, if you like."

She smiled. "Relax, Ricky. Flowers just remind me of my mom."

I sat down beside her. "You never talk about your family."

"Can you blame me? I heard you met my charming siblings. I wish I had been conscious for that."

"Which part? The part where your sister doubted that you'd have anything to do with me? Or when your brother offered to slam a lawsuit and a restraining order on me—if I ever saw you again?"

She faced me. Her brown eyes had purple shadows below them, but they still seemed to see right through me. "Yet here you are. I had you pegged right when I said you were a masochist."

I laughed in sheer relief. A car accident wasn't enough to dampen Josie's spirits. I'd rather have her insulting me than a million other women paying me fake compliments.

A nurse came in and took Josie's temperature and heart rate. She eyed the flowers. "How pretty. Did you want me to find a vase for those?"

"That would be great," I said before Josie could announce she was going to toss them. The nurse returned and made a fuss about removing the cellophane and arranging the flowers.

"Aren't you lucky to have a bouquet from such a handsome visitor?" she said.

Josie nodded. "Horseshoes up my butt. Of course, he's the one who put me here, so he figures that flowers are cheaper than getting sued." The nurse gave her a horrified look and scurried out of the room.

"Wanna bet they discharge me early?"

"When are you getting out?"

She pointed to the contraption on her side. "Once my lung is clear, they'll take the Alien out. I should get out of jail by Friday morning."

"How are your ribs?"

"You know what it's like when you get doored and you go ass-over teakettle off your bike, hit the pavement and scrape

189

all the skin off your knees and elbows and bang up your head?"

"Uh, no."

"Well, it hurts a hundred times worse than that."

"Look, Josie—if you do have extra medical expenses, I want to cover them. It's the least I can do."

"Welcome to Canada—home of socialized medicine. I'll be fine."

I wasn't quite sure where to begin. There was a short silence. Josie said, "Spill. What's up your ass?"

"How come you didn't even tell me your real name?"

She turned away and looked out the window again. "You never asked."

I pulled a chair over and took her hand. She looked at me with narrowed eyes.

"Josie, come on. We're together, aren't we? Am I the only one who feels everything here? You're amazing—you're smart, you're funny, you're beautiful. Being with you makes me feel so good, like I can take on the whole world. But you keep shutting me out. You dole out bits of your life like it hurts to talk. I want to know you."

"Could we not do this right now? I'm in a little pain here."

"No. We have to do this now. There isn't going to be a better time."

"Why not?"

"Because I've got stuff going on."

She frowned at me. "What?"

"First we talk about you, then we talk about me."

Josie blew out a big breath. She pulled her hand out of mine. "What do you want to know?"

"Tell me about your family."

"Well, you met my brother and sister. My dad's a big deal

lawyer at a downtown firm." She closed her eyes. "You're lucky you missed meeting him."

I waited, because I knew there was more.

"My mom… is dead."

"I'm so sorry."

She opened her eyes and made a dismissive gesture. "You didn't even know her."

"Of course I didn't, but I'm sorry because I can see how bad you feel about this."

She shrugged and then winced at the pain. "Anything nice about me came from my mom. Dad thinks that sympathy is for losers. We all used to idolize him and want to be like him —and now we are—assholes. I was a daddy's girl though, his little princess right up to the day he left.

"Our mom was the glue. She loved us unconditionally. But when she got pancreatic cancer, everything fell apart. Richard was a big important lawyer so he couldn't take time off. Cyn was in the middle of a difficult pregnancy, so she couldn't do much. My dad already had a brand new family, so we couldn't count on him either."

She tried to keep her voice unemotional, but Josie's whole body was trembling as she spoke. I wanted to hear everything, but I could see what an effort it was for her. "I quit university to stay home and take care of my mom. I was happy to do it. I loved her so much—she was the kindest, sweetest person."

Her voice caught, and I thought for a moment she might cry. I sat beside her and tried to hold her hand again, but she brushed me away.

"They thought she'd only live for three months, but she lived for a year longer than that."

"Oh, Josie."

"At the funeral, everyone said how lucky we were that she

lived longer than we thought. But you know what?" She looked up at me, her eyes blazing with anger now. "All the extra time she was in so much pain—pain that the drugs couldn't dull— that she became this whole other person. She was so angry and unhappy. She would complain constantly and scold me. I was only twenty, and I didn't know anything about nursing."

"That's terrible. Your whole family should have helped too."

Josie looked away, exhausted. "They did. If you ask them, they would point to all the things they did. Dad hired a nursing aide to come in daily. Richard took care of the finances and household stuff. Cyn made arrangements around food and groceries. And they visited a lot. But they had their own lives."

I nodded, but I didn't say a word in case she would stop.

"I was the only one without a life. But it was my own fault. I should have asked for the help I needed—insisted that I needed a weekend off to goof off with my friends and act my age. Instead I did everything because I was this nice person who wanted to make everyone happy. I was sweet JoJo, just like my mom had been this sweet person who made all these sacrifices in her own life for her husband and kids."

Josie straightened her back and winced. She shook her head. "Early on, Mom would have good days when she was pain-free. And she loved to watch these travel shows and see all the places she wanted to visit. She had dreams of her own, and I had never known.

"Once she died, I was ready to change. I was going to enjoy every day and not put things off for the future. And I was going to stand up for myself and stop telling people what they wanted to hear. I never deliberately hurt anyone, but I won't stand for bullshit either."

This was the most Josie had ever told me about herself. She was free because she was honest to herself. I realized that when she told me her life philosophy, she was telling the truth.

I reached over and took her hand again. She tried to pull away, but she was too weak.

Her voice took on a familiar brittle tone. "Was this your plan? Put me in a hospital bed and then force me to answer all the stupid questions you've been dying to ask."

I groaned. "Get real, Josie. I know you hate hospitals. I'm really sorry."

"Did you mean to do it?"

"What do you mean?"

"Do I need to spell this out? Well, did you enter the intersection, calculating the laws of physics so that the oncoming car would T-bone us at precisely that moment?"

"Of course not! I didn't even see it. That car must have been speeding."

"It was. I talked to the R.C.M.P. officer. They're going to charge the other driver."

I hadn't heard that yet, but I'd been pretty busy for the past 24 hours. "But now you need to be looked after for a month—and you're so independent. I feel terrible about that."

Josie looked out the window again. "You should feel worse now that you've met my sister."

"Okay, I have to tell you—I got cut from the team today."

"Why?"

"Because of the car accident. It's not my first one, right? They're worried about their team image, you know, publicity stuff."

"A team that has bar brawls is worried about their image. Yeah, right."

"I was thinking, maybe it's for the best. I could look after you now. I've got the time, and then you wouldn't have to go with your sister."

Josie looked away. "That's insane."

"Why is it insane?"

She didn't respond for a long time. I felt the warmth of her hand in mine, but her mind and spirit were far away. The sensation of remoteness between us made me shiver.

Finally, she asked me, "What about your life? What are you going to do?"

"I don't know. This gives me time to figure things out. I guess I could go back to Switzerland." But last time I went to Europe with a purpose. This time, it would probably be for the rest of my career.

"Is that what you want to do?"

"I guess." So much had happened in the past 48 hours, I really hadn't had any time to think.

"No, Eric, for once in your life, why don't you figure out what *you* want?"

"What I want?"

"Yeah, deep down, if you could have your life any way you wanted—what would that be?"

"Well, I'd be playing hockey."

"Where?"

The first answer that came into my mind was the NHL. If anything, this summer had raised my hopes. I felt like I was as good as Bomber or Reeds, and they had made it. But shit happens. Sometimes success had nothing to do with how good you were.

I shrugged. "I don't know."

"You do know, but you're too chickenshit to say."

I was sick of her pushing me when she didn't understand everything I'd been through. "You know what, Josie? It's easy for you. I've never met anyone with as much confidence as you."

She laughed. It was her hollow, sarcastic laugh. "I told you, I wasn't always like this. I used to be the quintessential nice girl. Too bad you didn't meet me then, we could have had the normal relationship you've been trying to force on me since the day we met."

"Is that how you see me? I'm not trying to force you into anything, or change you. I like how strong you are. I like everything about you. And that's why I want to see you more. Is that a crime?"

When I looked into her dark eyes, everything I felt for her came welling up. "I love you, Josie."

I waited for her to say something—anything. The silence was punctuated by the machine beeps and rolling carts in the hall.

She pulled her hand out from mine and finally spoke, "I don't want to be your next boss."

"What are you talking about?"

"You like people to boss you around. Your dad, your trainer, your shaman. I don't want that responsibility. You need to man up and decide your own life."

"It's not up to me!" I knew what I wanted, but if I couldn't even make the AHL, I'd never make the NHL. And now it seemed like I couldn't even get the woman I loved.

She raked a hand through her short hair. "You worked so hard to make the team, and you're letting them cut you for nothing."

"Nothing? Look at you! I fucking punctured your lung."

"A speeding BMW punctured my lung. It's not always about you, Eric. I don't know what happened in your first car crash, but this was an accident. Why are you letting an accident change your life?"

Cynthia walked in at this moment. Her eyes widened at the sight of me.

"Oh my God, you're back. Did you not hear what Richard said? Do I have to call security or something?" She held her large purse in front of her like a shield.

Josie scowled at her. "A restraining order requires my consent too. And he's not filing a lawsuit against Eric either. I'm fine."

"Really, Josephine? You're the last person I thought would get taken in by a pretty face." Cynthia boxed me out of the conversation. "Besides, you're not fine. You're going to have to move to my place for at least a month."

"That's not happening. I'm going back to my condo. If necessary, I'll hire a nurse."

"Where is all this money coming from?"

"I can pay for the nurse," I offered. They both turned and stared at me.

"No," Josie answered. "I'm not taking anything from you."

"Why not?" Cynthia asked. "The whole thing was his fault."

"It was actually the other driver's fault," Josie repeated. Cynthia began to argue with her.

I interrupted, "Or I can take care of Josie myself."

Josie shook her head vehemently. "That is not happening."

"Why not? You said I should decide what I want. This is exactly what I want to do—to be with you. To take care of you."

"I don't want to be dependent on anyone. Least of all you —the world's biggest pleaser."

"Why are you being this way? Can't you believe that it would make me happy to do this?"

She closed her eyes, and I watched her long lashes fluttering on her cheeks. Even Cynthia shut up, sensing the tension of the moment.

Josie took a deep breath, and then spoke in a flat voice. "You're too damaged to look after anyone else. Go to Switzerland. I think what you really want is an excuse to avoid your daddy issues."

I was speechless. Everything I had confided to her was being laid out in public.

"It's pretty clear that she doesn't want your help," Cynthia said.

"Off you go," Josie added. "Like a little puppy with his tail between his legs. That's your real spirit animal."

I couldn't believe this. Josie was always tough, but she'd never been deliberately cruel. She had lied about never hurting anyone, because she'd gone straight to everything vulnerable I'd shared with her and smacked me in the face with it. Her betrayal pierced me and filled me with anger.

"Bitch."

The word sprang instinctively from me.

She laughed. That sound I'd always treasured was now mocking me. "Took you long enough to figure that out."

25

THE WEIGHT OF A BUTTERFLY

OPERATING ON AUTOMATIC, I packed a bag and hit the road. It was late in the day to start the long drive home, but I couldn't stay in Vancouver any longer. All the trust that Josie and I had was shattered. Had she been laughing at me behind my back the whole time? Everything spiritual that I had shared was meaningless to her.

I didn't belong here. I needed to get home. I was drawn there like a salmon returning to spawn.

Nelson had a history of sheltering people who didn't quite fit in elsewhere or were looking for someplace special. Like back in the Vietnam War days, a whole bunch of draft-dodgers had settled here. Even today, on our main street, there were more holistic businesses than chain stores. It was a healing place. And right now, I needed healing. My mind kept coming back to Josie—I loved her, I trusted her, and to have her turn on me like that hurt so much; the physical pain was worse than anything from hockey.

If I thought I had hit bottom before, now was the lowest of the low. I had worked so hard for the past two years. Arizona, Switzerland, training with Tony—everything I had done to get this one last shot. Getting cut from the Vice meant I had no realistic shot at the NHL. I had only the slimmest of chances anyway, but now there was none.

The last time I'd felt this low was when I got cut by my last AHL team in San Antonio. I thought I'd hit rock bottom that night.

I had gone back to the team hotel and booked one extra night. I threw my hockey gear in the closet, went out and got completely wasted. Even to this day, that whole night was a blank. I woke up in my hotel room, and there was this strange girl sleeping beside me. That wasn't a huge surprise, in those days waking up alone after a party night would have been a bigger shock.

A beam of sunlight was coming through a gap in the curtains and shining on her face. Her makeup had worn away in the night, and she looked young—way too young to be out all night and sleeping with a total stranger. But I had been too drunk to see that and do the right thing.

I stared up at the popcorn texture of hotel ceiling and thought about how much I hated being inside my head. But it was a cycle; I hated myself, so I did stupid shit like getting drunk or blunted or laid, which made me hate myself more.

Then the girl had woken up.

"Good mornin', baby," she drawled. And I could tell from the tone of her voice that she had already worked up this whole fantasy where we were in love. I always had a ton of intuition, but in those days I never used it to stay out of trouble.

But I smiled at her anyway. I didn't say a word because I couldn't even remember her name. She kissed me and then she got up to go the bathroom. When she turned, there was a tattoo of a butterfly on her shoulder. It was a tiny pink cartoon drawing. That tattoo looked more like a sticker. It was exactly what a young girl would get. And there was something so sad about that tattoo that tears welled up in my eyes. That sadness was for her, but also for me—that my life was so completely in the shitter that I had ended up here. No job. No future in hockey. Hungover and sleeping with teenagers. I was only 21, and everything was over.

Later my shaman would say that was the first sign. That the butterfly had come to me to lead me out of that life and into my new one. And he was right. I had no big plan, but I decided to follow my intuition and do something different. Something better. I packed up all my gear and shipped it home. Then I took my knapsack and hopped on a bus and headed to Arizona. The first step on a long journey.

A long journey that led here? To bumper-to-bumper traffic as I fled yet another city after being cut by yet another team. If that night in San Antonio was worse than now, why did I feel so completely destroyed? Maybe because when everything was my own fault, at least I could change and fix things. I could stop drinking. I could straighten out my game. I could stop humping kids.

The traffic finally cleared out, and I drove mindlessly for hours. I stopped at a McDonald's drive-through just because it was open. Nutrition didn't matter if I wasn't playing. I could hardly taste anything anyway. Then I looked down at the half-eaten burger and remembered Josie's teasing promise that I could take her out to McDonald's. Only two nights ago, we were laughing and joking around. I had made the team, I had lost my interlock, and I had the woman of my dreams.

I drove on until the familiar landscape of my hometown appeared—the mountains loomed even in the darkness and the highway wound along the water. As I crossed the bridge, Kootenay Lake was a shimmering darkness beneath me.

I parked in front of my mom's place, and I could see that my dad's car was in the driveway. I had texted her that I was coming home, and she had probably told him. News travelled fast around here anyway, especially bad news.

I walked in the front door. Downy ran up to greet me with yips and jumps, but he was the only one happy that I was home. Everyone else was sitting in the living room. My mom looked worried, my dad looked pissed, and Dino looked— well, he always looked a little stoned. My mom got up and hugged me.

"Are you all right?" she asked.

"Yeah, I'm fine." I had soreness in my chest, but right now I wasn't sure if that was from the airbag or heartache.

"We were just celebrating you making the team, and now this. What did you do this time?" my dad demanded.

"Chuck," my mother laid a warning hand on his arm. "Don't assume anything."

"I wasn't drinking and driving if that's what you think. It was an accident, and not my fault."

"Then why did you get cut from the team?" he asked.

"Because I brought bad publicity to the Vice. My, uh, passenger was the daughter of a prominent Vancouver lawyer. I might get sued or something." I wasn't exactly sure what would happen next. I still trusted that Josie didn't want to do anything legal, but who knew what her father or brother would do.

"Goddamn it, Eric!" My dad jumped out of the chair and got in my face. "How many times have I told you that women are a distraction? Can you not keep it in your pants for one night?"

"It wasn't like that. She's my girlfriend. I mean, she *was* my girlfriend."

"The stakes were so high, and now you've screwed up again. This was your big opportunity." He shook his head like he couldn't believe my stupidity.

Why did my dad always assume it was my fault? It was

like no matter how much I tried to turn my life around, I was never going to get a goddamn break. "How the fuck do you think I feel? I did all the work—I'm in the best shape ever. I was the best player in camp. The coach hated me, but I was so good that he *had* to put me on the team. I told you—it was an accident. I did nothing wrong. Nothing."

My mom inserted herself between the two of us. "Both of you need to calm down and get into a more peaceful space, so we can really communicate. Let's sit down and have some tea first."

She gently pushed both of us into separate chairs, and Dino disappeared into the kitchen. We quietly steamed in our corners until he brought in a tray with Japanese tea cups, a pot of green tea, and seed cookies.

"Look, Eric—" my dad began, but my mom held up a hand.

"Chuck, I think it's important that we listen to our son first, and let him explain what happened."

I took a deep inhale and felt the soreness in my chest. But it only reminded me that Josie had a tube draining her lung. Whatever I felt was nothing compared to her pain.

"Okay, you don't have to lecture me. I know exactly how badly I've screwed up." I held my head in my hands and stared at the floor. "Every day, it's the first thing I remember in the morning, or when I go to start my truck, or when I get to whatever crappy rink I'm playing at—all I can think about is how I messed up. So you don't have to tell me."

I looked up, my mom had already started crying but my dad still looked angry... and disappointed. That was how he always saw me: a failure.

"If I could go back and do things differently—don't you think I would? Then Gary would be in the NHL... and I would too. You and mom would still be... together. And now, this time—Josie would be okay too. I keep trying, but—" I could feel a lump in my throat, but I was determined not to cry.

"I try... I try to do the right thing, but I fuck up. But this time, it wasn't my fault. I wasn't driving drunk or speeding or anything. All I was doing was being... happy."

That sounded so pathetic, but it was true. For the first time in years, I had pure joy and hope inside me. All I'd wanted was for that evening with Josie to last forever.

I felt a hand on my shoulder. It was my dad. He perched beside me and awkwardly slipped his arm around me. "Don't worry, son." His voice was choked. "You're okay... and that's what really matters."

"Thanks, Dad."

"I'm sorry if I put too much pressure on you. I know how much you love hockey, so I wanted you to be able to play—at the highest level."

He squeezed me with one muscular arm. When I was a kid I thought my dad was the strongest man in the world. When I looked up at him, he smiled. He wasn't the type to make big emotional declarations, but I got him.

"It's what I wanted too." As much as his nagging bothered me, deep down I knew he was right.

He sat back down on the couch. My mom was still crying, but now she was smiling too. Dino had placed a box of tissues in the middle of the coffee table.

My dad was already making new plans. "Eric, let's get Lance on the case here. He can find you a new team. You liked Switzerland, right?"

"Wait," my mom interrupted. "What did you mean when you said your dad and I would still be together?"

That was something I had never dared to ask, but we were letting everything hang out tonight. "Well, you guys decided to split up right after the draft. Was it because you were disappointed that I didn't go higher?"

My mom stared at me. It was like what I said didn't compute at all.

"Of course not. Baby boy, is that what you've been thinking all these years?"

"I don't know. I just didn't get it. It was so weird that we were all happy when we went to the draft, and then two weeks later you guys split up. I couldn't help thinking that the two events were related." It seemed stupid once I said it out loud, but I had worried about that for years.

She leaned forward and took both my hands in hers.

"When you moved away to play junior hockey in Kelowna, it became very clear that your father and I were no longer in the same headspace. Having you as our focus helped to mask our issues for years." She squeezed my hands tighter, "Now, don't start feeling guilty about that. We were young when we got married and we changed. Your dad is a wonderful man, but we have very different souls."

She smiled at my dad, and he managed not to roll his eyes.

"Your father insisted that it was important for your hockey career that we present a strong family image when the scouts interviewed us. So I agreed—reluctantly—that we should remain together until you were drafted. I felt honesty was the best policy, but...." She didn't finish the sentence, and my dad looked a little sheepish.

I nodded. They'd always fought, but that was what marriage was like. My mom was certainly happier now. My dad seemed the same as ever. But it was a relief not to feel guilty about it.

Now my mom moved onto a happier topic. "Tell me more about your new girlfriend. Josie?"

"Yeah, Josie. She's still in the hospital. She has broken ribs and a punctured lung."

"Eric, what are you doing here if she's in the hospital?"

"I told you. She broke up with me." I hated saying the words. It was like saying them made things more real. I couldn't deal with the pain yet.

"At the hospital?"

"Yeah."

"Oh my goodness, pharmaceuticals can have a huge effect on anyone's personality. Don't believe anything she might have said under the influence of drugs."

I began to laugh. It was funny to hear my pot-smoking mother lecture me about the evils of drugs—legal ones. My dad snorted and chuckled, and even Dino was smiling. Eventually my mom saw the humour and joined in the laughter.

"Isn't it nice when we've all got this mellow vibe on?" Mom declared. She hugged each one of us in turn and then passed out cookies while Dino refilled our teacups.

26

SAME AS IT EVER WAS

IT WAS AFTER ELEVEN, but I wasn't tired. I felt more peaceful inside after talking to my parents, but I was still restless. I put on my shoes and jacket and went for a walk. It was cool out. The leaves were changing, and it was fall. For the last seven years, I'd only come home in the off-season, so Nelson was in perma-summer in my mind.

I wasn't even aware of where I was going, but I found myself in front of Gary's house. His landscaping truck was in the driveway and a sliver of light showed in his basement bedroom.

I hesitated for a moment, then walked across the lawn and tapped on his window. He yanked open the curtain and looked at me in surprise. Then he opened the window.

"Goldie. What the hell are you doing here, man? I thought you were in Vancouver."

"I got cut again. Can I come in?"

"Uh, sure." He slid the window all the way open, and I began to slide in—like we did during high school when his parents were asleep. But halfway in, my jacket caught on something and I was stuck halfway.

"Shit." I couldn't even fit my arm in to reach back.

Gary instantly saw the problem, slipped his hand in, and released me. I propelled myself all the way in.

"Nice entrance, superstar," he said. We both laughed, and it broke all the tension. Why had I even worried about Gary being angry with me? He was never the type to hold a grudge about anything.

"The window's a tighter fit now," I confessed.

He nodded. "No duh. You're pretty jacked."

I pushed aside his clothes and sat in his desk chair. He sat down on his bed. Gary was wearing a t-shirt and boxers. I could see the long scar on his thigh.

"So, how's it going?" I asked him.

He nodded. "It's good. The usual stuff, y'know. Work, sleep, repeat."

I chuckled. Even though it had been a couple of years since I'd really talked to Gary, he seemed totally down with it.

"You wanna smoke up or anything?" Gary asked, motioning towards his desk drawer.

I shook my head. "No, thanks." Suddenly, I realized that throughout this entire crisis, I had never once craved alcohol or weed. Maybe I was finally learning to deal in other ways.

Gary nodded. He was easygoing. He always went along with whatever I wanted to do. We talked a little about a couple of buddies from high school. People always filled me in on the latest gossip when I got back to Nelson. But lately, I didn't even know all the names anymore. New people were moving in and others were moving on.

After another long silence, Gary spoke up. "So, what happened? I heard you made the Vice, for real."

"Yeah, I did. But this thing happened the other night—" Was Gary the right person to be telling this to? "I was in a car accident."

His face froze. "Shit."

"No, it's not like that. I wasn't drinking or anything. My truck got T-boned in an intersection. Not my fault."

"So, why'd you get cut?"

"There's this girl. She's, well, she used to be my girlfriend —" I blew out a noisy breath. "Anyway, she got hurt in the accident and her dad's a big deal in Vancouver. The coach found out and said I wasn't a good model for the team. To be honest, he never really liked me." I realized that Coach Panner was probably happy to have any excuse to cut me.

Gary was looking down at his hands and didn't say anything. Unlike my parents, he didn't question the rightness of my getting cut. Maybe he was used to life being unfair.

"Sorry, Gar. You're probably the last person I should be dumping this shit on. But when the accident happened—it took me right back."

He nodded. We were the only two people in the world who shared that memory. Being in that flipped car at night with not a soul around. But his memories were far worse than mine, because of the pain and the finality of what happened.

"I was hoping you were going to make it this time, Goldie."

I knew that. That had been the huge fucking weight that was always on my shoulders every time I skated on the ice. When Gary got out of the hospital, I used to visit him. Mrs. Lysenko had recovered enough to forgive me, and before I left for camp, she told me, "Now you must make it for you and Gary both."

He continued, "I feel kinda, I don't know, guilty."

I stared at him. "Are you kidding me? Why would you feel guilty?"

"Because what happened to me screwed up your head."

"My head? What about your leg? We were both supposed to go—the dream, remember?"

Gary looked down at his hands again. They were rough and calloused and darkly tanned from being outside all day. There was a black rim of dirt under each fingernail. They looked like the hands of a much older man.

His voice was quiet. Almost like he was talking to himself. "I was never going to make it."

"What are you talking about? You got drafted too."

Gary stretched his neck and looked off in the distance. "I was picked in the last round. I didn't even go to the draft because Lance Bertrand told me it might not happen. Fuck, I wouldn't even have had him for an agent without your dad arranging it.

"You know, Goldie, my numbers were good because I played with you. You fed me the puck a hundred times a game."

"No way. We were good together."

"We were good because we had played together for so long. But you were legit."

"My numbers in Kelowna tanked the year you were gone. I needed you too."

Gary looked up at me, and his eyes looked a little watery. "You tanked because you were messed up. I know what happened when you broke Buchanan's ankle."

I shut my eyes. I hated thinking about that night. It was the first round of the playoffs. I had had a shit season, but my game seemed to be picking up a little. During game five, I had missed on a breakaway. This big stupid winger skated by me and said, "Too bad for Kelowna, the wrong fucking guy got crippled." All I could see was red, and I went after him. He wouldn't fight though, and he kept taunting me all game long. Finally I took my stick and two-handed him—right in that spot where there are no pads or protection. He went down like a tree. I got suspended for the rest of the playoffs.

"How did you know?"

"Alex Trunch told me. He played for Tri-Cities, and Buchanan was bragging on the bench that he had gotten to you."

That was something else I felt terrible about. It wasn't enough that I shattered Gar's leg. I had deliberately injured another player. And then I had to sit and watch my team lose that round. Those days were like a blur now. I had so much rage and anger that I couldn't control. My coaches always wanted me to be more emotional and angry on the ice—but not like that.

Gary scolded me. "You used to float above all that crap."

"I know."

He nodded, and we sat in silence a while. Maybe that was one reason I liked being with Josie, it reminded me of the old days with Gary. If it rained hard and we couldn't play road hockey or soccer, we'd stay inside and listen to music. Sometimes we talked, but mostly we just sat around.

"It was an accident," he said.

He sounded like Josie. But he was wrong. "No. I shouldn't have been driving."

Gary yanked at his hair. "Fuck that. You and I both know that we drove in way worse shape. It could have been me driving. I don't blame you, man. I never did. I tried sometimes, because it would have been easier on me."

"How?"

"I dunno. Sometimes I'd think, like what if? If I called my dad for a ride. If you wanted to stay with that chick, so I got a ride home with someone else. If I walked home." He laughed, but it was a sad laugh. Then he concluded, "But none of that would have happened. It was us—doing what we always did. It's a waste of time to think about what ifs."

That was something Josie had said to me just before the accident: *You spend too much time in the speculative past*. It was funny that Gary and Josie were so different, yet they were both practical. I was the one with too much imagination and too many romantic illusions.

"Did you know you can get PTSD from a car accident?" Gary asked.

"Of course I know. I researched all this stuff while I was trying to get better." In between escaping my anxieties by drinking and smoking up.

"I thought I was being a wuss. It's not like we went to Afghanistan or anything. But it's a real thing."

"Yeah." I realized that I never knew if Gary went for counselling afterwards. We had still been good friends, but we hadn't talked about that night much. First it had been too raw, and then it had been too late. "I'm sorry I haven't been around much."

He shrugged. "No big deal. I get it."

"It's not that I didn't want to see you."

"Forget it. We're good."

That was what your real friends were like. No matter where I went in the world, I could come back here and some things would be the same.

"What's she like?" Gary asked.

"Josie?"

He nodded.

"She's amazing. She's so different from other people. I have no clue what she'll say next. And she's brave and confident." I didn't say the best part though, the fact that she never put any demands on me. Well, she made sexual demands, but that was nothing to complain about.

"But what's she look like?"

I grinned. "She's hot. Beautiful and hot."

"Do you have a photo of her?"

I frowned and pulled out my phone. Josie wasn't exactly the selfie type. Then I found the photo that Margie had sent me. "Okay, this is her at work, she works in movies. She doesn't always look like this, of course."

Gar whistled. "Wow. She's gorgeous. Not the kind of girl I would have thought you'd go for though."

"She's not like Sunny, if that's what you mean."

He stood up. "Look, is this Josie chick your new girlfriend or not?"

"It's a mess right now. She's complicated."

"What are you talking about?"

"Josie doesn't think I should let the team cut me. That this accident and our accident were two different things, and I should confront them."

"They weren't different things, Goldie. Neither one was your fault. Maybe you drank some, but you could drive okay. It wasn't like we were weaving all over the road and hit a tree."

I didn't totally agree with what he was saying, but maybe it was his way of dealing. So he didn't have to wonder about whether he made the wrong choice by getting into my car. There were many different realities. "If it's not my fault, then they can't cut me. An accident can happen to anyone. I never drink and drive anymore."

Gary nodded. "So you're going to go back and tell the coach that?"

"Yeah, sure. I'm going to claim the beautiful woman, get my spot back on the team, and then ride off into the fucking sunset."

He smiled. "You better hurry, asshole. The season starts on Monday."

"Fuck me. I drove eight straight hours, and now I have to drive back." I'd crash at home and head back to Vancouver tomorrow.

"Next time, just call."

I laughed, but then I realized Gary had been pacing. That slight hitch in his walk always bothered me before, but now it was only a part of what made him unique.

"What's wrong?"

"Since you've got Josie now, I wanted to tell you—I asked Sunny out."

"You did?"

"Yeah. I like her, well, everyone does. But I've liked her for a long time. Not while you guys were going out, but we've hung out and stuff. Then at a party two weeks ago, we kinda hooked up."

"Wow." It was hard to imagine the two of them together.

"I wanted to tell you in person."

"Go for it. Sunny's great."

"And so beautiful," Gary added.

They would be a good couple. Gary worked hard, but he didn't have a ton of imagination. Sunny had enough drive and ambition for both of them. And yeah, she was beautiful —in that conventional way. Not like Josie, of course. Nobody was like Josie.

I nodded. "I can see it, man. I can see it."

27

MAKING A SAVE

By the time I drove back to Vancouver, I was too exhausted to do anything but fall into bed. But when I woke up in the morning, I felt more optimistic than I had since the accident. I caught myself singing in the shower. I got dressed in a blue t-shirt that Josie had said she liked. I looked in the mirror and saw this goofy grin on my face. I laughed and said aloud, "Okay, let's do this."

When I got to the hospital, I could hear the arguing before I even got in the room.

"Cyn, I'm not going to your place. I want to go home."

"Believe me, I'd like nothing better. But the hospital will not release you without me signing a paper that states you're going to be supervised. They don't want you bleeding out alone, or whatever it is that's going to happen."

"'Bleeding out' sounds like something that zombies or vampires do. If I have to spend a month at your place, I'll be trying to bleed out."

"That's very insulting. We have a lovely home, and there's lots of room."

"You also have a very full schedule with the kids and your

social life. I'm not going to fit into that and you know it. And I need my own space. Why don't you guys chip in and get me a nurse?"

"Believe me, I'd love to. But Richard and Daddy won't pony up. Anyway, don't you have anything left from the money Mom left you?"

"Nope. Spent it all on my condo."

"If you had listened to me, you would have gotten a cheaper place and saved some money for a rainy day."

"It never rains in Vancouver, sis. Gosh, what do people who aren't born into loving families like mine do?"

"They go home with their boyfriends," I said as I walked in the room.

Josie's eyes widened. For a moment I saw something flash over her face. Was it relief? That made me feel like I was right—she did care about me. And maybe she'd been testing me. Then her protective mask fell into place.

"What are you doing here? Shouldn't you be on the next Swiss Air flight?"

"I came to take you home. Looks like I'm right on time."

Cynthia shook her head. "Didn't JoJo break up with you the other day? Are you one of those concussed hockey players?"

The whole family was gifted with offensive honesty. Well, I could be honest too.

"Look, I seem to be the only one who actually wants to look after Josie. I will sign any necessary papers and make sure she doesn't bleed out. Or in."

"What do you know about looking after sick people?" Cynthia asked. Josie didn't say a word, but kept watching me.

"Josie can tell me what she needs, and that's what I'll do for her. That's how our relationship works —communication."

Cynthia turned to her sister. "Is this what you want? Do

you want this big... athlete to change your tubes or whatever?"

Josie shook her head. "No. Absolutely not."

I smiled with maximum charm. "Sorry, Cynthia. Do you think that Josie and I can have a few minutes alone to talk?"

She eyed me suspiciously, but nodded. "You haven't got long. The nurse is coming back in a few minutes to go over her at-home care."

"It won't take that long," I assured her.

"Someone's overconfident," Josie muttered.

She was sitting in a wheelchair. I pulled up a chair and sat beside her. Her hands were folded in her lap and I reached over and took them in mine.

"I missed you," I told her.

"It's only been a couple of days." Josie sounded scornful, but there was a tiny smile on her face.

"It's an eternity if you don't know what the future will be."

"Stop talking in zen koans."

"I'm talking about our future." I took in a deep breath. "We don't have much time, so I'll get right to it. I took your advice and did a lot of thinking about what I want. I've decided what I want most is to be with you."

She rolled her eyes. "That's not a career decision."

"But it is a life decision. And everything else falls out from that. Do you want to be with me?"

She didn't answer right away. I noticed that she was wearing makeup, and looking more like herself. She still looked fragile and vulnerable though.

"I don't want you to look after me."

"That's not an answer to my question. I love you, Josie. Maybe you don't love me today... but do you think you could... maybe someday... feel the same way?"

Her gaze dropped, and all I could see was her long eyelashes trembling over her cheeks.

"Yes."

The word was so faint that I could barely hear it. But my soul expanded in that moment.

I squeezed her hands. I wanted to hug her, but I knew her ribs were too sore. And I also knew not to make a big deal out of her answer. "Okay. That's settled. Let's get you home. If you don't want me to look after you, we'll make other arrangements."

We kept sitting there, wordless. Josie's hand crept out and caressed the top of mine. The whole sterile room was bathed in a golden energy for me. Whatever happened next, we were going to be together.

The nurse walked in. It was the same one who had put my flowers in water.

"Oh goodness! Your handsome boyfriend is back. Is he going to be taking you home instead of your sister? Lucky you."

Cynthia appeared at the door. "That's a matter of opinion. What have you decided, JoJo?"

"I've decided that the guy who put me in the hospital can take me out."

I laughed. "Seems only fitting."

Cynthia snorted. "Well, I'll listen to all the aftercare instructions anyway. In case you change your mind later."

The nurse went over everything I would need to do to look after Josie. The main things were to look out for signs of an infection and to make sure that Josie didn't exert herself.

"At night, try to make her as comfortable as possible. She's going to have a lot of trouble sleeping, so you might want to consider a body pillow."

"What about sex?" Josie asked.

"What?" The nurse's eyebrows disappeared into her bangs.

"Can I have sex right away? That helps me to get to sleep."

"Josephine, don't do this," Cynthia said in a pained voice.

The nurse shrugged. "Well, you didn't have any trauma in *that* area. But no strenuous exertion which puts too much pressure on your ribs and lungs. And I think you'll find a lot of discomfort in positions that put any kind of pressure on your ribs."

Josie nodded. "He's very flexible. We'll be good."

Cynthia groaned. The nurse handed Josie a bag with her belongings in it, and I wheeled her out of the room. When we were in the elevator, Cynthia pulled out her cellphone.

"Well, I should get your number, Eric. If you're going to be looking after Josie, we need to stay in touch. I'm sure there will be things she needs."

Cynthia seemed to have accepted that I was going to be around, and she warmed up a little. We exchanged numbers. As we got out of the hospital into the sunshine, I noticed how oddly Josie was dressed. She was wearing a very feminine dress and flip-flops. I'd never seen her in a dress before.

"What are you wearing?" I asked her.

"Isn't this awful? I can hardly wait to take it off. And you haven't even seen the granny panties yet."

"JoJo! It's a Tory Burch dress. It's gorgeous, and the only reason I brought it was that it's too small for me. If you'd only given me the keys to your place, I could have gotten your own clothes and shoes. And underwear."

We got to my loaner car, and Josie got out of the chair and eased herself slowly into the passenger side. I could see she was in a lot of pain, but I let her do it herself. My eyes met Cynthia's, and she gave me a slight nod.

"I'll take this wheelchair back," Cynthia offered. Then she

leaned down to the passenger door. "I'm going to come by and see you tonight after James comes home."

I couldn't hear Josie's unenthusiastic response as I went to the driver's side. I waved at Cynthia and started up the car.

"Why do I feel that every time I let you drive, I'm taking my life into my hands?" Josie groused.

"And yet you keep doing it." I reversed and pulled out of the parking lot. "Must be love."

"Or insanity. But really, what's the difference?"

28

HOME ALONE

"Ahhh, home."

Josie's face lit up when she walked into her condo. She still moved slowly, but looked more natural and relaxed. "You know what I'm going to do? First, I'm taking a long shower. Then I'm going to get dressed in real clothes. Then food."

She went to the kitchen and poked around. The chocolates I'd given her were still on the counter, and she popped one into her mouth. Her eyes closed, and she swayed. "Yum!"

"Man, you're happy," I said.

"I love being home. Don't you?"

I shook my head. Sure, I liked going back to Nelson, but my mom's glitter den didn't make me act like this. But then, I hadn't created a nest for myself as Josie had. And I kept putting things off until I had made it, which might be never. "Teach me how to enjoy every moment like you do."

She shook her head. "At the risk of sounding like a shoe commercial—just do it."

"Okay." I gently placed my hands on her shoulders and kissed her. Her lips were soft, and she tasted like chocolate.

Kissing her again made me feel great. It also made me horny, but I didn't think I should push that.

I leaned my forehead against hers. "So, are you okay to take a shower alone?"

She squinted at me. "Is that an offer?"

I blushed. "Oh no. I didn't mean sex."

Josie grinned. "I'll be fine."

"Okay, I'll go and get some groceries then. I can make dinner later."

I went home first and packed a bag so I could stay over. Then I got some groceries. When I got back, the place was buzzing. Cynthia was already there with her two children.

"Uppy-uppy," called out a little toddler with outstretched arms in front of Josie. She was dressed in a tiny striped dress and matching shoes.

"No, Cordelia," Cynthia said. "Auntie JoJo can't lift anyone for a while."

"I can pick you up," I offered. She hid behind her mom at that suggestion. One suspicious eye glared at me from behind Cynthia's skirt.

"Who are you?" A little boy demanded. In his blue shirt and khaki pants, he was better-dressed than me.

"This is Eric," Josie explained. "He's my boyfriend."

That was a first. I beamed, and Josie introduced Cordelia and Zachary.

"Nice to meet you guys." I held up the bags. "I'm going to put the groceries away."

When I came out to the living room, Josie was sitting on the couch with her nephew and niece around her. She was reading a picture story from her iPad, and making funny voices for each character. Her genuine sweetness with the kids was unexpected but heart-warming. Josie had revealed so many new layers of herself this week.

Cynthia was watching me watch Josie. "They insisted on coming to visit. It's probably too much for her."

"I'll make sure she gets to bed early."

Her eyes narrowed, and she hissed at me, "And gets rest. No monkey business."

I chuckled. "Don't worry. I want her to get better as much as you do. I think the biggest problem will be getting Josie not to overexert herself."

"There's still a lot I'd like to know about you," Cynthia said. "But Josie said it's not my business."

"Ask me anything," I offered.

"Okay, how come you—"

Josie interrupted, "Down, Cyn."

"Auntie Jojo," Zachary scolded. "That's what you say to dogs, not moms."

"Well, tell your mom to behave then."

He giggled. "Behave, Mom."

Cynthia frowned. "We better get going, James will be home soon. I just wanted to check and make sure that everything was okay. And drop off the basket." She motioned towards a large cellophane wrapped basket with various gourmet foods in it.

"Oh, wait. Come on, guys." Josie got up slowly and went to the kitchen with the kids trailing behind her. There was whispering and then the kids emerged with bulging cheeks.

"You didn't give them treats, did you? They'll never eat their dinner."

"Noof," said Josie. Her cheek was bulging too. The three of them began giggling. A little dribble of brown ran down Cordelia's chin.

"Jojo, not chocolate! Now they'll be wired as well as not hungry."

They left with Cynthia still clucking in disapproval.

"I'm the bad aunt," Josie declared happily.

"The kids seem to enjoy it."

"Cynthia is kind of an intense mom. I figure that they need some balance."

"She is pretty tightly wound. She seems to think I'm going to do something criminal to you now that we're alone."

Josie groaned. "Richard and Cynthia aren't really the jerks they seem to be. I'm the youngest, so they look out for me. I've done things differently from them, so we clash a lot."

"Well, I assume that they care about you, but you guys sure have weird ways of showing it."

"That's our family in a nutshell. But if I ever need them, they'll be there. Even my dad. I just try really hard not to need them."

"Depending on someone is not the worst thing."

There was a little smile on her face. "You're here, aren't you, Ricky? I must be depending on you. And speaking of that, let's see what groceries you got."

She began poking through the food. "Seriously, dude? All these groceries, and there's still nothing to eat."

"While you're recovering, it's important to put good food into your body. Healthy meals will aid your body's healing."

She stuck out her lower lip. "When you're sick, everyone's supposed to be nice to you and give you treats. Like ice cream."

"There is ice cream."

"Oh boy!" She yanked open the freezer drawer, pulled out the container, and held it up. "Are you kidding me? Eric, this is made of avocados. Who eats frozen avocados?"

"You should give it a try before you diss it. It's got great texture, and this one is chocolate."

"I don't even know where you get this crap. Is there some magical raw foods superstore with hippie staff and spirit animals tied to posts in front?"

"I'll do the cooking. Let me make you meals for a week, and if you really hate them, we'll get whatever you want."

She scowled at me. "I'm not used to having someone around all the time. Don't you have to play hockey somewhere?"

"Well, that's something we need to discuss. Let's sit down."

We went back to the living room where it was more comfortable for Josie. I watched her ease herself down. Every time she used her pectoral muscles it hurt.

"So, you know I got cut right?"

She nodded.

"I was wondering how you feel about Switzerland. Where there's lots of chocolate."

Josie tilted her head at me and narrowed her eyes. "No. Forget it. I said I'm not going to tell you what to do."

"I told you what I want—to be with you. If you won't come to Switzerland, why should I even investigate it?"

She shook her head. "It doesn't work this way. You need to find a job you want first. Then we settle the next part."

"I want to play hockey."

There was a long pause. Josie leaned forward and put her hands on my cheeks. She turned my face towards her, and stared at me. Her gaze was so intense that it felt like x-ray vision. "Where?"

"Anywhere that'll take me."

"That's not what you want, that's still letting other people run your life. Where do you want to play hockey?"

I could feel the answer rising up inside me before I even consciously knew it. The response was like a word bubble that popped out of my mouth. "The NHL."

"Ahhh." Josie nodded and let go of my face. "That answer makes sense. That's why you've been doing all this work. Because you want your shot."

I reached down and held her hands. "If you knew, why did you make me say it?"

"Because I wasn't sure if you knew."

"But I'm kind of fucked right now."

"Explain the whole deal to me again."

"I have to get into the AHL, because it's one step below the NHL. Scouts and GMs can see me there. And the Vice were the only team who would even consider taking me. The only other option would be to go down to the ECHL, and maybe get a shot at moving up once teams have injuries and stuff."

Josie put her fingers up to her temples and rubbed them. I felt shitty for bothering her with all this.

"Let me see your contract," Josie said. I found it on my phone and handed it to her. She scrolled through, reading and shaking her head. "This morals clause is crap. It's so vague that breathing wrong could be cause for dismissal."

"So that's bad, right? Even if I haven't done anything too wrong, it's enough to fire me."

"No, it's good. A decent lawyer could demonstrate that it creates an unreasonable standard of conduct."

"How come you know so much about this stuff?"

She made a face. "I had to live with a lawyer who thought that mealtimes were the perfect opportunity for debate. My father had me tagged to become a lawyer—just like him. And join his firm, like Richard did."

"What happened?"

"Well, first off, he left my mom for another woman. That didn't exactly endear him or the profession to me. And then once my mom died, university didn't seem so important anymore. I wanted to live and do active things while I'm still young. I could do law school anytime. But now I'm not sure I ever will."

"What about Cynthia? How come she didn't become a lawyer?"

Josie laughed, but it wasn't her full, throaty laugh. "Here's a direct quote from my father: 'Cynthia, you're the pretty one—just like your mother. Richard and Josephine are going to law school, but you won't need to.' How to insult four people at once. It's a skill."

"I wish you could be there with me when I talk to Panner. I could use someone who knows the law like you."

"Sure. Someone who looks like a bike courier is not going to cut a lot of ice with your coach."

I kissed her on the forehead. "You look like a superhero to me. And you could wear your pretty new dress from Cynthia."

"Already burned that," Josie replied with a laugh. "No, Eric. For a job like this, you need a real lawyer."

29

LAWYERED UP

We paused outside Panner's closed office door.

"Okay, Eric. Let me do the talking."

I nodded, that was fine with me. I had a hollow feeling in my stomach. After all, getting to stay in Vancouver had become a lot more important in the past 24 hours. I knocked on the door.

"Yeah?" Panner's voice sounded irritated before he had even seen my face. I opened the door, and we walked in.

"Mr. Pankowski? I'm Richard MacMillan of MacMillan, Brunswick, Carr." With one smooth motion he shook the coach's hand and then slipped a business card onto the desk. We all sat down in the cramped office. In his expensive suit, Richard looked extremely out of place.

When Panner saw me, he scowled. I straightened up in my chair and stared him down.

"What are you doing here, Fairburn?"

"I want back on the team."

Richard kicked me in the ankle.

"Mr. Pankowski, I understand that you released Mr. Fairburn from his contract on the basis of a recent car accident."

"Yeah, but—how exactly is this your business?"

"Sorry, did I not explain that Mr. Fairburn is my client?"

"Why does he even need a lawyer?"

"Let's start off with the facts." He passed Panner a file folder. "This is the police report I got from Constable Vinci, the officer assigned to investigate Mr. Fairburn's accident. If you read it, you'll see that he was completely not at fault. The driver of the other car was speeding and ran a stop sign. She's been charged with reckless driving causing injury."

Panner kept leafing through the file. I realized he had no clue what it all meant. He had probably read only that one web article and never really investigated my accident. That made me even angrier. Players got cut all the time, and they didn't have a high-powered lawyer to try to save their asses.

"Are you related to this Josephine MacMillan?" Panner asked. He rotated his neck several times.

"Yes. She's my sister." Richard fixed the coach with an ice-cold glare. I had experienced that glare myself, and it was scary. "I understand that you slandered her. But hopefully I won't have to file suit on that account. The main issue here is one of wrongful dismissal."

Panner had stopped chewing gum or even blinking.

"A thorough investigation would have revealed that Mr. Fairburn was not at fault, therefore the so-called morals clause that you added to his contract should not have come into effect. By the way, you should consult an attorney because the morals clause as it stands is not defendable in court. It lacks concrete definition."

Panner finally recovered some of his bluster. "What about the bad publicity he got for the team? You know he's done this kind of thing before."

Richard shook his head. "If you reread the article, I think you see that all the 'bad publicity' was generated by last season's Vancouver Vice team. Which you were in charge of,

I believe. And if you're referring to Mr. Fairburn's DUI conviction, he has fully discharged all the penalties for that and is beginning with a clean slate." Richard raised his eyebrows. "Fresh starts are a good idea. Don't you agree?"

"Well—" Panner's eyes darted from side-to-side, as he tried to weasel his way out. "Unfortunately, we've already filled his roster spot."

"Really? Because I have it on good authority that you still had an opening as of 9:00am this morning." Under pressure from Richard, I had called Brenda. She was all too happy to supply me with the roster information.

"Back to the issue of wrongful dismissal suits." Richard paused, leaned back, and tented his fingers. This guy was a master S.O.B. And right now, he was *my* S.O.B.! "In my experience, most of these suits could most easily have been settled by reinstating the employee early in the process— before the costly issue of damages to reputation have arisen."

He smiled, and I was reminded of a snake charmer with a snake. "I think you'll find the damages that Mr. Fairburn might receive would be well in excess of his original contract, and then there are lawyers' fees. And unfortunately, those fees can add up." He chuckled in a completely humourless way.

The idea of paying me more money for not playing had caused a sweat to break out on Panner's forehead. "Well, I'll have to talk to the GM before I can do anything."

"No need to do that. We already have an appointment to see him this afternoon. I was only hoping that since you hadn't filled the roster spot, and since Mr. Fairburn is such a skilled player—we might settle this matter right here and now. But if you don't have the power to reinstate him, that's fine. We'll involve your boss and apprise him of the whole situation—your erroneous dismissal of the player and the resulting exposure of the organization to a lawsuit."

Panner didn't say a word. You could see all the scenarios running through his head.

Just then someone rapped on the door, and Coach Lee stuck his head inside.

"Rob, I was just—" He stopped talking and stared at us. "Oh sorry, I didn't know you had a meeting going on. Oh hey, Eric." He gave me a head nod and started to leave, but Panner called him back in.

The head coach glared at me. "So, Ian, it looks like Fairburn here has sorted out his, er, issues, and he can rejoin the team."

A big smile broke out over Coach Lee's face, but after noticing Panner's scowl, he quickly hid it. "Uh, okay. I guess we can still fit him in somewhere. I'll be in and around the training room, Eric. You can come by and see me later, and I'll get you set up." He backed out of the office.

Richard opened up his briefcase. "Well, it's great that we could come to this understanding. But before I go, I'd like to get this all in writing. Here's a memorandum stating that you agree to the new terms."

Panner signed it without reading a thing.

"And here's a new copy of Mr. Fairburn's contract. It's exactly the same as his previous one, except the morals clause has been removed. As I mentioned, in its current state, the clause is not actionable. So there are really no material changes."

"Okay. But I'll have to get the General Manager to sign off as well."

"That's fine. As a representative of the Vancouver Vice, your signature is binding. Any paperwork required on your end, you can fulfill. I'll take this copy for Mr. Fairburn's files."

Panner nodded. I'd never seen him so quiet before.

Richard stood up and extended his hand again. "Thank

you very much, Mr. Pankowski. Glad that we could settle this matter so easily. We appreciate your time and effort."

I got up, nodded at the coach, and thanked him as well. He scowled.

Richard was already checking his phone as we walked down the hallway, so we didn't speak until we left the building.

"You know, Eric, when your lawyer tells you to shut up, you need to shut up."

"Yeah, sorry. Panner gets my back up."

"I've seen cases like this before. He's going to make your life hell from now on, you know."

I shrugged. "He was already. How much worse can it be?"

"You'll find out, I'm sure."

"I can handle it. Hey, how did you get a meeting with Mr. Richardson so fast?" The team GM was notoriously hard to reach. Unless you were a beautiful woman, or so the rumours went.

Richard smiled. "The lawyer is the one who should ask the questions. I prefer to keep my methods to myself."

Son of a bitch! He never had a meeting. I laughed loudly.

"Okay, I have to go now." He hit the remote, and his Mercedes beeped open. He held out his hand and shook mine.

"Good luck, Eric."

"Thank you so much. What you did today was huge."

"You're welcome. But I didn't do this for you. It's the first favour that JoJo has asked of me in ages—" He didn't finish the sentence, and again I was struck by how every one of the MacMillans seemed unable to express affection normally. To find out that Josie was the warmest member of her family was stunning. But they all seemed to care in their own ways. Richard put on his sunglasses and turned to me. "Be good to her."

His tone made that sound like a threat. But he didn't have to worry, and I was pretty sure he knew that.

As I TURNED to go back into the arena, I noticed that Rams was standing in the entranceway. He had been watching us. Now I'd have to deal with him daily, and I didn't want to waste energy watching my back every moment. What Would Richard Do?

"Hey, Rams." I ran up to him. "Great news. That was my lawyer, and I'm back on the team."

He looked less than thrilled to hear that. "Really? Well, we'll see how long that lasts."

"Don't worry, I'm going to stick." Then I leaned in closer. "But you want to know something really interesting?"

He nodded slowly.

"In all that free time I had, I did a little investigating on my own. I went back to that pub we were at. I was talking to this waitress—you remember the one with bright red hair? Anyway, she saw something weird. Someone put something into the shots we drank. No wonder a lot of guys got sick."

He flinched a little. "That is weird."

I pulled a folded paper out of my jacket and waved it at him. "I asked her to sign a statement verifying what she had witnessed. Once we get a team photo, I'll go back and get her to pick out whoever it was that did that. According to my lawyer, that's a prosecutable offense."

Was "prosecutable" even a word? I must have heard it on TV, but whatever—this was working. Rams looked very nervous.

"You know, Burner, maybe pushing this thing is not the best idea—you know, for team unity."

"D'ya think? Maybe it was one of the guys who got cut. Anyway, the most important thing is how things go from now on. If bad shit keeps happening, it will be important to sort out who the asshole causing the problems is."

I watched him swallow and nod. "Yeah, I think you're right. Hey, welcome back, Burner."

"Thanks."

We both headed inside. He was a huge fucking phony, but at least I had called him on his shit. I tucked my new contract back into my jacket pocket.

30

CELEBRATE GOOD TIMES

AFTER CALLING Lance and meeting with Coach Lee, I rushed home to see Josie. She was still lodged amongst the living room pillows where I had left her, but on the table there was an empty container of chocolate avocado ice cream.

"Well?" She looked up at me with wide eyes.

"I'm back!"

"Woo hoo!" She tried to high-five me but ended up wincing. "Ow, my ribs."

"Oh no. Don't hurt yourself." I sat down beside her on the couch.

"But we have to celebrate." She stuck two fingers in her mouth and let out a shrill whistle.

I shook my ears. "Jeez, Josie. That hurt."

"I am a woman of many talents. So, tell me all about it."

"Richard was phenomenal. He made me want to go to law school."

She held up her fingers in the sign of the cross. "Stay away, bloodsucker."

"He had Panner cowering by the time he was done. And he completely snowed him into thinking we had a meeting with Richardson. It was magnificent. And all because of you!" I leaned in to kiss her. We had developed a new kissing system that didn't involve our bodies touching at all.

"Richard can be all right," Josie admitted. "I'm sure he was in his element. Now I'll have to be nice to him at the next family reunion."

"You have family reunions?" That would be scary.

"No. But now they might start so they can dissect you."

"Your brother started by finding out the worst stuff about me, so things can only get better from here."

Josie laughed. "Who cares what people think?"

I squeezed her hand. "Well, I do. But I'm trying to make sure it's only important people."

"Like me?"

I nodded. "The most important person. How are you feeling today?"

"Better. I was walking around and doing a few things today."

"No lifting, right?"

"Nope. What's to lift? But I had to turn down a job today."

"Oh no, really? A stunt job?" Of course it was. She could do the courier thing whenever she wanted. I sighed.

"Do you feel guilty?" Josie asked.

"Of course I do. I did this to you, and now you're missing out on a job and a paycheque."

"I could feel better if we had pizza for dinner. Like real pizza—with mozzarella, mushroom, and pepperoni. Not healthy pizza made out of cardboard and kale."

"Josie, you're manipulating me!"

"Is it working?" She nestled further in the pillows and giggled.

I bent down and kissed her again. Then I stroked her hair. "Why are you so flipping adorable?"

"I think it's the pain meds. I feel like I'm having an out-of-body experience." She giggled again. "And I didn't even have to go to the desert."

I laughed and carefully put an arm around her. "You're cute."

"I'm also happy you got back on the team."

"It's going to be tough. Panner looked like he wanted to strangle me right on the spot." I dug out the paperwork I'd gotten from Coach Lee and H.R. "I've got my schedule. Practice tomorrow. I'm home for the next ten days, and then we leave on a road trip. I'm going to have to find someone to take care of you when I'm gone."

"Maybe I'll be better by then. Anyway, I can find someone myself. I appreciate your doing all this, but I'm not your responsibility."

"Okay." It was great to get to spend all this time together, but I still had to navigate around her independence.

She was reading through my schedule. "You go away for weeks at a time?"

"Yeah. We have road trips—on a bus. So we hit all the teams in the area. Is that a problem?"

"No, it's great." She patted my hand. "Nothing personal, but I like being alone sometimes."

Was this an invitation to keep living here after she got better? I wasn't going to presume, but I could hope. With Josie, taking things slowly was key.

She pulled out a large pink post-it. "What's this? *'Eric, so happy you're back on the team! I'd love to take you out for lunch and give you the inside scoop on how things work around here. Brenda.'* And there are hearts all around this! Does this chick have a crush on you?"

I blushed. "Yeah. I guess." Then I braced myself for what was going to happen next. Sunny used to go ballistic when crap like this happened.

Josie threw back her head and laughed. "Owww, my ribs. Oh Eric, you crazy ladies' man, you."

"It doesn't bother you?"

She snorted. "Why? When you're not into me anymore, I assume you'll have the decency to tell me. But I am pretty awesome."

I kissed her. "The awesomest. I'm hungry. Did you want dinner?"

She smiled at me and nodded.

"Okay, where's the pizza menu?"

"Ahhh, perfect. This means I'm still into you," she declared.

"You'd get rid of me if I didn't feed you pizza?"

"I have executed men for less."

JOSIE WAS STILL WEAK, so after dinner we settled for watching a movie on her laptop. But even then, she started to doze off.

"Hey, sleepyhead. I'm going to tuck you into bed now."

She nodded and went off to her bedroom. When I came in, she was already in bed.

"I'll put your water and pain stuff here. Do you need anything else before you go to sleep?"

"Are you sleeping in the living room again?"

"Yeah, I was planning to."

She rolled her eyes. "What's the point of having a hot guy look after me if he sleeps on the couch?"

"It's for your own good." If I slept beside her, it was going to lead to something that would hurt her ribs.

"Have you done this before—looked after someone?"

"Nope. Only for you, babe."

Something softened in Josie's expression, but her voice was still mocking. "That's pretty fucking sweet."

I lay down on the bed beside her. I put a hand on her hip, and she rolled to face me, wincing a little.

"So, you think I'm a hot guy?"

"Don't start, Eric. You know."

"I want to hear it from you."

She snorted. "Okay, Mr. Needy. When I first saw you, I thought you were totally gorgeous. I wanted to rip your clothes off and do you right on the table at the pub."

I laughed. "There. Was that so hard?"

"Yes. It hurt me. My ribs hurt."

"Your ribs hurt whenever I make you do something you don't want to. You're a wimp."

"Nobody has ever called me that before. I'm a freaking stunt woman—taking pain is my job."

"Mine too," I pointed out.

"Great. We can have a pain-off to see who's tougher. Fire up the branding irons."

I laughed and tried to cuddle her without touching her ribs. Squeezing her ass seemed to work—for me, anyway.

"Josie, can I ask you something? If you liked me so much, how come you practically ran away the first times we saw each other?"

She didn't answer right away.

"I don't know. When I saw you guys, I wrote you off as assholes. You all had this physical presence—like you owned the space around you. It reminded me of the jock table in high school. Then you started betting on picking up women."

"How did you know? You couldn't have heard us from where you were sitting."

"I could tell by watching. That's why I like to go to bars. Instead of TV, I get to see all the sex and drama live."

"You know what I don't get—why didn't I see you when I came in? Because once I saw you...."

"That's easy. It's this aura thing. I learned it from being

on sets—all the good actresses can do it. You project confidence and you're visible. Or you act shy and you disappear into the background."

"Seems like magic. But let's get back to the part where you wanted to rip my clothes off."

Josie laughed—her full-throated laugh that I loved. Then she winced. "Well, I thought you were good looking, and your body... oh yeah. Jocks are usually jerks though. But you had this detached quality even amongst your buddies." She put her hand up to my cheek. "It was like you were lonely too."

Had she even noticed that she admitted she was lonely? That only made me love her more. I kissed the hand resting on my face.

"So you turned on your magic aura and drew me to you?"

She smacked me in the chest. "You, of all people, shouldn't make fun of auras."

"I wasn't. It's what happened."

"Yeah. Like a butterfly to the light."

I caressed her hand. "I'm pretty sure you're the one who came on to me."

"Maybe. You were hot so I thought, why not? It's just one night."

"But then you backed out when you saw the interlock."

"I bet that was a first for you, getting turned down."

I shook my head. I'd been turned down before, but never once the woman had agreed to come home with me.

"I was going on intuition. I thought you were a good guy under all the macho posturing. But when I saw you blow into that thing, it gave me second thoughts. I knew nothing about you, and you could be some criminal with a handsome face who was going to strangle me after we had sex!"

"That's crazy."

"I know. My inner nice-girl comes out at the worst times. I could hear my mom's voice telling me to be careful."

I had more questions, but I could hear the fatigue in her voice. I kissed her on the forehead.

"Good night, Josie." I started to get out of bed.

"A forehead kiss? And now you're leaving me alone in bed? Does a punctured lung make me less attractive or something?"

I laughed. "You are as gorgeous as ever. But if I spend all night lying beside this body, something's gonna happen.

"What if I want something to happen?"

"You heard what the nurse said."

"She said it would be okay if you didn't contact my ribs. You could go down on me...."

"I could." That sounded like fun. "But what about me?"

"You could get naked and jerk off in front of me. That's always been a fantasy of mine."

"Josie!"

"What? I'd do it for you—if I was well."

That was a debt I wouldn't mind collecting. I took off my t-shirt and got back into bed with her.

"You comfortable?"

"Yes. Except I'm a little hot." She was a lot hot in my opinion.

I undid her flannel shirt. Josie was wearing button-down clothing because it was more comfortable to get on. Underneath she was naked and I pulled the shirt to her sides. She raised herself to let me take it off completely.

"Well, look at that. Peach fuzz." I ran my hand over the dark hair where the V of her legs met.

"I know. The Vancouver General doesn't have a waxing bar. Can you believe it?"

"Mmmm." I blew on her hair and she shivered a little. I

carefully pushed up her knees so I could access her pussy. "You okay?"

"Not yet…."

I ran my tongue slowly over her pussy lips, and she sighed with pleasure. "Yes, I'm feeling better now."

I used my fingers to spread her open and popped the hood off her tiny clit. Not fucking Josie for a week had made me extra-horny, and I wanted to get her off before I exploded. I poked the little button with the tip of my tongue, then sucked on it. Josie wriggled a little, but I could tell that she wasn't able to move around much. I watched to make sure she was okay. Judging from the sounds she was making, everything was fine.

It didn't take Josie long to come. I got off the bed.

"Where you going?" she murmured.

"Nowhere." I put my hands on her hips. "Can you move your hips to the edge of the bed?"

She gingerly crab-crawled over, trying not to move her upper body much. Once she was sideways on the bed, I put a pillow behind her head, and a couple at her sides.

"What's happening?" she asked.

"I'm going to help you get to sleep." I pulled down my jeans and boxer briefs. Josie smiled lazily at the sight of me naked.

"This is more like it. When a hot guy wants to take care of me—this is what I had in mind."

I waved my boner at her. "I'll take care of you, baby."

"Could you be any cornier?" Josie started giggling. "No, owww. Don't make me laugh, it hurts."

"You're not supposed to laugh at a guy who's naked and ready to do you." I took a condom from her bedside table where we kept them. Then I knelt on the floor between her spread legs. She was watching me with half-closed eyes.

"Okay, tell me if it hurts anytime, and I'll stop." But could

I really stop? Once I was inside Josie, all conscious thought went out the window. I eased my aching hard-on into her hot depths. It felt so fucking good that I pushed in deep and fast and then pulled out. I could see Josie trying to meet my motions by rising up.

"No." I put a hand on her stomach. "Lie there. Really, I want to make it good for you—I want to do everything."

She fell back, and I moved my hand down until my fingertips were resting on her clit. I pushed my whole hand down and started fucking her again. In and out—this glorious sensation of being inside her was so fucking incredible. For Josie, having to stay still was intensifying the sensations. The pressure of my hand on her and my cock inside her was unreal for both of us.

"Oh God, yes," she panted. Her eyes were tightly closed, and her hands gripped the sheets. Was she coming? I fucking hoped so. I stroked in and out of her, and the pleasure was intense. I started to come and come.

Afterwards, my legs felt weak, but I carefully lifted Josie up and tucked her back into bed. She moaned a little, and I kissed her on the mouth. Then I slipped into bed beside her. I leaned over her to see if she was asleep yet. Her eyes were closed, and her breathing was regular. I lay back down and slid one hand over her hip.

What an incredible day. I was back on the team and things were perfect with Josie. Again I felt joy surging through me. Maybe I hadn't made the NHL, and maybe I never would. But it was hard to imagine how things could be better. I had set my own goals, gone after them—and won! Now I was going to enjoy every moment—just like someone else in this bed.

"I love you, Josie." She was asleep, but my excitement was uncontrollable.

Josie shifted slightly, and her words were only muttered. But I still heard them.

"Love you too."

I waited for more reaction, but there was none. She seemed to be fast asleep.

Maybe it was the post-orgasm high, the pain meds, or the fact she was semi-conscious. But she loved me, no matter how cool she acted. I hadn't thought I could feel any happier, but now I did.

I closed my eyes and relaxed into that good feeling.

31

THIRD STAR

Two months later

"AND THE THIRD star of the game, from your own Vancouver Vice—Eric Fairburn."

I skated out to the faint cheers of the remaining fans. Most of the crowd had left early, reasonably assuming that we weren't going to come back from being down four. And we hadn't, but I had scored both our goals. Being a star in a 5-2 loss wasn't a huge personal achievement, but tonight's game was a special one for me.

Back in the dressing room, the guys weren't particularly upset about the loss. Unfortunately, losing was something we had gotten used to. And it was only December. Coach Panner came in and ran down all the issues we'd had tonight. I wasn't really listening because he'd repeat the same speech tomorrow while we watched the game lowlights.

I got changed quickly. I was sitting beside Marty Devonshire. At one time, I was going to live with Devo, but I hadn't needed to. I managed to parlay my stint looking after Josie into permanent roommate status. My regular road trips gave her all the time alone that she needed.

Or maybe it was sex. Luckily, Josie's ribs had healed quickly and we hadn't had to wait that long to have intense sex again. We had tried to achieve the Tantric ideal of long sex sessions without male orgasms, but being inside Josie felt too good and I'd never succeeded. But we were having fun trying—trying all kinds of new things. Sex with total trust was the best.

Still, between road trips and Josie's convalescence, this was the first time she'd been to one of my games. Her first hockey game ever, and I could hardly wait to hear what she thought of it.

I hurried out to the concourse where I'd asked her to meet me. No way I was putting her anywhere near where the players came out.

"Eric! Eric!"

A couple of preteen girls spotted me and wanted autographs. I signed their jerseys and then they wanted selfies with me too. As I posed with one, my eyes were drawn to Josie. She was leaning against the counter of the closed concession. We smiled at each other, and then I noticed she was wearing these high black motorcycle boots with buckles that I hadn't seen before. That looked really hot, and my cock started to harden.

Click.

The shutter sound of the phone brought my attention back to the young girls. Shit, I hoped my hard-on wasn't in the photo. Oh, what the hell, maybe that would bring more fans to the games.

They continued to talk non-stop. "Oh my God. This is incredible. Thank you so much, Eric."

"You're our favourite player."

"You're welcome. Thanks for supporting the team."

As I walked towards her, Josie immediately noticed my excitement and smirked.

"Hey, beautiful."

"Hey, handsome."

I kissed her on the cheek.

"You can do better than that."

I kissed her on the mouth, parting her soft lips and pushing my tongue inside. She tasted like artificial spices.

"Josie, you didn't eat a hot dog here, did you? They're filled with chemicals."

"Oh no. It's the food police. Arrest me, officer." She held her wrists up mockingly, but I grabbed them in one hand and raised them above her head. Then I kissed her again, this time with an open-mouth and a lot of passion. I heard giggling and a click behind me.

Josie looked up at me, with eyes clouded with desire. "Mmmm. Tastes better than a hot dog."

"Yeah, I'm jealous. I don't want any hot dogs in your mouth but mine."

She laughed. "You're bigger than the one I ate tonight. You're a smokie, at least. Maybe a Jumbo."

I put an arm around her, and we started walking towards the player parking lot. Josie looked over my shoulder.

"So, is our photo going to be reblogged on a hundred Tumblr sites tomorrow?" Her voice went up an octave. "Eric Fairburn is such a hottie!"

"A dozen sites maybe. We're not that big a deal. Does that bother you?"

"Naw. I'm getting to go home with the third star of the game."

"That is impressive."

"Yeah, I got an offer from the first star, but he's not that good-looking."

"What! Really?"

She cackled. "No. I sat alone at the game, and the only person who talked to me wanted to sell me 50/50 tickets, whatever they are."

"You shouldn't have been alone. Next time I can seat you with some of the wives and girlfriends."

"Eric. Really?" It was kind of hard to imagine Josie making nice with the other women. "I like being alone. If I want company, I'll bring Cyn and Zach."

"That's nice of you."

"Not really. When you guys started losing, I learned some new words. I can hardly wait to see what Zach can pick up. He's at that stage where he repeats everything. Cyn will have a fit."

Josie had already bought a drum kit for Zachary's Christmas gift, so it was exactly the kind of thing she would do. I still didn't understand her family dynamics.

"So, if you're coming back, that means you liked the hockey game, right?"

"Meh."

"A meh from you equals five gold stars from anyone else."

We got her bicycle from where it was chained up and put it in the back of the truck. Once we got in the cab, I turned to face her and held both her hands.

"Okay. Tell me what you thought of the game."

Josie's eyes widened, and she actually hesitated before blurting out her opinion. She was definitely getting sweeter these days.

"You guys sucked."

Well, maybe not that sweet.

"I'm sure that's not news to you. But watching the other team, I think you need to move the puck around between each other more."

"It's called passing, and yeah, you're right."

Great, someone who had never watched hockey before was able to identify that we needed more teamwork.

Josie squeezed my hands. "But, Eric, you were the best player out there. I love the way you skate. You're so smooth and fast. You're flying—just like a butterfly!"

She *was* sweet. I kissed her. I ran my fingers through her short hair, and she leaned into my touch.

"It may be time to quest for a new spirit animal," I said.

"Why? I like that my spirit animal can eat yours as an appetizer."

"A butterfly symbolizes movement and change. I'm becoming more settled." With hockey, trades meant that there could be change at any time. But whatever happened, Josie and I would find a way to be together, and that grounding made me comfortable.

"Well, if you get something bigger, I want something even bigger than that."

I laughed and kissed the top of her head. "Thank you for coming to my game. I hope you'll come to some more."

"Maybe next time, I can come to a game against a bad team and you'll win."

"We *are* the worst team in the league." I didn't talk hockey much at home. It was better for me to have a place to get away from the rink.

"Oh." Josie cleared her throat and changed the subject. "You didn't even notice that I dressed up for the game."

"Really?" I looked over. She was wearing her usual uniform of leather jacket, faded jeans, and tiny t-shirt. Today's accessories were those boots and a low-slung belt that looked like a medieval weapon of torture. When I looked closer I noticed that her t-shirt had a Vancouver Vice logo on it. It was really worn out and looked like it had been sized for a five year-old. The logo was our old one, a rip-off of the Miami Vice logo that looked a lot less lame across Josie's chest. I reached out and ran my fingers over the logo and felt her nipples rising to meet my touch. "Looks hot on you."

Car headlights swept over the truck, and I stopped feeling her up. No point giving Panner a reason to insert a morals clause again. I liked fucking Josie everywhere, but not in public. I was beyond the days of post-game blow jobs. I started up the truck.

"How did you get that old t-shirt anyway?"

"The fact that you're the worst team explains why there are so many Vancouver Vice t-shirts in Value Village."

"Hmmm."

"Does it suck to lose all the time?"

I nodded. "Yeah. Winning feels good. Not only the points, but the room feels good afterwards—like you've done something together. That's what can bring even a dysfunctional team together. Whereas our team is splitting further into cliques because all we get is negativity. And that doesn't lead to better teamwork."

"So, a vicious cycle."

"Yeah. It's tough to break."

I had ideas on how to break it, but they were never going to happen under Panner. He had never forgiven me for forcing him to take me back on the team. He felt I had humiliated and undermined him, and he had tried to get back at me in a hundred ways. I'd been healthy-scratched, demoted to the fourth line, played out of position, blamed, and constantly harangued.

But what he didn't realize was that this treatment was exactly what I wanted. The Vice were the perfect team for me. We were going to go through a ton of pressure, with none of the highs of success. There was going to be temptation to drink with the guys, most of whom were major partiers. I figured that if I could make it through a season here, I would be genuinely healed and ready for the next step.

Besides, I was already the leading scorer on the team even after all of Panner's antics.

And there were a lot of advantages to living in Vancouver. The city was beautiful and exciting. And it wasn't that far from Nelson. My mom and Dino had come out at Thanksgiving and stayed at Joe's place in his newly reno'd suite. Then all of them, including Margie, had come to my games. My mom loved Josie, but then my mom loved everyone. It didn't matter though; all that mattered was how Josie and I felt about each other.

My dad had come to our first games, and he was coming back soon, but he'd be staying in a hotel. And Gary and the boys were coming—as soon as I broke the news to Josie that there'd be guys sleeping all over her sectional. Or maybe it was a better idea to see if Joe's place was free for a weekend.

I had mentorship going in Vancouver as well. I could still train with Tony and get his guidance on my playing and my mental game. I was keeping in touch with the other guys from training, and we had plans to see each other when they were in town for games.

Of course, there was Josie. Beautiful, unpredictable Josie. I reached over and held her hand. I lifted it up to my mouth and kissed it.

"I love you, babe," I said.

"Of course you do," she replied.

The End

ACKNOWLEDGMENTS

I hope you enjoyed this book. If you'd like to read more about the Vancouver Vice hockey team, please check out the *Also By Melanie Ting* section at the back of the book.

I'd love to stay in touch with you through my newsletter. If you sign up, I'll send you a free short story about hockey and a dating app entitled *Sunny Side*. You can sign up here.

I want to thank the supportive community of writers and readers who help me create every book. For *Tao*, the lovely Kate Willoughby and Jaymee Jacobs both beta-read this novel and listened to me brag or whine—depending on my mood swings. They also write wonderful hockey romances that you should check out.

To make my books as realistic as possible, I need all the help I can. Thanks to Jamie Plume, who read over the medical sections of the book for me. Any medical errors are my fault and not hers! And thanks to Daisy M., who became a lawyer just in time to read over the legal bits and tell me What Would Richard Do.

ABOUT THE AUTHOR

When not assuming Cat Pose with actual cats underneath her, Melanie Ting is watching hockey in beautiful Vancouver, British Columbia. The U.S.A. Today best-selling author began writing hockey romances during the 2010 Olympics, inspired by both the extraordinary athleticism and the crazy party atmosphere. Her aspirations include winning the Stanley Cup of hockey romance writing, finding the perfect little black dress, and world domination.

Learn more at www.melanieting.com.

ALSO BY MELANIE TING